NAPI'S DANCE

NAPI'S DANCE

Alanda Greene

Second Story Press

Library and Archives Canada Cataloguing in Publication

Greene, Alanda, 1947-
Napi's dance / Alanda Greene.

Issued also in an electronic format.
ISBN 978-1-926920-87-0

I. Title.

PS8613.R432N36 2012   C813'.6   C2012-904027-4

Edited by Colin Thomas
Copyedited by Lynda Guthrie
Designed by Melissa Kaita

Cover photo © iStockphoto

Printed and bound in Canada

Second Story Press gratefully acknowledges the support of the Ontario Arts Council and the Canada Council for the Arts for our publishing program. We acknowledge the financial support of the Government of Canada through the Canada Book Fund.

 ONTARIO ARTS COUNCIL
CONSEIL DES ARTS DE L'ONTARIO   Canada Council   Conseil des Arts
for the Arts   du Canada

Published by
SECOND STORY PRESS
20 Maud Street, Suite 401
Toronto, ON M5V 2M5
www.secondstorypress.ca

NAPI'S DANCE

PROLOGUE

SUN WOMAN DREAMED. Before her stood a large, beautiful woman. "I am in danger," she said. "Will you make the long journey for my rescue?"

Sun Woman knew this was one of the Above People, a spirit person, and she knew it was not a good idea to refuse such a request. "Yes, I will," she replied. She also knew that the people of dreams could be confusing and were not always what they seemed. She would wait to see if the woman came again.

She did. The beautiful, tall woman appeared and spoke once more as Sun Woman slept. She said Sun Woman and her husband, Sees Far, must travel, and she gave the signs they must follow on their long journey.

Sun Woman woke and told Sees Far, and both of them were fearful of the journey to be made. They were good and generous and did much to help their people: they gave meat to the elders who could not hunt anymore; they offered horses and travois to those in need when it was time to move camp; and they had learned the teachings of the holy ceremonies so they could help their people more. But now they must travel through the lands of the Sioux and Assiniboine, who at that time were great enemies. Worse, they must travel through the land of the longknives with their ghostly pale skin who lived to the south and were even greater enemies. Worst of all, they must travel on water, where the Underwater People live, who ever seek to lure the land dwellers into their liquid world.

Sun Woman said to her husband, "I will wait for one more dream, to be sure this spirit woman is truly an Above Person."

When the beautiful, tall woman appeared again, she reminded Sun Woman of her promise. "It is time that you go."

So it was that in the season of melting snow, as the ground softens and the cottonwood buds swell and fill the air with perfumed restlessness, Sun Woman and Sees Far left their lodge to follow the way told by the dream woman.

They journeyed far, day after day, wearing out moccasin after moccasin. When they met the great river that the woman told of, they found the paleskins had lodges that floated over the water carrying horses, cattle, and white-faced women in long dresses. Sun Woman and Sees Far floated with them until it was time to again walk on land.

Finally, in the season that chokecherries ripen, Sun Woman and Sees Far arrived to a camp where the people lived in mounds made of earth. Then they knew they had come to the end of their journeying. In the center of the camp people waited to welcome them, for the people had been told in dreams of this coming.

Sun Woman and Sees Far remained one full winter with the Earth Lodge People and learned much of their ways. They learned the mystery of their holy ceremonies and the mystery of dwelling in a lodge that never moved. When the Earth Mound People saw that the two visitors were true, they spoke of what was to come.

"Every year, as it is with all the people of the Sun, we gather for our ceremonies. Every year we mend the tear in the fabric that connects us all. Every year we restore the pattern in the ways given by the Creator with our prayers and sacrifices. Even so, the time for the Earth Lodge People nears its end. You, Sun Woman, and you, Sees Far, have also kept true to your ceremonies and teachings. Sun Woman, with your husband's help, you must take our sacred Bundle where she will be safe."

Then Sun Woman knew that the beautiful, tall woman who spoke to her in dream was a Bundle Spirit.

When the time of swelling buds came again, Sun Woman and Sees Far said farewell as the Earth Mound People wept to know the Bundle would be taken far away where they would never see it again. Yet they also rejoiced, knowing it would be kept holy in its new home. "May your people endure and keep the holy ways alive," they prayed, and said good-bye.

Sun Woman and Sees Far were full of sorrow to leave these friends, but they were eager also to return to their own lodge, to move again across Napi's great body, under his great, blue sky-lodge overhead. So it was that they made the long journey again, on the water, through the paleskins' land, through the land where the Sioux and Assiniboine roamed, until they came to the lodges of their own people.

The Sun Dance Circle had gathered three times since their return and preparations for another gathering were beginning when three thin and weary women, in ragged clothes and worn moccasins, walked into the camps of the great Okan Circle. Sun Woman recognized them as ones from the Earth Lodge Peoples and gave them food and rest, tending their worn feet with salve and new buckskin.

"After you left," the women told, "a terrible sickness came to us. Only a few were spared from death. We are scattered with different tribes now. We three had a great need to see our sacred Bundle once more, to know she is kept safe and honored with prayer and smoke and ceremony."

During the Okan Circle, these three joined the women of the holy Women's Society. They sang the sacred songs, danced the sacred dances, and smoked the holy pipe.

They felt then at peace and returned to tell the few who still lived from the Earth Mound People that they could have hope.

SECTION ONE

Disruption

◇◇◇◇◇◇◇◇◇◇◇◇◇◇◇◇◇

Ears stretched forward, necks strained, nostrils flared.

What's moving there?

The brown mare snorted and stamped. She and the others stood in the pre-dawn like horse shadows scattered over the prairie.

Just the old woman. Brown recognized her first, exhaled relief with a snort, and tore off a clump of grass. The others swished tails, brushed noses against shoulders, shifted weight to other feet.

She's still singing for that flower.

I saw it yesterday, by the buffalo trail. Early to find it so.

Things are out of pattern.

She's been singing it up for two suns and two moons. It had to come.

What's the old woman's big want, to call it out of rhythm like that?

The child won't come.

What child?

You know, inside the big-bellied one wandering around here for days, slashing her arms and legs, cutting off that soft black hair, moaning and crying.

They mourn that way. Her man was killed.

Either the child won't come, or she won't give it up.

So the old one's calling it.

The flower will call it.

There. She found it. She's putting little bits in the corner of her blanket.

She's going back to her lodge. We'll be hearing a newborn soon.

◇◇◇◇◇◇◇◇◇◇◇◇◇◇◇◇◇

CHAPTER 1

MOUNTAIN HORSE BENT, lifted the flap, and entered the lodge. At first, only dim red coals were visible. The air, in contrast to the cool freshness outside, was heavy with smoke and sweat and grief. The old woman's eyes adjusted quickly to the darkness, but she needed no light to image the body lying left of the entrance, its rough-shorn hair, lacerated limbs, sunken dark eyes.

She knelt to place a small, flat rock near the woman's head and set a glowing coal in the stone's center. Her blanket corner, folded in her lap, held the pale purple flowers she had finally found. Breaking off petals, she dropped them on the coal and began to sing.

The song was given to Mountain Horse long ago by her aunt; it belonged to the flower. She rocked gently as she sang, while the smoke drifted up, recognized the sound, shaped itself to it, coiled over the unconscious body, and wound into the nostrils of Owl Woman.

Mountain Horse continued singing as she dropped bits of the plant on the coal until every piece was burned. When the smoke and the song were finished, only the sound of the sleeping woman's regular breathing remained. The old one sighed and leaned against her backrest, drawing her blanket close.

For two days she had not slept and had hardly left the side of Owl Woman, who lay exhausted from pain and birth struggle. Now, Mountain Horse sighed relief as her foster daughter rested easily, calmed by the spirit of the flower. She murmured a prayer of gratitude to the plant for rising up to help this young mother, so dear to her heart.

Images of the day that brought Owl Woman to the old woman's Otter Lodge rose clearly, as if fresh from last year's summer. It was a day that seemed fine, but wasn't. Owl Woman – Owl Child then – was going with her mother and aunt to pick chokecherries. The girl often came to the lodge to play with Mountain Horse's son, who then still lived. When Owl Child laughed in pleasure as she spoke of going to the coulee, Mountain Horse felt her belly tighten inexplicably. Something was not right.

She should have called to them, warned them to stay. Warned them of what? Her uncomfortable belly? Then suddenly she had called, "Owl Child, stay here with me." The girl looked back, waiting for more. Mountain Horse could find no words, no reason to entice her to remain. So Owl Child had waved and run to catch up to the others. Moments later, her scream had brought Mountain Horse running. She reached the girl just as three Crow horse raiders galloped up the far side of the draw, brandishing spears above their heads. The two women who had surprised them in the thicket lay dead, throats slit.

Owl Child had joined Mountain Horse in the Otter Lodge then, and had grown close as if formed of the woman's own body. They had become four women's hands that skinned and dressed, tanned and stitched, cooked and packed.

Memories of the young girl mingled with those of her own youth and all of them thickened in Mountain Horse's numb drowsiness. Her head fell forward, and her breath joined the slow, deep rhythm of Owl Woman's.

What memory was this now in her mind? A bright day, the sun flashing brilliant before her. Two beings, twisting round and round, entwined in a strange slow dance. "Who?" she asked, and both turned their heads to face her. Snake Beings. One a deep blue-black, the other shimmering gold. Round they coiled, a spiral dance, twining like a rope, higher and higher. "Who are you?" Mountain Horse asked again, her voice languid and far away.

They leaned their heads back, mouths agape, red serpent tongues flicking and touching. They laughed and rose in their twirling. But now the bright sun shone in her eyes and she could not see them anymore, twisting into the light as they laughed and laughed. An odd laugh, that sound, more like the cry of a child, like a newborn's first wail.

Mountain Horse opened her eyes. Before her squirmed the infant, bloodied arms and legs tense and waving, face scrunched in plaintive protest. Owl Woman lay panting, knees drawn up, head toward the lodge wall. The old woman leaned forward to examine the child. She smiled broadly. A girl child. "Owl Woman, you have a daughter." She lifted the infant so the mother could see it. "While I dozed, she slipped in here."

Owl Woman turned her head and her eyes found her child, but when she tried to lift herself, the effort was too much. She collapsed and her head rolled back on its side.

"No sleep yet, little mother. Not yet. Soon." Mountain Horse set down the baby and stroked Owl Woman's face, shook her gently, and called her name until she groaned and opened her eyes. "On your knees, little mother. Roll over."

The old woman pushed downward on the mother's abdomen, in spite of groans and weary protest. "Almost, my Owl Woman, a little longer. Then you can rest."

The afterbirth came cleanly. Mountain Horse's strong arms eased her foster-daughter onto her back, and turned her attention to the child.

Days earlier she had prepared the bits of cloth and soft hide. Now she wiped the baby free of slime and blood, and tenderly touched every portion of the tiny body as she sang and hummed a welcome. When the child was clean, she massaged the sinewy cord joined to the afterbirth and squeezed it between the thumb and forefinger of each hand to clear the blood. She severed it with one strong bite, then coiled the remnant over the infant's belly and wrapped soft hide all around to hold it in place. She lay the child in the hollow between Owl Woman's arm and chest. "Here's your new daughter, little mother."

A moment of a smile flickered on Owl Woman's face, drawn in exhaustion, while her eyelashes trembled in an effort to open. She leaned her head until it touched the baby, and she relaxed into sleep.

Mountain Horse gathered the afterbirth on a plate of twigs and moss, then cleaned the body of her foster daughter, who slept unaware of the ministrations. Her own tiredness had been forgotten since the child came, but she now looked at the two who slept before her and felt weariness return, heavy and dense. She wanted to join them in sleep but could not, not yet, not until she knew the two were truly safe.

She covered the sleeping pair with a soft calfskin robe and leaned again on her backrest. She must not sleep, just watch in relaxed wakefulness. Only then did she remember her dream. Was it a dream? The vision of the entwined Snake Beings returned to her, and she heard again their strange laughter, saw their upward coiling dance and the brilliance of Sun. The image of flicking red tongues disturbed her, and she pulled the edges of her blanket over her shoulders.

It is a good omen, she assured herself, that Sun blessed the child's arrival, and that the Snake Ones danced. She wished she understood the meaning, for they had not spoken. Only that laughing. She would name the child for the dream. Snake Woman. A good name, carried by her grandmother's sister. The Beings had come for the child, not her. She didn't need to know their message.

She was so tired. Her mind was numb like her body. But she must rest, watch, and only later sleep.

Mountain Horse woke clammy and hot, to a lodge lit golden by a spring sun already high. She loosened her blanket and tried to breathe deeply, but the air was dense, sticky, and unsatisfying. Why was it so stale? Her eyes closed, reluctant to leave the dark ease of sleep.

Something bothered her. She shifted her weight and muttered silently at dogs squabbling outside the lodge. Shifted again and listened to sounds of the camp. Quiet mostly. The boys would be out on the fields, guarding horses, practicing riding skills and war games. Most of the men were off hunting. It was a day like the one when Owl Woman's husband, Little Bear, had gone out.

She opened her eyes briefly to gaze on Owl Woman and the new child, lying peaceful after the days of struggle.

Perhaps now her daughter would release the grief of these past weeks. With a child to nourish and love, light would return to her black eyes.

That Napi, that trickster being. It was all his doing. Sending the wind to call out the young men to hunt at the end of a winter when they were restless and eager for adventure, to raid for horses or scalps, to ride over land newly free of crusty snow.

The wind comes, the men dream, they gather and strut, recounting the exploits of war heroes. Daring, courage, and victory. They ride out. They do not all return. Little Bear did not.

Owl Woman had wandered across the grass, slashing her arms and legs, cutting her hair, moaning in bewildered loss. Mountain Horse knew that grief. She too had walked far from the lodges, the pain of her own knife wounds a welcome relief from the sorrow of a heart bereft with emptiness.

The old woman kept her eyes closed following the scenes of her recollections. Why did she resist opening them? The mother and child still slept. She could sleep again also. No one disturbed her. No one knew yet that the child had come. That she had a name. She must tell her dead husband's mother, Yellow Star, of the snakes who welcomed the birth. Yellow Star understood such visitations. She could help Mountain Horse understand the meaning.

Why did she feel so listless? What was the discomfort in her belly? The afterbirth and the rags. That's what the smell was, bloody and thick and sweet. Sticky sweet. The warmth of the daytime lodge made it so. She must give a prayer and take them out to the high branches. Then the air would be cleared and she could rest again.

Mountain Horse leaned forward, began to rise and stopped. Her throat tightened, her chest would not move to breathe. Something was wrong. She carefully lifted the calf robe that covered Owl Woman, then groaned and sank back. The new mother lay in a pool of dark blood. Mountain Horse had dozed off, had not heeded the warning in her body, her instinct to keep awake until the two were out of danger. Owl Woman's peaceful stillness was not sleep.

The old woman reached to touch the thin face. Cold and hard. The child opened her eyes. Mother and baby lay so at ease, Mountain Horse could not bear to disturb them.

◇◇◇◇◇◇◇◇◇◇◇◇◇◇◇◇◇◇

WindMaker blew hard, rippling the buffalo grass, ruffling the feathers of Magpie where she sat on a hummock and watched the women skin and cut carcasses. She would rather have sat in the lee of a stone, but wolves and dogs were all about, also waiting for the women to finish. *Just like one of them to pounce on poor Magpie.*

A grasshopper lifted its legs and stroked them together, just in front of her. She scooped it quickly and tossed it back down her throat.

A bit of fresh meat would be good. Why don't they work faster? She stroked her beak through her shoulder feathers in three neat swipes. *The Sun Gathering's coming. That's why they're cutting those tongues. Magpie never gets to taste tongue. Maybe when they're drying, Magpie will swoop down and grab a piece.*

She knew she wouldn't. It was enough to keep clear of the four-footed enemies, the winged ones, and also the underground threats like Snake, without taunting the people too.

She would have liked to perch higher on the wolf willow scrub that crowded gray-green along the coulee rim. But the snake dens were there. The snakes made her nervous. *That old big one has sunned himself all morning with his eye on that little person. Why's he got such interest in her?*

Magpie hopped to a rock that improved her view. *There. The old woman's standing up. She must be finished. No. She's just bringing the little one back close to her. That one doesn't like keeping still. Now Old Man Snake is lifting his head to keep watching her. What's he got in mind?*

◇◇◇◇◇◇◇◇◇◇◇◇◇◇◇◇◇◇

CHAPTER 2

MOUNTAIN HORSE SET the scraper down and rose slowly to her feet. She pressed her hands into her back, leaned into them, and smiled at the child's chubby legs lurching in chase of a grasshopper. "Come back here, little one. There are wolves out there just waiting for a careless child to wander."

The girl turned back, grinning, and wrapped her small arms around the woman's leg. Mountain Horse hoisted her up to her hip. "Are you tired enough yet, my little Snake Child, to go peaceably into the cradleboard?"

Mountain Horse wished she had sent the child along with her newest foster daughter, Pretty Crow, and her close friend White Feather, when the girls went that morning to gather fat Saskatoon berries along the edge of the coulee bottom. Her work would be done now.

The child was a mystery and often a challenge. In the weeks following her birth and the death of Owl Woman,

Mountain Horse had found solace in the company of Yellow Star. She loved her dead husband's mother like her own, like a sister and a friend, and sought her counsel for knowledge that ranged from removing a swollen tick to healing despair. She had needed insight that would make sense of Owl Woman's death and the feeling that would not leave her that she had played a part. Why had her eyes refused to open? Why had the tightness in her belly brought listless refusal to move instead of the action required?

Yellow Star had asked for every detail of the child's birth and of the appearance of the Snake Beings. She had listened, asked more, listened more. Finally she advised, "You must watch her closely, daughter. She surely has a special path, and it is you chosen to guide her on it. Her own mother was taken away."

"Taken? Or lost because I dozed and did not watch carefully?"

Yellow Star sat in silence again, then added, "With the Snake Ones, you never know what is planned. You'll need to keep her safe and discover what path the two of you have been given."

"Do you see a path marked for her?" Mountain Horse searched the deeply creased face of Yellow Star, as if clues to the child's destiny were mapped there.

"Who can know why those Snake Ones have come? We can only know that they do not come without meaning. When the Snake Beings visit, it is bigger than just ourselves, daughter, more than dozing or not. They do not choose their helpers randomly. And they have chosen you. We do not know yet for what."

Mountain Horse was not convinced. She returned to watching the girl, who squatted near her leg, intently burbling at a large, iridescent beetle. The beetle scurried under a stone, and the girl sat back in the grass. A long-tailed magpie hopped from rock to rock, tail feathers glistening like the beetle's back. Mountain Horse lifted the child and carried her to the cradleboard, eager now to lead the sorrel back to camp, eager to be out of the wind.

The lodges were spread along the river's edge where the bottom land widened and steep sandstone walls bordered the water. Beyond, the Sweetgrass Hills rolled along the horizon, rising from the plain, their dark, forested hillsides surrounded by flat, brown land in all directions.

When Mountain Horse's family was new and the band camped as they did now, close to the hills, her husband, Lame Eagle, had enthralled their son with the story of how Napi set the hills there on his great walk northward when he created the world. How Napi had drawn, with his finger, the pathway of the Milk River that wound beside them. In hushed tones Lame Eagle would speak slowly. "Napi is fond of those hills. He filled them with spirit."

Whenever they camped in sight of the hills, her husband had been at peace, less angry at the halfbreeds, the paleskins, the Crees – whoever it was who trespassed on the land of the People, on Napi's own body. Perhaps if they had set their lodges here that late summer, Lame Eagle would not have joined the war party that attacked the Crow encampment to the south. He would not have returned on a travois darkened with his blood. Would not have died three days later.

It could have been much worse. Lame Eagle had time to speak with her, to ask her wishes. Did she want to stay with his people or return to her parents' camp? She wanted to stay. Become his brother's wife? No.

Lame Eagle could have died far away when the Crow spear pierced his chest, and she would now be the fourth wife of his brother, Prairie Owl. But Lame Eagle had lived three days. Enough time to transfer his own lodge to her. Time to speak with his father and hear Calf Shield assure Lame Eagle that his family would be to Calf Shield as his own, protected from enemies and given their share of the hunt. The Otter Lodge would continue with its place ever near Calf Shield's own Wolf Lodge.

So it stood today. It could have been much worse, indeed.

Mountain Horse loosened her arms from the cradleboard where the little one now slept and propped it in the shade next to the lodge entrance. She released the travois poles and padding and smacked the sorrel's rump, sending it at a trot to join Calf Shield's herd grazing near the river, guarded by his young men. She sat to rest while the child was quiet, her mind still wandering the past.

The buffalo tongues she and the others had collected would be part of the coming Sun Gathering. They expected a rider to come any day now, and the call to ring through the camp, repeated through the camps of all Napi's people scattered over his body, to come together in reunion, in the rituals that gave strength and survival.

Many years earlier, she had noticed Lame Eagle at another Sun Gathering, watched him as he slowed his pinto when riding past the group of young women who tended the children.

She had seen him glance quickly in her direction when he danced at the evening's fire. She had wakened that night to soft singing outside her father's lodge, singing she knew belonged to his voice. Each night for the remainder of the Okan, he sang, and she wondered how the pounding in her chest did not waken her parents. Then her parents enquired; has she noticed the young man, Lame Eagle? Yes, she has. Does she find him pleasing? Yes, she does. She knew then that her parents and his had spoken of their daughter and son. When the clans gathered the next year, she and Lame Eagle became husband and wife.

Mountain Horse's memories were cut short. The child was already beginning small noises, warning she would soon holler for freedom. Why didn't Snake Child enjoy the cradleboard as most young ones did?

"Perhaps her path is one that takes her wandering far. She feels it. Feels discontent when she stays in one place, even as a young one." Yellow Star offered this comment when Mountain Horse had brought the same question to her months earlier. As soon as Pretty Crow returned, Mountain Horse would put the young one in her care. For now, the toddler could play in the grass.

The child laughed with pleasure at being released and slapped her pudgy hands against Mountain Horse's shoulder before resuming the grasshopper chase.

The old woman stretched her arms and listened to the child babble happily in the grass to her left. The girl waved her hands up and down, absorbed with something in front of her. Had she found one of the leathery horned toads? Or managed finally to catch a grasshopper? The child squealed in pleasure. What did she have there? Mountain Horse leaned to her left for a better look. She froze.

A huge snake curled around the neck of the child and glided across her small shoulders. Its tail draped just beneath her wispy black hair. Its row of rattles hung like an ornament. The little one squealed again. The snake's head rose above the girl's right shoulder as the creature continued its slithery caress. The girl seized the snake just behind its head and giggled as it wound and twisted itself free.

Mountain Horse had never seen a snake so large. She sat like a stone that soaks up the cold ooze of night.

The girl had her back to the sun, her lap in shadow. The snake glided over her leg onto the grass, into warmth and light, where it coiled and faced Snake Child. She lurched forward and crawled to where it waited, sitting herself again with one leg stretched out, the other bent. The snake resumed its intimate slithering touch.

Stiff with tension, Mountain Horse dared move only her eyes, slowly scanning for anything that might startle the snake. It moved again into the clear sunlight. When the girl fell forward to follow it, she turned her head to Mountain Horse. Grunting and grinning her pleasure, she stood and waddled to the woman, wrapping her arms around Mountain Horse, who released a slow sigh and pulled the child close.

Snake Child's tiny head turned now to the snake. She reached her hand toward it, opening and closing her fingers, and tried to squirm free, babbling sounds of wanting.

The snake slid toward the embankment and disappeared in the grass. It raised its head and looked back at them. The baby wailed and leaned both arms toward it.

Mountain Horse finally stood, clutching the child close. "I don't know what to think about you, little one. Those Snake Ones visited for your birth and might be checking up on you now, but I'm the one who's got to keep you safe. You stay close to me." The child whimpered and reached her hands in the direction the snake had disappeared.

◇◇◇◇◇◇◇◇◇◇◇◇◇◇◇◇◇◇

Coyote sat on the hillside above the camp. He yawned. *Thunder's coming back. You think they know?*

His wife lay in the grass beside him. *Of course they know.* She shook her head to dislodge a fly sunning itself on her ear. *Raven flew over at dawn in the direction of Ninastako.* The fly circled in front of her nose, and she snapped half-heartedly at it. *And the air's full of his coming. That Ksisstsikomm always lets the whole world know what he's up to.*

Then why are they getting ready to move? Coyote leaned forward to keep in view the young men gathering horses along the river.

His wife stood up and shook the grass out of her coat. *To be where he wants them. They better move fast. He gets ornery if there's no welcome ready.* She turned and trotted away from the camp, toward the sun.

Coyote raised his nose in the air and sniffed. *He's coming fast.* He trotted after her. *You think they know how fast he's coming?*

◇◇◇◇◇◇◇◇◇◇◇◇◇◇◇◇◇◇

CHAPTER 3

MOUNTAIN HORSE WRAPPED the girl in the center of the travois and snugged the cradleboard between rolled-up hides. Snake Child scowled and stuck out her lower lip. The old woman chuckled. "You don't like being still and not able to see what's going on, do you, little one?" She lashed the board securely with a long strip of rawhide laced between the travois poles. "Next thing you know, Eagle will be landing on that lip, thinking it's a good ledge for a nest." The lip retreated.

Mountain Horse was among the last to leave. Busy with packing for the move, the woman had not noticed the girl wander. Yellow Star, hoisting a hide on the travois, saw. "There she goes again, off to where the coyotes watched earlier. Go and get her. I'll finish here and you can catch up. Pretty Crow's already gone with White Feather's family."

Snake Child did not want to ride in the cradleboard.

"I'm not a baby. Why am I in a babyboard?" The scowl had returned.

Mountain Horse brushed a strand of hair from Snake Child's face. "It's true. You are not a baby. But today we must travel quickly." Her hand lingered on the girl's cheek. "If the horse stumbles or bolts, you'll still be safe." Five sun cycles since the huge snake had caressed the newly walking child in their camp far to the southeast, and Mountain Horse had been chasing after her ever since, keeping her safe, close, protected.

"Did you hear Thunder holler this morning? He surprised us this year, coming back so quickly. He told grandfather in his dream last night where he wanted his welcome to be. It's a long ride." She stood, the child's round, black eyes staring back accusingly. "We'll stop to visit Old Man Buffalo Stone on our way. Rest well, little Snake Child. Tonight there will be feasting and stories."

The old woman mounted a dark bay mare and, as the horse moved out quickly to follow the others, she looked to where the lodges had stood that morning along the river's bend. For a full moon cycle, the cookfires had blazed here while people, dogs, and horses ate, played, worked, and slept. Raven flew over in the early light, toward Chief Mountain to the southwest, and now the camp followed his path. Spring filled the air with scents of melting, new grass, and Thunder; it felt good to move, feel the sun on her back, see the mountains before her.

Sun was already high when she finally caught sight of the upright stone, black as Raven's wing, shimmering like his feathers. Mountain Horse could not remember a time when the great stone had not been on his windy hilltop that today was tinged bright green with just-emerging grass. Far beyond jutted the peaks of Napi's backbone, still white beneath deep gray rolls of cloud.

The grandmothers of her tribe told of the long ago time, the time of the grandmothers of the grandmothers, when Old Man Buffalo Stone lived in the sky. He looked below and saw the People, their bellies aching in hunger, their lodge hides worn and thin, their hearts in despair from war and loss. In compassion for their suffering, the Iron One fell to earth from his heavenly home to land on this hilltop, to live in beauty among all the beings of the land and like them, to grow. He gave the People of the Blackfoot Confederacy – the Blackfoot, Piegan, and Blood tribes – his promise that they would have health and strength, abundant herds and victory over any enemy who dared enter their territory. In exchange for his protection, he required a promise in return: *Never disturb me from my new dwelling. If this should happen, war, disease, and famine will follow.* The People gave their promise and brought him gifts: tobacco, meat fresh from the hunt, clothing, beads, tender touches, and always, always their prayers.

Year after year they came. Year after year the Iron One continued to grow. Now, Old Man Buffalo Stone was so large it would be impossible to dislodge him, impossible for his home to be defiled.

Mountain Horse shivered and drew her blanket tight. The Black Stone was part of her. From earliest introductions in childhood to the regular visits as the band of her youth passed close, following the buffalo, he was a living presence. When Lame Eagle died, she had walked two days and nights to Old Man Buffalo, her hair cropped in short tufts, her arms and legs scabbed and swollen from the lacerations she gave herself. She curled at his base and slept another day and night as his strength seeped into her heart and restored her mind to balance.

This spring day, she again drew close to the assurance of the stone, the promise of his existence. Though buffalo herds to the south were rumored small and weakened, though disease destroyed whole tribes beyond the powerful Medicine Line, and though paleskins encroached relentlessly to the north and east and south, here Mountain Horse's people remained strong. Their warriors fiercely kept all intruders at bay. When disease came, it left quickly. The buffalo returned plentiful each year.

Mountain Horse dismounted a short distance from the stone where a group of women and children, their offerings completed, sat chewing dried meat as they rested on the warmed hillside. She loosened the thongs holding Snake Child and the girl squirmed free, running onto the grass to join two other children who chased each other around the women.

She opened the pouch belted at her waist and took a piece of tobacco from it. Kneeling at the base of the Black Stone, crowded with offerings from those who had passed earlier, she felt his familiar hum, the deep vibration in her chest, the way the earth rumbled when a great herd drummed over the land. She sang and hummed with the stone's drone while she scraped away a piece of ground, carefully placed the tobacco, and covered it.

The child appeared beside her, head to one side, looking intently at the stone. Mountain Horse guided the girl's right hand to the rock. "He likes to feel our hands when he hears our prayers."

The small hand spread flat and lingered on the black surface. "Singing," she said, and grinned broadly at Mountain Horse.

A rumble from the west jarred them. "Do you hear, little one? Thunder's calling. Come, we have far to travel yet today."

"Not on baby board. I ride. That's my prayer to Stone. He says yes."

The girl's determined voice and the fact that they could be underway more quickly if the girl rode checked the woman's protest. "You shouldn't tell your prayers to others. Ride with me, then." The bay horse was strong and would hardly notice Snake Child's weight.

The others also spurred themselves with Thunder's repeated growls, and they set out together on the trail of flattened grass where the camp had passed earlier. Mountain Horse turned for another look at the Stone, in sudden reluctance to leave its sight. She felt the urge to stay longer, absorb its presence and the sense of all-is-well that came when near it. She raised her hand to the Stone. Thunder rolled again, and she urged the bay forward on the trail.

She wished, now, that the ride was finished. She wanted to be in the Wolf Lodge, to share the berry soup Yellow Star would make for tonight. She wanted to be pulled into the rhythm of Thunder's pipe ceremony with drums, whistles, song, dance. Thunder's ceremony reassured her the same way the Black Stone did.

She turned once more for a last glimpse of Old Man Buffalo, but he was gone from sight.

◇◇◇◇◇◇◇◇◇◇◇◇◇◇◇◇◇◇

Can you hear it? Can you hear it? Listen, Rock. Listen. There it is again. Do you hear it?

River, where she narrowed at the bend, tended to babble.

Rock liked it. He had his whole family scattered around him, but they mostly slept. He enjoyed conversations with River. He didn't always know what she went on about. But he listened and tried to understand. *No. I hear only wind. And you.*

Listen again. Listen again. It's getting louder. Louder, yes. Clear. Can you hear it now? She was more excited than usual.

Rock listened a long while. *There is something.*

Yes. Yes. Singing. There's singing. Something's happening. Something's calling, Rock.

Sometimes River talked too fast for Rock. It was hard to follow her quickness. But she was right. There was something. He listened deeper. *The Stone. It's the Stone. Farewell. Singing farewell.*

Yes. Yes. Farewell song. You hear it. But why, Rock, why? Why farewell? Something's happening.

◇◇◇◇◇◇◇◇◇◇◇◇◇◇◇◇◇◇

CHAPTER 4

MOUNTAIN HORSE WOKE to singing. Who would be singing at this hour? No, it was the ringing silence of the dark that she heard. Or was it? She listened deeper and night sounds erupted: the nicker of a horse; the slow breath of sleepers around her; the pop of a coal in the fire as it cooled.

The ringing persisted, more than the song of the quiet night. It reminded her of the Black Stone, that kind of song. But sad.

She rolled over, moved an arm under her ear. Perhaps, she thought, a ghost wanders through the camp, lonely for loved ones who still live. So much misfortune, so many of her people gone to the Sand Hills. Why had Lame Eagle died so young? Why was her only son killed as a young warrior? Where were his bones? Did his ghost wander lost because no one gathered his body at death? Owl Woman dead. Snake Child to raise, and now Pretty Crow, her family all dead.

Mountain Horse sat up. What had brought these sorrowful thoughts? She put branches on the white ash where fire had blazed earlier, waited for hidden coals to ignite the flame, then lay again on her back and watched the flicker of light and shadow against the lodge covering. Smoke rose through the top where a single star glistened in the black space. Why were her thoughts so dreary this night?

Her vague feelings of late, a sense of dread and worry, intensified with this sad singing. Fear seeped through her, for her people, for young Snake Child and Pretty Crow. How would their land and their life be kept sacred and safe? Each day, news arrived of another whiskey fort, or battle with the Cree, attacks by the blue-coated soldiers to the south, or wild slaughter of buffalo by the half-breeds in their lines of two-wheeled carts.

She sat up again. This sound fed misery and fear. What was it? A desire to see the Black Stone welled up in her chest. More than two years had passed since she and the child had visited Old Man Buffalo, when the girl first laid her hand to it and heard his song. Mountain Horse wanted to kneel again where he rested in the golden prairie, feel WindMaker blow above the grass with the blue sky-lodge arching above her. She longed for the comfort of the Iron Stone in his place of beauty. Holding this image, she lay down once more and slept.

On the third day after the troubling night sound, message riders galloped into camp on horses breathless and flecked with foam. When she heard them speak, Mountain Horse understood the singing she had heard and the sorrow she had felt.

The Black Stone was gone. Taken. A hole where he once sat. Nothing left but dusty, pale earth and bits of decayed offerings.

She stood numb. People ran to the three riders where they panted fragments of the news. A woman began to keen. Men stood bewildered, anxious face seeking face, mirroring the unspoken question: How? Then disbelief. Impossible. A lie. It cannot be, cannot be done. Who? Anger swelling.

Calf Shield composed the confusion. "Listen, all. These friends made a hard ride to bring this news. We will show respect and see first to their needs. Later we will hear what they have to say." Addressing the three riders, he said, "Come now, to my lodge. One Spot here will care for your tired horses." To the group, "Call in the herders and scouts. Tend to what is needed for the children, food, guards. Then come to the Wolf Lodge."

By the time eating and smoking had finished, Calf Shield's lodge was dense with sitting listeners. Shoulder to shoulder, blankets wrapped tightly, they waited quietly. Mountain Horse squeezed close to Yellow Star.

The riders sat on Calf Shield's left; the man nearest him prepared to speak. He wore a well-stitched shirt and moccasins; if he didn't yet have a wife, one was in preparation. A thin braid curved over each shoulder, and three black feathers hung from a twist of hair at the top of his head.

He spoke at last in slow, measured speech, like a man who must report defeat in battle. "My name is Rough Hair, from the Lone Fighters band. I had visited the Blackfoot camp of my mother's people to the north. Two days ago, as I returned, I met the red-haired parson, the one known as John."

Nods of understanding rippled through the lodge. This man, his trader brother, and preacher father were well known to the camps. The sons were braggarts with a zeal to compete that earned them good-natured tolerance in the tribes, also respect. They boasted wildly and often won the challenges they set. In the lands of the Cree to the north, the family built a mission post where father and son persuaded many to accept the parsons' Great Father and give up their own sacred ways. Their efforts to convince Napi's people in the south met no such success.

Rough Hair continued. "Parson John drove a team of four large, black horses that strained to pull the wagon. Blankets covered their load. Three halfbreeds rode alongside, another paleskin sat on the seat. Using his hands to sign, the parson told me he wanted to show what was in the wagon. He lifted the blanket." Rough Hair paused, his eyes on the earth in front of him. He breathed deeply, slowly. "There lay the Black Stone."

The listeners gasped.

Rough Hair stood and imitated the posture he described. "Parson John puffed up his chest, his arms folded across it as he stood smiling in the wagon above Old Man Buffalo, his chin stuck out." Rough Hair sat again. "I tried to touch the Stone, thinking it is a trick. But that red-haired one wouldn't let me. Instead he signed that I should ride and tell the camps what I saw. Tell them the Great Stone is gone. Tell them Parson John is stronger than the Stone. Stronger because his Great Father is stronger than our ways."

Bodies in the lodge shifted position. Faces scowled. Eyes flashed.

"I thought – I will kill him right now," Rough Hair continued. "But the riders held rifles at the ready, and I would have been dead before I brought my own from its sheath. Then I thought – perhaps he lies. I will ride to the Stone and find if the preacher speaks truth."

Scowls adjusted. A possibility remained. Everyone who knew of him also knew that Parson John was a great liar.

"When I saw the hill where Old Man Buffalo stood, I saw the top of it flat. Empty. No Iron Stone glinting as he does – as he did – in the sun. I saw that this time the parson spoke true."

Heads dropped, shook back and forth. The impossible had happened. Rough Hair shook his own head. "I mounted my horse and rode south, finding the camp of Heavy Runner of the Fat Horses band. It was he who sent riders in each direction to bring the news to every camp. At the Sun Ceremony, a council will determine what is to be done."

The crowd within the Wolf Lodge dispersed. Mountain Horse stood outside with Yellow Star and watched the blue-black western sky speckled with flashing stars above the jagged black ridge of mountains.

"I heard Old Man Buffalo sing farewell," she told Yellow Star. "His song woke me, filled my heart with sorrow and troubled thoughts. I did not know the cause then. Now, I do not grasp the meaning."

Yellow Star shifted her weight and linked her arm through Mountain Horse's. "Indeed, now that it is done, what will come of it? This is our important question. Will Old Man Buffalo see that the Real People had no part in this and not bring the prophecy upon them? Or will he only see that he has been moved, and the promise he exacted has been betrayed?" She squeezed her daughter-in-law's arm gently. "There's young Snake Child's voice bubbling, Pretty Crow and White Feather are laughing, dogs are barking, just as they have done for seasons before. They do not know this terrible deed has happened, that the pattern of our being has been torn. Yet, they may reap the consequence. This year's Okan, daughter, will demand great prayer and sacrifice. Our hope lies with those of good character and noble intent who are willing to make the effort, make the sacrifice. You are such a person. You can be part of your People's hope, of Snake Child's hope."

Mountain Horse set her own hand over Yellow Star's, taking comfort in the strength she felt there, hearing the invitation to join the Women's Lodge. But Snake Child was also a particular responsibility. She could not bear to lose another one dear to her, as Owl Woman had been, because she neglected her duty to safeguard the child. "I hear you, Mother. Yet the young one holds me. She remains a mystery, restless to wander beyond where she is safe. I must be her mother and keep her safe."

Yellow Star gazed west. Though she spoke no word aloud, Mountain Horse heard her clearly. 'If the prophecy comes to pass, my daughter, there will be no place safe for her, for any of us.'

In the weeks that followed, Mountain Horse sometimes wondered if Old Man Buffalo had in fact chosen to spare them. Abundant herds gave fat cows with glossy, thick hides. This meant good trade for guns, powder, blankets, and knives.

She skinned, cut, dried, and tanned through long days. The bountiful hunt meant parfleche stuffed full, and this meant winter bellies kept full. War, disease, starvation did not seem possible.

But loss of the Black Stone had also not seemed possible. Like a wind, disbelief swept once again through her, as if the loss was only truly comprehended in that moment, cutting raw, rising up to surprise her anew, over and over.

Yes, they had a good hunt. But her foreboding was not appeased, no matter what stories she tried to tell herself. Every few days, riders arrived with news from other camps, news that fed anger in the young men.

"The talk over all the land is war," Yellow Star said as the two worked side by side that morning. "Calf Shield is our chief and counsels patience, but Shaggy Bull is our war leader. He still hungers for the thrill of war, and he lets his son, Big Plume, fuel hatred for the Crees and their encroachment on Blackfoot land, and for the whites whose presence has brought sickness and disorder. Their anger sees only one solution, and that is war."

"What news did yesterday's riders bring?" Mountain Horse asked, sitting back on her heels to let the wind cool her sweating face.

"Blackfoot and Piegan war councils send invitations to all the southern bands. The Crees grow bolder each day, backed by the paleskin support. The talk is to act swiftly and drive the intruders out of Blackfoot land." Yellow Star stopped her scraping also and wiped the back of her hand across her forehead. "I tire too easily with this work. My efforts are better placed in prayer."

"I do not have your certainty, Mother, in the strength of prayer. We were true in our prayers to Old Man Buffalo, yet the white preacher carried him away. War against these pale-skins may be our hope."

Yellow Star rose with effort to her feet and gathered her scraping tools. "The men do not know the ways of the Women's Society. They cannot. You can, my daughter. You can learn how to be of use to your People in ways other than war."

Mountain Horse did not respond. She watched Snake Child chasing a pup in circles and could not find the certainty to trust that the girl would be safe without her protection.

"Perhaps you will find comfort at the Okan, daughter," added Yellow Star. With that, she left the hides and returned to her Wolf Lodge.

Mountain Horse kneeled and leaned her weight to push the scraper along the hide staked before her. Its network of white fat laced through lenses of flesh lifted smoothly with her deft strokes. Ahead, Snake Child now tried to wrap a black pup in a child's cradleboard. The pup squirmed free and scrambled to join the litter with the girl in chase behind it.

The old woman realized that she was looking forward to the coming Sun Gathering and did seek its comfort, as Yellow Star foresaw. The work of the spring hunt would be finished, and long days would emerge for friendships and catching up on the news from other camps. The child could be in the care of the young women. Mountain Horse wanted the easy company of old friends like her childhood companion, Weasel. She wanted to sit with someone who knew the Black Stone and grieved his loss, to talk with those who also had made offerings in the dusty earth and touched his black body in prayer as they felt him sing.

She wanted the solace of friendship, but she wanted also the renewal that the ceremonies gave. They were the framework of the Okan. At the end of the Sun Gathering, when each one stopped to look back at the central holy post standing alone, hung with offerings waving in the wind, each was restored. Whether inside the society lodges to enact the secret rituals, or in visits to them for blessings of paint, smoke, dance, drum, story, and song, it happened: the pattern of their being was renewed. She did not have the certainty of Yellow Star, but she knew there would be solace and comfort that nothing else could give, now that the Black Stone was gone.

Snake Child had chased the pup too far. "Come, child, give that little dog a bit of rest. I need you to help me fold the hide." No, until the girl was older, she would not have time to give what was demanded if she belonged to the Women's Society. The child herself demanded more than she sometimes felt able to give.

◇◇◇◇◇◇◇◇◇◇◇◇◇◇◇◇◇◇◇

They come. They come at last.

Hawk's cry of joy pierced the wind, right to the ears of the riders far below, who looked up, pointed to her, acknowledged her welcome. She swooped and glided ahead of the camp as its people approached from the east to enter the Great Circle forming in the midst of the wide land, as they did every year. Hawk banked north, then veered west.

Such joy to see them come again.

Over and over in the days that followed, Hawk flew high to watch for signs of arrival, the plumes of dust shining golden in the sun, the distant barking of camp dogs. With each band, she repeated her cry of welcome and flew ahead to lead them into the Sun Circle.

What joy that Napi has given me this song, this sight, these wings, and the honor to lead the arrivals.

Now, the last band had arrived. Hawk stretched her feathers wide and felt the wind push up beneath her as she sailed above the clamor of dogs, drums, horses, and shouts. She tipped her wing and spiralled higher and higher, following the circular pattern of lodges below, until they were as tiny stones set in the great, tawny land beneath her.

◇◇◇◇◇◇◇◇◇◇◇◇◇◇◇◇◇◇◇

CHAPTER 5

THE GATHERING did not satisfy Mountain Horse's longing.

The Black Elks arrived with pounding drums, jingling harness, firing guns, prancing horses, and songs of welcome. Hawk flew overhead as escorts guided the bands to their assigned site in the great circle. Weasel and others from the Many Children's band, already camped for two days, stood before their lodges and joined in the wild sounds of welcome. Mountain Horse was grateful for her friends' help in setting the Otter Lodge and sharing news of family. But the anticipated days of slow conversation would not be, for Weasel had joined the Women's Society at the last Okan, and her time would be given to its duties.

Pretty Crow and Snake Child quickly sought others of their age, and Mountain Horse joined Yellow Star to prepare for feasts in the Wolf Lodge in the days before ceremonial duties began.

In his days as a young warrior, Calf Shield had established considerable influence in the Black Elks, demonstrating skill, prowess, and courage. He was now the acknowledged leader of the band, but as he aged he emphasized the teachings of the Bundles and Societies more than those of war. It was White Feather's father, Shaggy Bull, who had risen as the band's warrior leader, and in his lodge the voices through the long night talked of horse raids, counting coup, and the threats that grew on the borders of Blackfoot territory.

Calf Shield offered the first feast and served his guests from other bands the choice ribs and tongue of fresh kill brought that day by his hunters. Mountain Horse and Yellow Star offered berry soup to each, and Calf Shield moved with slow, deliberate care to light and pass the pipe.

Then he spoke. "The talk of war grows within lodges of the Black Elks and in other lodges of the Blood tribe. War is not the solution to mend the indignities and harm of these last years. We have made changes in the past to adjust. Long ago, the People lived without horses to pull our loads and gallop into the herds of buffalo. We changed and brought the horse into our life. Once we had no guns. Then we learned to hunt with rifles and increased the wealth of our lodges. We are asked to make changes again, to use our minds and hearts, turn to the wisdom of our holy ones, to the Bundles and visions and dreams that have ever given guidance."

Shaggy Bull sat to Calf Shield's left, jaw tense and lips tightly pressed as Calf Shield spoke. Now, he countered in a loud, resonating voice. "Horses and rifles we adopted because they made us strong. They helped us remain rulers of this land, given to us by Napi to hold sacred. Now, to stay strong we must destroy our enemies, the paleskins and the Crees. We must drive them all out of the land we were given to protect."

Beside Shaggy Bull sat his son, Big Plume, the largest warrior of the Black Elks, with a reputation as a wild and fierce fighter. "My father says what the courageous ones of all the bands here say. Our hope is to kill the whites. The old men grow soft and counsel peace. There can be no peace if the paleskins and Crees are not destroyed."

Calf Shield showed no response to Big Plume's insult of cowardliness. He turned his pipe and knocked the ashes to the ground. The feast was over.

In the following days, Mountain Horse assisted in the feasts and councils of Shaggy Bull's Badger Lodge, where the war leaders from assembled bands recounted disturbing events of the previous year. But the most important event, the theft of Old Man Buffalo, was far down the list of grudges.

Those who had hunted beyond the Sweetgrass Hills and traded at Fort Benton told of water-spoiled gunpowder, moth- and disease-ridden blankets received in exchange for the People's hides, meat, horses. Inferior guns were traded to the Blackfoot, while their enemies, the Sioux, Assiniboine, and Crow received the best. The whiskey now traded stained lips red, blistered tongues, and called a demon spirit into their midst.

As another spoke, Mountain Horse recognized it to be Rough Hair, the rider who had brought the news of the Black Stone. He spoke of changes in the northern forts. "The Crees, like dogs, lick every part of every trader in the area, and every paleskin has a Cree woman in his bed. Their halfbreeds swell in number like geese in spring. The whites supply our northern enemies with guns and powder, and our enemies grow strong. If we want to continue in our land, we must kill the whites who strengthen the Cree."

It vexed her that no one spoke of the theft of Old Man Buffalo as something more than these other atrocities. He had promised to keep the People safe if he was not moved. War, disease, and starvation would come if he was. Why did these words not ring in the ears of those gathered as it did for Mountain Horse? Must they cooperate with what was forecast? She did not want to hear any more. Yellow Star was right. If they did not find a way to avoid the prophecy, nothing would keep the People safe. War would not keep them safe from war.

The following morning, Mountain Horse walked to the Women's Lodge and asked that her training begin.

That night, she returned to the Otter Lodge with at least one question – whether it was time for more involvement in the Women's Society – answered.

Her training was simple. She helped with preparations, watched, did as requested. When not occupied with these duties, she listened to the escalating outrages in the warrior lodges.

Mountain Horse feared that when the morning arrived for the Great Circle to disband and each of the camps rode out, the Black Elks would not depart as one band, but two. Shaggy Bull's open opposition to Calf Shield appeared more and more as a leadership challenge. It was not uncommon to resolve a challenge by the challenger's riding out in one direction as those who wished packed their lodges and rode after him. She had heard of it but had not experienced it, and the idea of the Black Elks dividing pained her.

Again, she sought counsel with Yellow Star, but her mother-in-law refused to discuss the matter. One of her first lessons was that the men's affairs and the talk of the camp did not come inside the Women's Lodge.

On the last day of the gathering, after the Women's Lodge ceremonies had finished and the men who had pledged to pierce themselves and dance at the pole had completed their gruelling sacrifice, only the night's celebration remained. Mountain Horse visited Weasel to share farewells. The Many Children would be leaving early the next morning. They would travel to trade with the Nez Perce and after would settle at one of the Mountain Horse's favorite childhood camps, the lake where the mountains rise up quickly.

In the center of the Many Children camp, Pretty Crow's laughter rode on the breeze from where Snake Child and another girl imitated the vivid gestures of a warrior acting out his exploits. The young woman's eyes flashed brightly, and Mountain Horse was struck with how beautiful she had become. Her black hair was carefully combed and braided, a line of light reflected across the top of her head. Where had she gotten those shells tied on the end of her braids? The old woman remembered the late night singing outside the Otter Lodge.

"Your Pretty Crow looks like a young woman ready for a husband," said Weasel. "Has she spoken of anyone?"

"No, not yet. I would miss her terribly."

"Your Owl Woman's husband came to your lodge. Perhaps Pretty Crow's would do the same."

"That's a rare event, as you well know. I'm glad it won't be soon, for Snake Child's sake as well. That one needs several eyes watching her."

Sun was gone behind the mountains and Nightlight, his wife, lay back like a luminous bowl above the ragged edge of the earth when the drums began their pounding, calling all to the dance. From the central fire, flames the color of the western sky already leapt in joy, and the dancers soon would do the same. In twos and threes they came from various camps to celebrate in one circle this last night.

Mountain Horse and Pretty Crow each held a hand of Snake Child who hopped between them to the drumbeat. They passed a group of young men standing together in the Many Children's camp. Pretty Crow glanced quickly to one on the edge of the group. The young woman's gaze went again to the child, and Mountain Horse did not know if it was the young man or the bouncing girl who gave the wide smile to her face.

At the dancing's end, White Feather returned to the Otter Lodge, her arm linked in Pretty Crow's. Side by side in the dark, they whispered long and shared the news of their separated days at the gathering. Was it the last time for the friends to share their secrets in the night? If Shaggy Bull chose to depart in a different direction in the morning, White Feather must follow her father.

At dawn, Mountain Horse woke to Yellow Star's voice as she faced Sun and sang, naming her children one by one as she invoked the blessings of his light. This time, Mountain

Horse joined her, looking east, arms upraised, eyes closed. "Let them be safe in Sun's blessing." Voices echoed her invocation through the circle.

When Calf Shield swung onto his black and white pinto, most of the bands had already gone. A gentle wind flicked the offerings that hung from the center pole. Soon it would stand alone at the site. Milling horses and dragging travois poles raised dust that floated like a pale fog where the tribal circle had been. A thin dog the color of the sandy grasslands, her teats hanging pink and swollen, nudged at a squirming bag of pups on Mountain Horse's travois.

Pretty Crow sat astride a black mare and looked to where White Feather waited with her family. Mountain Horse lifted Snake Child to a small pinto and climbed on the bay.

Calf Shield never looked back. In one hand he held his spear upright, feathers and skins hanging along it, swaying to the pinto's steps. His other hand guided the horse at a steady walk northward. Prairie Owl rode behind him, followed by Yellow Star, two other wives, his son's wives and children, and then the Otter Lodge. Mountain Horse rode with Snake Child to her right, Pretty Crow on the girl's other side. Dogs trotted beside the riders, happy to be on the move again. Even the sandy-haired mother abandoned her sniffs and whines and walked relaxed beside the travois that carried her pups.

Horses snorted and nickered. Yellow Star's black mare whinnied a high, long call. A young black colt galloped frantically to the front of the group, answering with his own anxious calls until he saw his mother and nuzzled in close on her left flank. Poles dragged, hooves pounded, dogs yipped. Mountain Horse strained her ears beyond the noises of the move to hear if they were followed. If Shaggy Horse was coming, it would be his lodges that came next.

She could bear it no longer and turned to look behind. Just as she did, Shaggy Bull urged his big gray forward and, holding his own spear upright, moved into the line behind Calf Shield's family. Singly or in clusters, his sons, wives, daughters, grandchildren, horses, and dogs took their places after him.

The Black Elks rode out as one band.

Raven clutched a thick cottonwood branch. He leaned his head one way, then another to give both eyes an equal view. He croaked his half bark, half chortle. He always did this when he was curious or uncertain. Right now he was both.

They don't see. No they don't. Raven sees. Clever Raven has sharp eyes. Raven sees something shiny near the small lodge. Something dropped. Raven could fly down and grab it. Raven would like to look closer before he takes it. Walk one way and then the other. Let both eyes see. But yellow dog lies close, in the sun. Maybe sleeping. Maybe not.

Is it something Raven would like to take back to his nest, to turn over with his beak, poke into the crack of a branch to save, so on a gray winter day Raven would have something pretty to look at? Is it a trick? Sometimes they trick Raven. They try. Catch Raven's feet. Raven cannot fly. The child and the older one sit near the lodge. Do they have a snare? They do not seem to see what is dropped.

Clever Raven sees. Raven is more clever than the camp people. Raven sees far in time. Raven sees the great change. They do not see what is coming. They do not see even a little shiny thing in the grass.

Raven croaked again. He lifted from the branches and glided silently to where the round shell lay. The yellow dog scrambled to her feet snarling and snapping. But Raven was already high above the lodge. The gnarled, black claws of his feathered foot grasped the shell tightly.

◇◇◇◇◇◇◇◇◇◇◇◇◇◇◇◇◇◇

CHAPTER 6

MOUNTAIN HORSE LAY in the dark. What had become of peaceful nights of rest? Yes, the Black Elks had ridden from the Sun Gathering as one band, had followed Calf Shield together to this new camp where for five days already the lodges had dotted the south base of a wooded hillside. But the easy rhythm of day-to-day activities, the good hunting, the horses growing sleek and fat on rich grass, could not erase the tension that hummed between Calf Shield and Shaggy Bull. Their tension focussed on trade, but it was as much about leadership and the future. Nothing had eased her own tension over the Black Stone and the prophecy.

The quarrelling of men is not new. Why does it disrupt the peace of the darkness? Why do simple actions of the day bring restless wondering and fear?

Today a raven flew down and seized a shell that had dropped from Pretty Crow's braid. Ravens do that. They like shiny things. They're curious. The raven liked the challenge of dropping right in front of the yellow dog and Snake Child, just to taunt them. She could not shake the feeling that it meant more than just a lost ornament. She knew it meant more, the same way she knew there was more to Snake Child's path than for the other children playing through the Sun Dance. The same way she knew the loss of the Black Stone meant much more than just losing his solace and refuge.

"Mother," she had asked Yellow Star while setting the camp here, "Will the ceremonies give the understanding and the answers I seek?"

"You will gain understanding, daughter, though not as you now conceive it. Our work is to serve the sacred ways and Bundles. Doing so, we serve the People by restoring balance. We sacrifice our own wants to follow the way given, the way that unfolds through the ceremonies."

Mountain Horse rolled to her other side. How long until Shaggy Bull and Prairie Owl return? They had ridden north two days earlier to propose that the Hudson Bay men bring their wagons south to trade where it is safer for the Black Elks.

"I will tell them," Shaggy Bull announced, "we will not trade where the Cree are well provided with arms. If they want our thick furs, they must come south."

"They cannot risk what we ask," Calf Shield objected. "The last time a Blackfoot camp proposed the same thing, the company men were caught in a skirmish and all their goods stolen. They were lucky to get back to the fort, but it was with empty wagons and no hides."

"We will promise escorts. We will give our word to protect them." Shaggy Bull was adamant.

"If we trade with the Kutenai," Calf Shield consistently returned to his preference for this autumn's trade, "we have no fear of attack. The Kutenai trade with the paleskinned ones and bring that trade to us. This year it is a wise choice."

But Shaggy Bull remained firm that the Kutenai must be avoided. "A council to discuss war has been called. All the tribes and bands will send representatives. Old Sun, Crowfoot, and Big Swan are ready to lead us in driving the whites far from our land. As soon as this autumn, if we are ready. By spring, for certain. We need good rifles and ammunition. We will not get this from the Kutenai. Who can blame them? There is peace between us now, but often we are at war. Who would arm a possible enemy and make them stronger than yourself? No, Calf Shield. We have good hides this year and must trade them well."

Mountain Horse shifted to lie on her back. Would she get any sleep tonight? Would she hear the arguments between Calf Shield and Shaggy Bull over and over in her mind, hear the words of those who supported one view and those who supported another? Behind their words she heard the prophecy. Shaggy Bull and his arrogant oldest son, Big Plume, had poor memories, she thought. They remembered only the glories of war. They had not known enough defeat to caution their pride and lust for revenge. It might have been better, after all, for the Black Elks to separate. At least she would get sleep.

Mid-morning of the following day, One Spot and another scout rode into camp. "We have met traders to the south, on Old Man's River," One Spot told Calf Shield. "Four paleskins, one with a Piegan wife."

"They send a request to trade with the Black Elks," he continued, "and send this tobacco to Calf Shield." He handed Calf Shield a package wrapped in gray cloth from the sorrel's shoulder bag.

Mountain Horse stood with other camp members to hear what would be decided. A single wagon of goods to trade would be a diversion, though it would not solve the needs for winter. But a diversion would be good right now, she thought.

Calf Shield stood silently, his head down, as he often did when he listened and pondered what was said. He has grown old, Mountain Horse thought, noticing for the first time that his hair, in three braids tied with wolf skin, had become completely gray.

Calf Shield nodded to Big Plume, One Spot, and three other men to follow him inside the Wolf Lodge. Mountain Horse shrugged. Whatever was to be decided was out of hearing. She would finish pounding the chokecherries and find Snake Child to help her make the cakes and place them to dry.

By the time Yellow Star approached, the cakes were laid in rows on the twig mats. "He has chosen to trade," she announced, "on condition no whiskey enters camp. One Spot and Running Fox rode out to convey the message for the traders to come in the morning."

A diversion would be welcome, yet Mountain Horse noted that on hearing Yellow Star's words, her belly tightened and her breath felt cold. Am I growing so fearful, she asked herself, that even a small trading wagon brings fear?

That evening, WindMaker carried chill mountain air all

the way to the camp, and Mountain Horse was glad to be inside the Otter Lodge, warmed by the cookfire and the light that reflected golden from the hide walls.

Snake Child held in front of her the make-believe child that Pretty Crow had shaped from a stuffed piece of hide, with braided black horsehair stitched to its head. "Maybe the traders will have shells and we can get some for your braids, Sun Woman," she said and gave the doll a pat on its head. "Maybe Pretty Crow can get one to replace the one that Raven took."

Pretty Crow looked up from the moccasin where she sewed tiny yellow beads. Her eyes had moved closer and closer to her work as the light inside dimmed. Now she stretched her neck and arms to relieve the stiffness. "It's the shell Raven took that I want, little one. It's special."

"Why is it special?"

Pretty Crow stared closely at the beads in her lap and poked through them in search of just the right one.

"I want to know," the child protested. "Where did you get it?" But Pretty Crow said nothing.

Mountain Horse recalled the young man who sang at the gathering, the same one, she was sure, who had watched Pretty Crow at the Many Children's camp. "Snake Child," she said, "you might be able to get some ribbon from the traders for your Sun Woman's braids."

"If the paleskins have such white skin, how do we know they aren't ghosts?" the child asked. "I don't like ghosts and I don't want any ribbon from one."

"Ghosts come at night," Pretty Crow offered. "They never ever come into a lodge if there's a fire burning."

Snake Child put a thick stick on the fire.

"That's why you have to make sure we have a good pile of fuel in here by dark," added Mountain Horse. "And ghosts don't bring ribbon."

The traders arrived the following day, Two wagons lumbered over the grass, swaying like drunkards, each pulled by a pair of dusty brown mules, a driver on the seat. Canvas covered the haul boxes, stretched over low, arched poles. Three riders, one a woman, rode alongside. Groaning axles and rattling cargo set dogs barking as children ran toward the sound. Snake Child, the yellow dog beside her, joined the throng. They stopped all at once, suddenly shy, the children grinning awkwardly while dogs trotted back and forth at a cautious distance, sniffing from different angles.

Calf Shield pointed to where the wagons should stop and welcomed the traders. Henry Dawson and his Piegan wife, Sings Alone, spread two red blankets on the ground. As Calf Shield and Dawson sat to smoke and exchange greetings, the Black Elk women carried hides and parfleche to the grass behind Calf Shield. Sings Alone carried bags from the wagon and set them behind her husband.

She kept her tan-and-black striped blanket close over her shoulders and her eyes down as she assisted Henry Dawson with his faltering attempts to speak in the Blackfoot tongue.

Mountain Horse had not heard a paleskin speak in the language of the People before. It was even stranger than when the People spoke in the paleskin tongue. In the Black Elks, only Big Plume had learned it, picked up at the forts over many years. But where his speech sounded harsh and grating, Sings Alone spoke softly, rhythmic like a stream in summer.

Her husband's thick black moustache and broad smile dominated his face. The drivers remained on the wagon seats, while the other rider leaned against the closest wagon box. The man had the same thin nose and moustache as Henry, but it was brown like the shabby hat he wore. A bright green kerchief wrapped his neck and his eyes scanned back and forth over the assemblage of traders and watchers.

Mountain Horse wondered how long Sings Alone had been wife to a paleskin. What will happen when he doesn't need her anymore to gain access to the camps, when he's made enough money and gone back to his own people? Gone back to a paleskin house and a paleskin wife. This was the story heard again and again: native wives left behind with nothing, often not even farewell. Now and then, a trader gave enough that his wife could return to her band with dignity. More rare, he took his native wife to live among the white-skinned people.

Mountain Horse could not understand how this could happen. She had seen the woman from their tribe's own Fish Eaters band, wife to the chief factor in Fort Benton, who lived in a house of four log walls and had done so for several years. How could she stay in one place when the breezes of spring came and the scent of new grass and poplar filled the air?

On the blanket where knives, pots, cloth, and beads were spread, lay a hank of brightly colored ribbon. Blue like the river on a bright day, green like new buds of pine, yellow like the buffalo bean blossoms that covered the hillsides in summer. Mountain Horse signalled to Snake Child, whose arms clutched Pretty Crow's leg tightly. The woman pointed to the colored strands. The girl moved closer and stared.

Sings Alone spotted Snake Child's fascination, picked up a bundle of red ribbons and reached them across to the girl who forgot her cautiousness entirely and stretched her arm to clasp the red prize. She smiled broadly to Sings Alone and to the man beside her, then leaned against Mountain Horse, suddenly shy again.

When Calf Shield's lodges finished, Shaggy Bull's family prepared to trade, and Mountain Horse helped carry the trade items back to Yellow Star at the Wolf Lodge. By the time she returned to the Otter Lodge, Sun had already moved high and now began his journey towards the west. The tightness in her belly had been with her all day, but she comforted herself with her unease by knowing the trading was nearly done. Snake Child was trying to tie a ribbon on the yellow dog's ear, but the animal shook her head each time the ribbon tightened. "Then you don't get any ribbon in your hair. I'm going to put it on Sun Woman instead." The dog yawned, stretched out on her side, and Snake Child went inside to find her doll.

"We need branches and chips for the fire, little one," Mountain Horse called from outside. "For dinner, and to keep those ghosts away. Is Pretty Crow still watching the trading? She could help you."

The girl came out and looked over where the traders sat. "She's going with White Feather to the Badger Lodge, carrying blankets."

"I'll go with you then. There's lots of dry wood just up the hillside."

"I'm leaving the ribbons inside with Sun Woman in case Raven gets the idea to steal them, too. Look. Big Plume and the man with the green scarf are going somewhere. I wouldn't go with a paleskin. Especially that one."

"What's wrong with him?" The two walked along the edge of the small cottonwoods and snapped off low, dried branches. "Does he look too much like a ghost?"

"He stares, like a mean dog who wants to fight," Snake Child answered. "This branch is too thick for me to break."

Mountain Horse pressed on the branch with her foot and it snapped.

The girl continued. "He stares at the girls, and he stares most at Pretty Crow. Do we have enough wood yet?"

Mountain Horse felt her belly turn cold. This fear is soaking into everything. Pretty Crow is with White Feather and the women of that lodge. The men are busy with men's things: horses, guns, rifles. She took a deep breath and put the anxiety aside. "We have enough wood. Let's carry it back. That man has probably gone to look at Big Plume's horses. These traders will be gone soon."

"Do we have enough wood for an all-night fire?"

"Might want to get a bit more. You can use the bucket and gather chips, just over there in the open grass. Take your yellow dog along."

The fire burned well and the pot hung above it when Snake Child returned, dropped the bucket of dry, flaky dung, and ran back to the trading area again. Mountain Horse soon followed her to the crowd, which was expanding in size now that the trade was nearly done. Running Fox's family had been last to trade, and the women gathered their stock from the blankets.

Calf Shield sat again with Henry Dawson, now at ease

and trusting his halting skill to speak the People's tongue. Pleased that the trading had gone smoothly, Calf Shield offered, with outstretched arms, a finely worked buckskin shirt, beautifully beaded in tight, intricate patterns on the front and back shoulders. "I thank you from all of us. Please take this gift in remembrance."

Henry held the shirt up, smiled broadly, and praised the quality. "I thank you for your generosity in letting us come to trade," he returned. "I would also like you to have a remembrance." He offered a blanket of soft white wool, and on top of it, a red checkered shirt.

Calf Shield immediately stood and put the shirt on, patted his hands to his chest, and looked down happily at the garment.

Sings Alone packed the remaining hides in the wagons and the drivers saddled the horses, but the brother, Conrad Dawson, still had not returned. Henry looked around repeatedly as they readied for departure. Sings Alone had tied down the last corner of canvas when a loud holler turned everyone's eyes to the southeast.

Big Plume rode his sorrel at a lively trot, Conrad beside him on a smaller black. They stopped in the grass beyond the wagons, slid from the horses, and Big Plume hooted again. He carried something on his left shoulder and sauntered towards them, leaning to the right with his load. The green-kerchiefed Conrad led his horse to the farthest wagon and hitched it to the back.

Everything became silent and still. Except for Big Plume who stopped face to face with Calf Shield.

"Hey, old man. Have you lost your manners along with

your youth? Would you send away these traders without feeding them? This is not the way we trade." He held a keg, a keg that could only be whiskey, on his shoulder.

Big Plume faced the crowd. "I, Big Plume, don't forget hospitality. All of you are invited to my father's, my brother's, and my own lodges." He swung his free arm around and gestured towards the Badger, Fox, and Many Stripes Lodges at the far east of the camp. We do not forget how to feast and celebrate when we have traded successfully. We do not forget how to show our guests respect for visiting us."

Mountain Horse tensed. Big Plume was already heated with whiskey, and the usual restraints to his surliness were gone. She wished again that the Black Elks had divided. This hot head was provoking a fight with her father-in-law.

Calf Shield turned to Henry Dawson. "Yesterday we gave our word to each other. We smoked to seal our agreement that no whiskey would come to the camp? What is this betrayal?"

Henry's mouth gaped as he looked from Big Plume to Calf Shield in bewilderment. "I swear," he stammered, "we brought no whiskey."

Big Plume hooted again. "Who are you, old man," and he moved his face closer to Calf Shield's, "to tell us what we can do? Trading has always meant whiskey and celebration. Just because there are only a few who come to trade, do you think we forget?" He moved then to stand before Henry Dawson. "Do you think this old man makes all the decisions? Do you think you have to do everything he says? Your brother has wisdom to see that a man like Big Plume will decide for himself." With that, he pivoted and strode towards his families' lodges. "Come now, my friends," he called over his shoulder, "and feast, and we will show our hospitality to our trader friends before they depart."

Henry Dawson's face transformed from shock to rage. He breathed quickly and his lips tensed in a stiff grimace. "I offer my sincere apology," he said to Calf Shield and jerked his arm to signal Sings Alone. "Come here, woman, and explain what I say. We had whiskey in our wagons but we left it cached back that way, to pick up after we finished here." He waited, breathing loud and shallow, while his wife translated, then continued. "My brother, Conrad, has gone back and brought one of the kegs. I will try to stop this. I am truly sorry." He strode in a long, jarring gait toward Conrad, who still stood where he had tied the horse. But when he saw Henry coming, he hastened to catch up with Big Plume and walked alongside him to his lodges.

Mountain Horse stood with others and looked in bewilderment from Big Plume and Conrad, to Henry and Sings Alone, to the drivers waiting on the wagon seats, to Calf Shield facing her. Nothing like this had ever happened in their camp.

After a long silence, Calf Shield spoke. "My people," he said, and Mountain Horse heard for the first time his voice sound old and tired. "You know what was agreed yesterday. Big Plume has offered a feast and celebration. You must choose for yourself." He walked slowly then toward the Wolf Lodge, and Mountain Horse wondered if when he chose this site for the Black Elk camp, where the lodges naturally spread in a line along the base of the hill, that he did so to have this distance between his own lodge and that of Shaggy Bull's family, camped at the opposite end.

Yellow Star followed her husband, and behind her followed the other women of the family, heads low and blankets clutched tightly. Mountain Horse signalled Snake Child to come also and scanned the group for Pretty Crow. She couldn't see the young woman and thought it likely that she was still with White Feather at the Badger Lodge.

"Little one," she said, "I need to go and get Pretty Crow. Go to our lodge. Put chips on the fire. Stir the pot. Don't leave." She had seen too many times what happened to men when whiskey came into the camps. It was always better to be far out of sight, away from the inevitable ruckus.

The Badger Lodge housed Shaggy Bull's wives, sons and daughters. Next to it was Big Plume's lodge with three wives and five children. A fire burned in front where strips of meat roasted. Fat dripped into the flames and sent tantalizing scents to a ragged half-circle of people standing around the blaze. Conrad Dawson pulled two tin cups from inside his vest. These Big Plume filled with brown whiskey from the keg and passed the cups to those assembled. Mountain Horse stopped when she neared the group and scanned for Pretty Crow.

"Don't hang back like a timid dog, old woman. Come and celebrate with a drink of whiskey," called Big Plume.

She pretended she didn't hear. The girl must be in the Badger Lodge. She walked toward its entrance.

"Old woman, I offered you hospitality from our lodge. Are you refusing my hospitality? Afraid your old father-in-law might not like it?" Big Plume walked to her and pushed the cup at her lips. The liquor aggravated his usual bad temper.

Mountain Horse needed to avoid offence. No red stain marked Big Plume's lips. A good sign, she thought. This wasn't the vile poisoned whiskey of recent years. She needed to appease him. "Big Plume, I thank you for your offer. But I am an old woman. I can't drink like you young warriors. I only came here to find Pretty Crow and bring her to Snake Child who misses her."

"Have a drink, old woman. You come from the family of Calf Shield to the lodges of my father where a feast is given. You insult my generosity and my father's if you reject my offer." He pressed the cup harder to her mouth.

She took it, drank a mouthful, shuddered as its heat seared her throat all the way to her stomach. "Thank you, Big Plume, and to your father who is away, but whose hospitality is still present through his son."

One Spot threw an arm over Big Plume's shoulder. "Let's keep that cup filled and traveling, my friend. There's empty mouths over here that need your generosity too." He caught Mountain Horse's eye and she realized he was not nearly as drunk as he was feigning in order to divert Big Plume's confrontation.

Big Plume has been belligerent since the Sun Gathering, she thought, and now, with his father away, he's pushing his weight around and looking for trouble. Shaggy Bull might be war-happy and powerful, but he would never countenance this open challenge or display such disregard for a promise given.

Inside the Badger Lodge, White Feather sat with her mother and the other women of Shaggy Bull's family, Pretty Crow next to her. "Come and join me at the Otter Lodge, all of you," Mountain Horse offered. "Eat with me there and leave the men to their noisy drinking."

Cloudy Woman smiled. "We're fine in here, my friend. My son behaves badly," she said. "Tomorrow his head will hurt and he'll be like a grizzly in spring. By evening he'll be quiet and ashamed."

"Sometimes it's safer where eyes don't notice you," Mountain Horse replied. "Pretty Crow, come back with me."

"I started to come, Grandmother, but Big Plume hollered to come and drink. I waited in here, as he will not bother his mother and sisters. Later, when they are busy eating, I'll slip away unnoticed."

Mountain Horse hesitated, reluctant to exit and encounter Big Plume again, reluctant to leave Pretty Crow. But the girl was right. In the midst of Shaggy Bull's family, she was as safe as anywhere.

Was it the fear created from the past that put the cold stone within her, made it hard to breathe, hard to think clearly? "Pretty Crow, come now, please," she entreated as she pushed the lodge flap aside and glanced outside for Big Plume's whereabouts. A group of young herders hung together at the fire. They lurched and laughed and staggered against each other. Henry Dawson, his face tense and sullen, stood beside his brother. Mountain Horse remembered what Snake Child had said about Conrad watching Pretty Crow. Bringing the girl out in clear view of that one would not be wise, either. Sings Alone was a few paces behind the revellers, holding her blanket at her neck. Her eyes darted from one raucous caller to another.

Conrad, his green kerchief bright in the low afternoon

sun, tipped back a cup, emptied it, and then tore a mouthful of dripping meat from the chunk held in his other hand. His feet were wide apart and he swayed to keep his balance. Still his eyes scanned the group and when he saw Mountain Horse, he gave the first smile she had seen on his face, but it was a smile with no kindness. She shivered.

Henry Dawson stepped close to Big Plume and spoke slowly and carefully. "Thank you for this feast. We have eaten well because of your hospitality to us. Now, we will depart and remember your generosity."

"Your brother isn't ready to go yet," Big Plume responded. "He wants to trade a little more, don't you?"

"He's free to stay on if he wants. Conrad can catch up to us when he wishes." Henry did not look at his brother. He made small steps backward from Big Plume's lodges, as did Sings Alone, while he talked evenly, calmly, the way one would ease a frightened horse.

Conrad tipped his hat to Big Plume. "Let's go then," he said, and turned his kerchief to the side. "You know what I want." He staggered off along the edge of the trees.

Mountain Horse guessed another keg was hidden close by.

Henry Dawson and Sings Alone continued to step back from the group, and now turned in a brisk walk to the wagons. The drivers had never left the seats and sat with rifles across their laps. Henry indicated he would lead one pair of mules and Sings Alone the other, while the men kept watch.

Good, thought Mountain Horse. They'll move out quietly and not draw attention. This was her chance to leave as well. She motioned to Pretty Crow to come with her, but the girl refused. "I'll stay with White Feather for now, and we'll both come when it gets dark."

"Please come with me," Mountain Horse entreated. The knot in her stomach was hard as a steel ball.

"We'll make sure she gets back safely, Grandmother," assured Cloudy Woman. "There are many women in the lodge to watch for Pretty Crow's safety."

There are more people here in the Badger Lodge than in my own, Mountain Horse told herself. Cloudy Woman is Big Plume's mother; he will not allow this lodge to be violated. I need to get back to Snake Child. Her thoughts circled around the cold ball of foreboding. Carrying it with her, she left alone.

At the Otter Lodge, Snake Child lay asleep, arms around Sun Woman, the doll's tresses festooned with red ribbons. The fire was nearly out and Mountain Horse knelt to build it up with chips. She was restless. Don't let your thoughts run wild, old woman, she told herself. Take Snake Child and wait in the Wolf Lodge with Calf Shield and Yellow Star.

A woman's scream pierced the air from the east end of the camp, followed by screams of two, maybe three other women. Mountain Horse bolted from the lodge and began to run toward the Badger Lodge, only to nearly collide with White Feather running toward her.

"Grandmother," she gasped. Tears streamed on each cheek. "Grandmother, my brother, Big Plume, has taken Pretty Crow. He came into the lodge and grabbed her. My mother tried to stop him and he struck his fist into her belly. While we tried to help, he struck Pretty Crow and pulled her out."

Snake Child woke and began to cry also.

"White Feather," Mountain Horse held the girl at each shoulder. "Listen. Where did Big Plume take her? Where did he go?"

"I don't know. Beyond the camp. East, by the trees. It happened so fast."

"Stay with Snake Child. I will find her." Mountain Horse reached and took the new skinning knife she had brought from trading that afternoon. She flipped aside the entrance and heard, far in the distance, the wagons' wheels groaning, thought with relief that Sings Alone and the paleskins were speeding their departure.

Sun had lain down behind the mountains but the light was still strong. She was grateful that she could still see well enough to move through the edge of the trees unseen. She approached the Badger Lodge and – with shock – recognized Big Plume at the fire's edge. Where was Pretty Crow? Back inside? She darted to the entrance. No Pretty Crow. Cloudy Woman sat hunched over her legs and looked at Mountain Horse with shame and sorrow, eyes swollen and a trickle of blood at her nostril. The other women of the lodge huddled together with her, like beaten dogs. Mountain Horse edged out, back to the trees and watched. Had the girl gone back to the Otter Lodge without being seen? Mountain Horse did not think she could have.

Where was the green-kerchiefed one? The man's saddled horse stood tied to a tree. He had not gone.

Mountain Horse moved quickly through the shadow of the trees' border. An argument at the fire grew louder. She moved further east from the camp; the words grew fainter, but what was that noise ahead? Did she hear a moan?

The noise was closer. Grunts. A snarl. More grunts. Faster. Nearer.

There, in the grass, she saw him. Mountain Horse raised her knife and ran. Conrad rolled just as she struck, his green kerchief bright at his neck. The knife gouged his shoulder but did not drive clean between his shoulder blades as Mountain Horse intended.

"What in hell's blazes? Christ Almighty, you've knifed me!" Blood spurted from the wound.

She lifted the knife again, but he turned and staggered off, grasping his shoulder with one hand and holding up his pants with the injured arm.

"Pretty Crow, little one," Mountain Horse knelt beside the girl who lay on her back, face swollen and bloodied, brows tensed in pain. Her upper lip had swelled huge, blood trailed from both nostrils and the corner of her mouth. She was barely conscious. "Can you sit? You must. Try." Mountain Horse reached an arm under Pretty Crow's neck and lifted her. The girl groaned. "You must get up. We must get away from here."

Pretty Crow leaned away from Mountain Horse and spewed out acid and blood. She spit and moaned, but she crawled to her knees and reached for Mountain Horse's hand to pull herself up.

"Lean on me, Pretty Crow. We'll move along the trees so no one can see us. To the Otter Lodge. Only that far, my sweet one." Step by step they moved behind the lodges. The voices sounded distant now. All her attention was on the young woman who stumbled and staggered in small steps. It seemed forever before they reached the west end of the camp.

While she was gone, Calf Shield had ordered that his lodges were to be struck and loaded. White Feather and Snake Child had the travois ready.

Mountain Horse signalled to White Feather. "Get another horse, and I'll get a travois for Pretty Crow. Get the roan. Snake Child, put the chokecherry cakes into the bucket." While White Feather ran to where the herders gathered Calf Shield's horses, Mountain Horse brought a travois and set Pretty Crow on it. The girl lay on her side and drew her knees up. From the east end of the camp, yelling and arguing grew more intense.

A rifle shot cracked the air. A strange silence. A galloping horse. A man hollering. "What have you done? Big Plume, what have you done?" Was that One Spot? Where was Calf Shield? The Wolf Lodge was almost ready.

A woman wailed. "You killed him. He's dead."

Dear Sun, what has happened? Who has been shot? Women keening.

"Snake Child, put a blanket over Pretty Crow. White Feather, can you see what has happened?"

Someone ran toward them. One Spot. "Grandmother. It's Calf Shield. Big Plume has shot him." He ran on to the Wolf Lodge.

White Feather clasped her hands over her mouth. "No, he wouldn't. He couldn't."

Mountain Horse listened. Angry voices from the eastern edge of the camp. Hollering and confusion. Then in her mind came clarity, clean and cool, like a mountain lake. Like the small lake where the mountains rise up quickly. She understood exactly what she must do. "White Feather," she said.

"Get a horse for yourself. We ride to the Many Children's camp. It is not safe here. You can return later if you wish, when Shaggy Bull is back. One Spot will take care of Yellow Star. Snake Child, what are you doing? Oh, little one, you've remembered the pups. Tie them on. White Feather, ride behind Pretty Crow's travois. Snake Child, ride close beside me. Let's go."

SECTION TWO

Recognition

CHAPTER 7

THE GIRL LEANED from the train window, strands of hair flicking across her face. Inside, her parents gathered bags and cases, busying themselves with last-minute frets at the end of a long journey.

"Eleanor, close the window," her mother called. "Your hair is all a mess. You don't want to arrive looking like a ragamuffin."

"I'm trying to read the sign. I nearly can." She drew back and pushed the window up. "We've been cooped up for days and days."

Stephen, her father, laughed while he stacked three brown cases on the seat, checked their locks, and stood them upright at the compartment door. "You'll soon have plenty of chance to be outside. But as a proper young lady. You're fifteen now, my dear, and coming to the Best West, not the Wild West."

He was of medium height and angular, and his eyes, like his daughter's were the same gray-blue color as the sky.

Eleanor gathered her hair into a tidy bunch at the nape of her neck, then dropped it to press both hands against the window. "I can read it now. Medicine Hat. We're finally here."

Her mother, more slightly built, deftly smoothed Eleanor's wayward strands to a single neat mass and tied it firmly with dark green ribbon. "There now. Here's your hat. And bag and coat. Mind the sill. Don't rush, dear. We've plenty of time. The train is still moving."

Eleanor side-stepped awkwardly down the narrow aisle to the coach's door, banging her bag against the walls and tripping on her long, brown skirt. Half a dozen men waited before her at the exit.

In one exasperated huff, the train stopped and spewed bodies onto the wooden platform where they collected trunks and boxes from the baggage car. Some carried bundles wrapped in cloth and twine, a few only a bag. Amid laughter and choked-back tears, two men in baggy pants and shirts of coarse, tan cloth hurried to embrace a third who waited on the platform. A small man in a gray suit offered rides to the hotel. "The American Hotel. Finest in town. Mr. Rudyard Kipling stayed here on his visit two years ago." An older woman and a young man took his offer and, as the buggy drove away, a haze of dust rose and quickly moved east in the strong wind that blew outside the protection of the station. Almost as quickly as the dust, most of the passengers left. Those who stayed milled about or found a place to sit.

Eleanor spread her arms wide and turned in a circle where she stood. "No more stuffy train compartment."

"One more yet; just a short ride," her father said. "Help me push these two trunks against the station wall. We can put our cases on top and sit out of the wind while we wait. There. Now, help your mother watch the luggage while I go into town for fresh bread and meat."

She inhaled quickly to begin a plea to join her father, to see her first western town, but he interrupted before she could speak. "No, Eleanor. Your mother can't be here all alone."

Releasing her breath in a sigh, she slumped her shoulders and sank onto the bench where her mother already sat. Immediately she stood again. "I'm tired of sitting."

"But stay on the platform, dear. It's terribly dusty and windy. Your skirt will get soiled."

No one here would notice if my hair was blown about by wind, she thought, and no one would think me a ragamuffin for it. It's different here, just like Uncle Bernard said.

Uncle Bernard had been three times in the west and had filled her imagination with stories of buffalo, Indians, redcoats, and horse rustling. *And a sky that goes forever, girl. The only thing big enough to hold that sky is your own heart, once it opens to that country. Don't you forget your old uncle when you get into that wide prairie where the wind blows through everything. It will blow all the memories right out of your head if you're not careful.* She had laughed and laughed while he puffed his cheeks and blew, waving his hands above his gray hair as if to catch escaping thoughts. *I won't forget you ever, Uncle Bernard. I'll write, and you'll come and visit, won't you?*

"I hope you'll find other young ladies to be friends with here. Perhaps when school opens." Her mother's fingers clasped and unclasped in her lap. "Look to see if Father is coming, would you dear?"

Eleanor's sturdy laced shoes thumped on the wooden planks as she walked to the end of the platform. "Yes, I see him."

They ate fresh bread and salted pork and drank from clear glass bottles that said "Mooney's Perfection Cream Sodas" in black writing. Her father described the town: new banks and hotels of red brick, streets dry and dusty that must be a mess when it rains, livery and lumber stores, and a general store with everything you need for a homestead. "What they don't have they'll order."

"Why is it called Medicine Hat, Father?"

"It might be an Indian name. This was all their land at one time."

"Where are they now?" Eleanor looked from one end of the station to the other as if expecting a band of mounted hunters to ride up from the river and into their midst.

"They live on reserves now, not everywhere like they once did." Her father reached for another chunk of bread and meat that lay on oiled paper on the bench between them. "With the buffalo gone, their way of life went as well. Part of the duty of opening the west, some say, is to uplift the native from primitive ways. By staying on reserves, they learn to cultivate the soil and reap the rewards. Just like we'll be doing."

"Are all the buffalo gone?"

"Every last one of them."

Her mother stood to brush crumbs from her lap, wrapped the remaining food and tucked it into the corner of a satchel on top of the trunks. "Just as well, isn't it, Eleanor? We'll have enough to do without herds of buffalo running over our grain and bands of Indians chasing after them."

"Couldn't there be some left? We traveled so far and never saw a single person out on the prairie. There could be a few out there."

Her father also stood, brushing his shirt and pants, his dark jacket over his arm. Although they sat in the shade, the air was hot and dry. "Our train to Seven Persons will be here shortly, my two lovely ladies. Come, Catharine," he said, reaching his hand to his wife, "and Eleanor. We move one step closer to our new home in the Last Best West."

In late afternoon, when the small train on its narrow track slowed for their station, both Eleanor and Catharine leaned out the compartment window to watch its approach. "But there's hardly anything there at all," Catharine exclaimed and pulled back into the car. "It looks like a pile of boxes that tumbled from someone's wagon and got left behind. What have we come to, Stephen?"

"There, there, my dear. You're tired and hot after our long journey. This will look much better in the morning."

At the Seven Persons station, a tall man, graying at his temples, approached and helped them pull trunks and cases to the platform for the second time that day. "Bernard sent a letter asking if I could assist you when you arrived. How do you do? I'm your uncle's friend, Tom Barton."

He loaded their baggage into his wagon box. "Climb aboard and we're off to the hotel and one of the finest meals you'll find this side of the Rockies."

CHAPTER 8

DAWN GLOWED like a flat crease of orange in a dull gray world. Eleanor's nose twitched in the chill air. The wagon bench seated three only, so she lay wedged between a brown trunk and a wooden crate, propped against sacks of oats and flour.

Two black horses rolled metal bits around their mouths and snorted vaporous plumes as they stamped first one foot, then another. Horses, wagon, and contents had been purchased in Seven Persons the previous day as Mr. Barton advised her father on what he needed to begin a homestead.

Stephen patted the neck of the horse on the left. "Yes, yes, Charlie," he said and adjusted the buckle at the horse's wide collar. "You're anxious to be off. So am I. Very soon, big fellow. Very soon." He examined the harness of the right horse in the same way. "There's a girl, Belle. What a fine pair we've got. No oxen for us. Tom's a horse man, too, Catharine."

Charlie tossed his head over and over, his harness jangling an eager rhythm. Belle flicked her ears forward and back and noted each movement of the two men who made last-minute checks to horses, wagon, and load.

Eleanor's mother waited on the seat and drew a checkered wool blanket tighter around her shoulders. "Why do some people take oxen, Mr. Barton?"

"They're slower but stronger. You might need to hire a team to break your sod. Two oxen could do it alone but never two horses. Horses need proper feed. Oxen do fine on just grass, and they'll drink any water. For your team, you'll need water that's good and clear. But you can travel faster with horses, and you can ride them."

"That's it. We're ready," Stephen shouted and sprang onto the wagon to sit beside his wife. Tom Barton followed, took up the reins and flipped them. "Hee up. Let's go."

The horses leaned eagerly into the harness and the wagon lurched forward with a creaking, heaving roll.

Thrown back, Eleanor settled against their newly purchased tent to watch the view from behind. The town grew small and disappeared into the dark, flat grassland. The sky lightened quickly, and the few stars that had been visible faded like the town.

The day moved in and so did a steady wind from the west. A pair of coyotes rose from grass as the wagon passed beside them, lifting their thin noses in the air. They trotted east on feet that never quite touched the ground. One stopped to look back over its shoulder, staring right at Eleanor before it continued.

Uncle Bernard had talked about coyotes. *Like small dogs, but a lot smarter. Coyotes hate dogs.*

Why would they hate dogs?

They hate anything that's tame. You can't chain them or make pets out of them. They're like the Indians. Can't hold them to one place. People try. It doesn't work. They pine away.

I'd like to have a dog when we move out west.

Keep it away from the coyotes.

She wished Uncle Bernard had come west too, wished he was here now, leaning against the oat sacks. He would know the bird that sang in long, plaintive trills, fading on a note uplifting and yet full of sadness. He would know if those were hawks that circled above. He would know where all these piles of bones came from.

You can't imagine, my girl, how huge the herds were and how the ground trembled when they were on the move. He had waved his hand from one side to another and before her eyes a vision of a great mass of brown shaggy bodies arose, moving like ripples on water. *Imagine, girl, the dust rising up as they passed, the earth shaking, rumbling, and grumbling. I'm glad I was there to see it, Eleanor. It's a glory gone, never to return.*

Where did the buffalo go, Uncle Bernard?

Buffalo coats for fashion, machinery belts for factories. Strongest hides in the world.

Who killed them?

Everybody. White hunters shooting from trains and boats and wagons, just for the thrill of killing. Indians and halfbreeds, bringing loads of hides to trade for whiskey and guns to kill more for more whiskey. He had shaken his head, as if he still did not believe it. *A lot of buffalo died in a short time, girl.*

Eleanor pushed herself up and looked at another pile of bleached bones with blades of dry brown grass between the ribs.

"Are you all right back there, Eleanor?" her father hollered over his shoulder. She could barely make out the words over the rattle of the wagon and steady hum of the wind. She smiled and waved and leaned back again. The sun had climbed steadily and she removed her shawl, then her coat.

The blue of the sky was pale along the horizon. Above, it cleared to the color of forget-me-nots, covering her in a giant, blue bowl like the inside of her grandmother's teacup. Visiting her grandmother, drinking sweetened milk in the favorite cup, she had held it high, drained the milk, and gazed into blue. Until her mother spoke. "Do stop playing with your cup, Eleanor. Hold it properly, dear, and mind your manners." Her mother didn't understand being lost in blue. Here, she didn't need a cup to lose herself in it.

She woke when the wagon stopped.

"Time for lunch, tea, a stretch. Give the horses their oats." Mr. Barton gathered large, dried flakes. "Buffalo chips," he said. "Dried dung. Gives a hot, quick fire. We'll have tea brewing in no time."

They sat in the grass by the wagon, the wind light. Even so, it pulled a strand of brown hair from the coil at Catharine's neck. She tucked the wayward bits back but, before she had time to pick up her mug, wind coaxed the strands out again. This time she pushed them under the brim of her hat and pulled it down firmly. Wind darted back to pull out another wisp and wrap it across her face. "This wind is provoking a declaration of war," she scowled.

"Best to call it a truce right from the start, Mrs. Donaldson." Tom Barton offered, snapping a dried grass stem and chewing one end. "You never can beat the wind out here.

In the coulees you get a break from it. There's a coulee not far from your land. *Coulee* is the Blackfoot word for valley," he added and stood. "If we want to get to your land by evening, we'd best be going."

The land did not look like the poster Eleanor and her father had seen nailed to a slat fence in Aurora. "The Last Best West" it read. A tanned man in a white shirt smiled at them, sleeves rolled up, his hair the color of the fields of grain stacked in sheaves behind him. The fields stretched all the way to the blue mountains on the horizon.

"Doesn't that look grand, Eleanor?" her father had said. "Look at the space and all that wheat. People say the west is the last frontier, the land of opportunity."

Her mother hadn't thought so. "We've plenty of opportunity right here in Ontario, Stephen. You've got good prospects with Mr. Darby. He told you that. And your Uncle Bernard said there's always room in his business if you want to work there. Why would we want to go to the frontier?"

"I'm only going to the meeting, Catharine, just to hear what they have to say. Why don't you and Eleanor come too? Just to find out. We'll all hear what this free land is about and whether it is an opportunity or it isn't."

Eleanor looked out at the flat, dry grassland that stretched the same no matter which direction she looked. At the meeting, they had seen other posters that showed more fields of grain and faces of happy farmers. One had apple trees thick with red fruit, another a blue lake where boats, their white sails full, listed in a strong wind.

The speaker at the meeting, in his enthusiasm, had

shouted to the audience. "Look at this grain." He shook a fistful of wheat stalks above his head.

"Look at the size of these seeds. Does this appeal to you? Does having land to grow your own grain like this sound good? Acres of it? An invigorating climate? Does it appeal to you to be a part of a great enterprise? You can be part of opening the west. You can turn its land to good use, grow food to feed the hungry world. It's a glorious future that awaits the man who can grasp the vision, put his shoulder to the wheel of a great cause, and civilize the western lands. It's land for the taking, if you have what it takes."

Another skeleton lay in the grass. The sun passed overhead, drawn now to the western horizon.

When Mr. Barton stopped the horses and stepped out of the wagon to walk ahead, Eleanor sat up on her knees and watched as he moved slowly and swept his eyes carefully over the ground, left to right, as if seeking a lost coin. With her parents, she sat on the wagon in quiet anticipation. Only Belle and Charlie dared, with rhythmic munching of dried grass, to disturb his quiet concentration.

"And here it is, Stephen." Mr. Barton knelt at a small white peg and pressed the grass at its base flat, leaning close to examine black numbers and letters on one side. "This is the northeast corner of your homestead."

Her father bounded to look carefully at the peg himself. He shook Mr. Barton's hand vigorously. "We're terribly grateful for your skill, Tom. We could never have found our land without your help." He reached one arm around Eleanor and the other around Catharine. "And now we are here, my dears. There is our land before us. Tomorrow we will walk its boundary while we still have our fine guide to lead us."

By the time the western sky shone like dark turquoise glass whose color bled to deep blue above, the tent stood and glowed softly, illumined by the oil lamp inside. Catharine's body was a brown shadow on the tent walls moving back and forth as she removed blankets and quilts from the trunk. Belle and Charlie munched invisibly in the darkness, tethered in the grass beyond the wagon where Mr. Barton had laid out his own bedroll.

He and Stephen lingered beside a small fire, its remains glowing dull red, and the low tones of their conversation reached Eleanor, who had walked a short way from the camp. Looking back now, she saw a small bit of light surrounded by darkness. No other light interrupted the vast space.

But one more light appeared and suddenly, as she looked up, a multitude. All the light missing from the land was scattered high from one horizon to the other. She gasped. She had never seen a sky like this, never seen stars in such brilliance, glittering like gems pressed into a dark bowl.

Eleanor lay down on her back. Brittle stems of grass poked through her blouse and shawl to prick her skin, but she hardly noticed. The vibrant, jewel-studded expanse enveloped her. Even the space between the stars shimmered and hinted at stars beyond the reach of her eyes.

How can it be that I have never seen the stars like this? she asked silently. How did I not know of such brilliance, that there are so many, that they reach so close to the earth? We have come all this long distance, through great empty space, to find this piece of land. But really, it was to find this sky.

The distance they had come was as nothing compared to the hugeness of space above her.

Back in Aurora she had seen stars, had stood on the wide porch and gazed up in wonder, had reveled in the joy of recognizing the Big Dipper and wishing on the first star of the evening sky.

But that was not this sky. This is where the stars are truly themselves, she thought. This is where they reveal what they are. Here, in this great and empty land. This is where I will also be truly myself.

What she could not understand was how these stars that shone above her in a brilliance she had never seen could appear to her now as something she recognized, something familiar. Something she had longed for without even knowing that she longed for it. The feeling of having come home filled her, as surely as it had when her father, on their return from a long day away, carried her half asleep to her bed, and her mother leaned over to kiss her forehead and whisper, "Sleep well, my darling." The same feeling, here on hard ground, cool and prickly against her back, where she had never been before. She felt at home. I belong here, as surely as I once belonged in the warm bed of the white house. These stars above are lighting the sky in welcome, to celebrate my homecoming. Like a birthday party. Her eyes were closed by the time her smile settled on her face.

"Here she is, Catharine." Her father's voice woke her. "Fallen asleep in the grass. Come on, my dear." He reached his hand to help her up. "You're exhausted with all this travel and excitement. Your bed is waiting for you inside the tent."

CHAPTER 9

"THOSE HILLS to the south, those are the Sweetgrass Hills. And do you see that tiny bump to the southeast?"

Eleanor followed the invisible line from Mr. Barton's finger to the horizon. "I see it. Is it a big rock?"

"It's a big mountain," he answered. "Chief Mountain. A holy place to the Indians." He dropped his hand and kept his eyes where he had pointed. "That's where the Rocky Mountains begin."

"How can a mountain be holy?" Eleanor asked.

"They have different ways." Mr. Barton leaned over to pluck a small pink flower from the grass and handed it to Eleanor. "Cranesbill, that's called. These places, Chief Mountain, Sweetgrass Hills, they were to the Indians like a church is to the white man. You only see the Chief now and then, usually in the early morning. They are good landmarks to find your way."

They walked together through night-chilled air, guided along the eastern boundary by Barton's skill.

"How do you find your way over this land, Mr. Barton?" Eleanor's mother asked.

"After awhile, you begin to see how it changes place to place. I worked with the survey crew who set out the posts through this land." He stopped again and turned right. "This is your southern boundary. Now, we walk west. If we'd kept on that way," and he pointed south where they had been walking, "we'd come to the coulee rim. Can't even tell it's there, can you?"

Eleanor stared but could find no clue that the land dipped down, that there was anything other than its level, brown flatness. This was how Uncle Bernard told her it would be.

"You've a lot of work ahead before the cold weather," Mr. Barton continued, "if you plan to live here the winter." He led them westward on the southern boundary. "You could stay in town, of course. But you aren't alone. The settlers already here will help with what you need to know. There's a family west of here, the Wagners, that you'll find to be wonderful neighbors."

He resumed his walk and turned north after a few paces. "This is the west boundary, and that ahead is the sky you'll watch for signs of blizzards. When you see it dark black, right to the ground, get inside, get the animals inside, and plan to stay there till it passes."

"Inside a tent?" Catharine stared at the clear blue of the north horizon, then to the white canvas tent, like a single whitecap on a brown, quiet sea.

Tom Barton laughed. "Sorry, Mrs. Donaldson. You'll

have your shelter built long before the blizzards come. The best house is sod. You'll lose too much time if you wait for lumber to build a wooden one this year. And you'll want to turn over as much sod as you can this fall, as it's better for planting if the ground rests open till spring."

As they walked the full boundary, Mr. Barton continued with bits of advice. "For water, dig down. It's not far below ground. Get old Ted Durham to witch it for you. To keep warm, you can get coal along the coulee. Get a load delivered before the snow comes."

They drove Mr. Barton to where he could meet the mail wagon going back to Seven Persons. It felt like the hardest good-bye of their whole journey west. They rode back in silence, the quiet broken only when Catharine blurted, "Surely, Stephen, we are not going to live in a house made of dirt?"

CHAPTER 10

ON THE MORNING the Wagners were to arrive to begin turning sod, Eleanor stepped outside to a thick glittering frost covering her world. Each blade of grass, the wagon, the tent, and the boxes and planks along its sides, glistened in a white coat.

"Oh, do come and see," she called. "Everything looks like sugar candies." Belle and Charlie exhaled steamy plumes, and Eleanor's own exclamations were smoke-like puffs that quickly faded in the crisp air. "It's all so clear and bright, but brrr it's cold. Here they come. I see the Wagners."

To the west, dust and steam rose in pillars of golden light, illumined by the sun just risen over the horizon. Gradually, the dark shape of horses emerged with jangling harnesses and a rattling wagon, soon joined by the thudding, like a chorus of bass drums, of twenty-four hooves pounding toward the tent.

Eleanor faced the advancing team, her heart in her throat at the beauty of the morning's scene. The sun warmed her back and, at the same time, dissolved the spell of the frost, except where shade kept its warmth at bay. Her silvery shadow reached westward over the grass in front of her, toward the magical vision that approached.

Three days earlier, Stephen had returned full of enthusiasm from his visit to the Wagners. "George Wagner hires out with his team of six horses. He'll come the day after tomorrow to begin breaking sod."

Catharine had looked intently at the tea inside her blue mug and exhaled slowly. The three of them sat on overturned boxes in front of the tent entrance. A wide plank with each end set on a bucket made a table where a plate of biscuits sat.

"A sod house," Stephen had explained as he reached for another biscuit, "is warm in winter, cool in summer, and costs next to nothing. The Wagners lived in one a whole year."

The wagon was close now. Eleanor stared at the two men on its seat. The driver looked her father's age, with a thick neck and wide shoulders, his face broad and arms large. Beside him sat a younger man, a son in a smaller, leaner version of his father. Both wore loose shirts, blue suspenders, and broad-brimmed hats. The younger man looked directly at her with a wide grin.

"Whoa up there, easy now," the driver coaxed. Steam wafted from the horses' sweaty necks and their rich, thick scent blended with that of damp dust. Eleanor had been holding her breath and suddenly exhaled to breathe deeply the earthy horse scent.

In a flurry of greetings and introductions, a woman, two

girls, and another young man rose in the back of the wagon and jumped to the ground at the same time as the two in front: George Wagner, his son Adam, nephew Carl, wife Ada, and daughters Hattie and Lydia.

The men immediately clambered back onto the wagon to head the team to the southeast corner. "It lies lower there," George explained while passing four large baskets from the wagon box to Ada, "and holds the water longer. That's where the best sod will be."

Ada, nearly as tall and broad as her husband, had light brown hair knotted on top of her head. Ruddy cheeks and wide-set dark eyes filled her face. "We've brought dinner fixings, Mrs. Donaldson. May I call you Catharine? Do please call me Ada." Her voice boomed like her husband's and filled the tent site. "Lydia and Hattie are going to show Eleanor where to find coal at the coulee." She pulled burlap sacks from one of the baskets and handed each girl a bag. "Off you go now."

And off they went. Hattie, golden hair loose and bouncing, skipped ahead. About twelve, Eleanor guessed, and her sister is probably my age. Lydia, tall and broad like her parents, walked beside Eleanor. Their long brown dresses swished with each stride.

The silence was awkward at first, but they soon exchanged bits of introductions that warmed to easy conversation, the way the rising sun warmed the air.

"The coal is all through the coulee walls. There's a man who digs it and sells it by the wagonload. But anyone can gather the chunks," Lydia explained.

"I'll show you some tipi circles," Hattie offered. "They're

close to where we get the coal, over there." She pointed as they reached the edge.

The coulee opened miraculously, sandy banks dipping in folds and troughs to a narrow, irregular bottom, green with thick grass and brush.

"Mother wants us to come straight back with the coal so we can heat the stove for dinner, Hattie," Lydia said.

"It will only take a moment." Hattie strode purposefully west along the coulee rim. Eleanor, then Lydia, followed.

What had Uncle Bernard said about the coulees? *There are whole other possibilities, my girl, that lie unseen just a moment before, and then lay out before you.* Eleanor breathed deeply and scanned the coulee bottom. What mysteries might hide there?

"Here they are," Hattie shouted triumphantly. Rocks mottled with rust and black lichen, shaped like round loaves ready for the oven, formed a circle, and another, and another along the coulee's edge.

"But what are they?" Eleanor gasped.

Hattie skipped around the circles. "It's where the Indians had their tipis and put the stones around the edges to hold the sides down."

"They camped right here?" Eleanor looked along the coulee to the flat grassland beyond it and the mounds of the Sweetgrass Hills, hazy and gray on the horizon. Here Indians stood and saw the same view, felt the wind blow against their cheeks as she did now, smelled the pungent grass crushed by their feet, watched the flicker of poplar leaves along the margins of the bottom land. Maybe they had seen buffalo here, huge herds the way Uncle Bernard had described them.

"You're not supposed to step inside the circles, Hattie, it's bad luck." Lydia scowled as her sister jumped back and forth over the rock border, first on one leg then the other.

"Have you ever seen Indians here?" Eleanor asked.

"Only in town sometimes," Lydia answered. "We're not to go near them. They're dirty and have lice."

"Last time," Hattie added, "an old Indian woman with a striped blanket and no teeth laughed and pointed at my hair. Indians don't have yellow hair. I gave her rock candy."

"You're not supposed to, Hattie." Lydia turned and angled down the coulee wall, while Hattie stuck out her tongue at her sister's back. "We can get to the bottom along here and pick up coal. It's time we went back."

Eleanor and Hattie lingered. "I would like to see the tipis standing and all the horses," Eleanor said, "Wouldn't it be wonderful to gallop over these fields with the wind blowing through your hair?"

"It would be," Hattie chimed.

They followed Lydia, who waited a few steps on. "I wouldn't like that at all," she said. "It would be uncivilized."

The coal gave sustained heat and, under Ada's direction, produced a well-cooked meal. The men returned to roasted chicken, potatoes, and shiny bread rolls that filled the tent with yeasty aroma.

"It's wonderful how the plough cuts through the sod, Catharine." Stephen reached for the plate of chicken and passed it to George. Adam and Carl sat on the ground, plates in one hand, and an overturned basin in front. There were not enough plates for everyone to eat together. The women waited.

"Let the men finish and get back to their work," Ada advised when they carried out the meal. "Then we can take our time." She spoke with the confidence of someone sure of what she knew and eager to convey as much as she could in the time available.

"I have a china teapot wrapped in my winter coat in the black trunk," Catharine said as Ada boiled water in the blue enamel pot bought in Seven Persons. "Eleanor, would you get it?"

"Don't bring out the special china, Eleanor," Ada called back and dropped the tea into the steaming pot as she set it at the back of the stove. "With these men about, Catharine, it'd likely as not get broken."

Catharine's jaw tightened, and Eleanor closed the trunk.

When Eleanor's father was last in Seven Persons he bought ten enamel mugs. Now, they all sipped at the hot metal edges. Adam was the dark-haired son who had smiled from the wagon seat. Carl, smaller built, with sandy-colored hair, was George and Ada's nephew.

Hattie moved to sit beside her brother. "I showed Eleanor the tipi rings. There's lots of coal pieces at the bottom of the coulee. Jacob Pacey isn't there right now." She chattered and Adam watched Eleanor. She felt awkward and unsure where to look.

"Did you see any snakes?" Adam asked Hattie.

"You're just saying that to scare Eleanor, Adam." Hattie moved to sit beside Carl.

"No, I'm not," Adam protested. "Hasn't anyone told you about the rattlesnakes?" He looked directly at Eleanor.

But it was Catharine who leaned forward and fixed her eyes on Adam. "What do we need to know about rattlesnakes?"

"There are lots of them," Ada answered for her son as she reached for the tea and refilled her mug. "But the ones you find in this country are surprisingly shy. They'd rather slither away down a hole than hang around where people are. Listen for their rattle – that's their warning. Watch where you step. They won't bother you if you're careful."

Catharine's body shivered, like the surface of a pond when a quick breeze darts across it.

"They won't bother you unless you're Billy Widdop and you bother them." Adam laughed as he said this, invoking the same from George and Ada.

"Billy Widdop is an idiot," said George. "And now, Adam, you have to fill in our neighbors with the story, since you brought it up."

"Don't, it's horrible," shouted Hattie.

Adam continued. "Billy Widdop worked for the Spencer Ranch, south of here. He had a favorite game where he'd grab the tail of a snake just as it went into its hole and couldn't turn its head around." Adam popped the last bite of bread into his mouth, chewed quickly, and went on. "He'd crack it quick, like a whip, and send the snake's head flying right off. He was real good with his bull whip and knew just how to flick the snake."

Hattie put her hands over her ears.

"But one time," Adam paused, staring at Eleanor, "Billy was slow. Or the snake was too fast. It whipped around and grabbed his thumb. Whole hand swelled up like a rock. He was sick for days."

George laughed anew. "Billy doesn't play that game anymore."

Eleanor's stomach churned at the image of snake heads flying through the air.

Adam went on. "Sometimes when we're ploughing, especially this time of year, when it starts getting cold, we'll overturn a den of them, all twisting and slithering. Turns your insides around for sure." Adam wove his fingers and wrists in the air to conjure the picture of the ball of coiling serpents. "We just throw coal oil on the bunch and set fire to it."

"That's horrible, Adam." Hattie stood up and stomped to face her father. "You don't do that do you?"

Lydia spoke up. "Well we can hardly leave them there, can we, Hattie? You don't want a bunch of snakes for neighbors, do you?"

Hattie held her gaze on her father, who did not look his daughter in the eye. "We do that sometimes, dear. There just isn't room for them and us too."

"But you won't do that, will you father?" Eleanor asked Stephen, who shared with Carl a grimace of discomfort and the awkwardness of not knowing how to respond.

"Let's hope we don't find any, my dear."

"This is not talk for a pleasant meal." Ada's voice thundered. "You men, off you go and let us have our turn to eat in peace – and with agreeable conversation."

Eleanor had no appetite. Uncle Bernard had told a snake story. *A man named Calf Shirt was given the power of rattlesnakes, my girl. Said he met the snake god in a vision in one of their ceremonies, and didn't it tell him he never had to fear a snake again. He carried snakes in his shirt, his pockets, hanging around his neck. They never hurt him.*

How could anyone do that, Uncle Bernard?

I saw it myself, girl, and I saw, too, what happened to a trader who thought the snakes were drugged and couldn't bite. He reached to grab one. Quick as lightning didn't it lash out and bite him. And didn't Calf Shirt just stroke that snake's head and talk to it all soft, then put it inside his shirt and walk away, while someone else rode for a doctor. The Indians will tell you snakes are powerful, my girl. Don't look funny at me like that. There's a lot we don't know about animals, and one thing for sure, the Indians know a lot more than we do.

That night, a terrible scream woke Eleanor, a high drawn-out howl. Her heart pounded against her chest like a fist. Though she opened and closed her eyes, she could detect no difference in the blackness. Had she dreamed that sound? Had it been a nightmare?

The pounding in her chest eased. Her breath came slower and deeper. A drowsy warmth came over her and Eleanor felt the numbness of approaching sleep returning when another scream shattered the silence. A third high, prolonged wail answered it.

"My God, Stephen, what is that?" Catharine whispered loudly from the other side of the blanket that divided their sleeping areas.

This is no dream, then, Eleanor realized. A chorus of howls, yips, yodels, and sounds she could not name erupted from all around the tent. We are surrounded, she told herself. There is no escape. Her mouth was dry and her breath caught in the back of her throat. Charlie whinnied and stamped. Belle snorted and nickered a soft snuffle.

"Stephen," her mother said again, louder this time. "What in God's name is making that sound?"

"I'm not sure, my dear." His voice was flat and low. "I'm wondering if it could be coyotes. I'd think it was wolves, but there are none left on the prairie." Silence again.

"Eleanor?" her mother whispered.

She did not answer. A cold weight pressed on her. Hearing her father say that coyotes made the sound brought a new awareness – a sense of their presence all around her, here in the dark, far from any other humans. They came to waken her, to make sure she knew that they, the coyotes, were the ones who understood the great power that ruled this land. They wanted her to know she knew nothing at all of its immensity and strength.

Another series of yips and howls resonated in the pit of her stomach. Silence again. I should answer my mother. But she did not.

"She is sleeping right through all this racket," her father whispered, his voice regaining some of its fullness. "It's a miracle how the young can sleep so soundly. I'm exhausted from our first day of breaking sod, yet I'm wide awake." The yipping began again, further away now, more clearly an animal sound. "Yes, I'm sure it's a coyote. Bernard once mentioned they give blood-curdling howls. I guess we've heard what he was talking about."

"Are the horses safe?" Catharine asked.

"They're fine. Wolves would be a problem. Coyotes would be no match for Belle and Charlie's feet. Makes me glad, nonetheless, that we'll soon have a sturdier shelter for the horses and for us."

Eleanor shuddered and turned on her side, curled her knees to her chest, pulled the blankets nearly over her head. The cold ball in the center of her belly gradually dissolved, but she could not rid herself of the feeling that the coyotes had come to howl at her. Where the stars had recognized and welcomed her, these tortured howls carried no pleasure in their greeting.

SECTION THREE

Confusion

Buffalo lay in the brown grass, half-dreaming in the luxury of late autumn sun. Close by on the hillside lay Wolf, her eyes narrowed with the pleasure of the afternoon. They looked below where River meandered like a green and blue snake, with Sky reflected on her surface and lush shrubs growing thick along her banks. Across the valley, where the hills rose again, aspen clumps had turned all at once to luminous gold and spilled leaves down the hillside, like liquid hardened in its flow.

Small, dark shapes grazed casually over the flat grass-land. Beyond, near a thicket of willow, wolf pups scampered and tumbled under the watchful eyes of the pack. Even WindMaker rested in the peace of the day.

Buffalo turned his great head to view the northern horizon and swept his gaze slowly down the valley to the dusty, deep-blue southern edge. *Our time is nearly done, Wolf. Our winter comes soon.*

Hawk cried a piercing call and floated in wide circles above them.

Wolf opened her eyes. *You and I, old friend, such a long time we have played out the story together.* She lay on her side and stretched her legs, then rolled up again and moved her head, like Buffalo had done, to take in the great expanse of land that lay before them.

Napi has another story in mind now, said Buffalo.

We are all in Napi's dance, old friend. We move and act out the parts given us. When Old Man says, 'No more,' we howl and bellow our lament, we struggle to extend our time of glory as long as we can, for that is the way given us to carry out our part. But when Napi sweeps his great hand to remove this bit of play, our story will go, the way a child builds a camp of mud in the sand by the river and sweeps it away with one playful gesture. Yes, this part in its beauty is nearly done.

Yet we never know what story Napi builds next, do we Wolf? Buffalo looked over to Wolf, who stood, shook herself, and sat back on her haunches. Buffalo spoke again. *Like Raven's feather, blowing this way and that on WindMaker's breath, where our story ends we do not know. He is one for capricious play.* Buffalo stood as well and shook his mighty brown body, sending a cloud of dust into the air. The motes glistened and sparked as they drifted, with no hint they would ever fall to earth.

We may dance again, Buffalo. That Napi always has surprises. Whatever play he gives us, my friend, let us take our roles and play them well, worthy of what we have been given, in honor of that trickster who bids us dance and sing his song to the last breath.

Let us, Wolf.

The two walked slowly, some distance apart but close in friendship and understanding, down the hillside to the land below.

◇◇◇◇◇◇◇◇◇◇◇◇◇◇◇◇◇◇◇

CHAPTER 11

DENSE, DARK CLOUDS captured the northern sky by late afternoon, followed by sharp, piercing cold. Horses sought shelter in hollows and among trees; dogs curled around themselves. The storm arrived with howling wind, and racing just behind, eager to outdistance it, the hard pellets of nipping snow.

Snake Child leaned into the fury, head down, blanket-shrouded, and hurriedly ducked into the Otter Lodge. Inside, poles moaned, lodge walls shivered, and the fire seemed weakened in the onslaught. The girl's arms clutched a makeshift sack of buffalo chips beneath the blanket and she released them to tumble in a pile next to a mound of dry branches. "It's so cold, Grandmother. I hope this is enough to last out the storm." The lodge was thick with the scent of stewing meat, and she felt suddenly hungry.

"We'll be warm." Mountain Horse poked the coals and

moved the stew pot closer to them. "A small lodge is good. Easy to move, easy to heat. Hand me some chips and we'll get this blaze strong." The cakes of dried dung burned hot and clean. The stew bubbled quickly. "Anyway, this storm won't last. Too early. ColdMaker's warning us to get ready."

"I wish we didn't have winter at all," Snake Child said. The cold, dark time was only starting. Not a good time to leave their people of the Black Elks and begin with a new camp, even if it was the band of Mountain Horse's youth. They were still strangers.

"Then the lessons of winter would be lost to us. Great teachings come from the north, little one. Uncomfortable ones, sometimes. Hold your bowls out, all of you. This meat's ready." She ladled a mass of steaming brown stew into Snake Child's dish, and then White Feather's, who sat opposite. "Pretty Crow, hold out your bowl. You need food to keep warm."

Pretty Crow stared into the fire and gave no response. Folds of blanket were layered at her neck; she looked frail under the thick, gray wool. Snake Child moved close, picked up Pretty Crow's dish to be filled, and handed it to the young woman, touching her knee to get her attention. Pretty Crow looked at the bowl with vacant eyes, as if she didn't recognize what it was. She took it slowly, glanced up at the girl and nodded. Her left eye was discolored and swollen, although much improved from a week earlier when only a thin slit showed between puffed lids. Her nose was thick along the center, where it used to be thin and smooth, but this too was less than previous days, as was the swelling of her mouth. The cut across the top of her lip had scabbed over. Still, when she did eat, the movement was awkward, and she frequently winced.

"First her body will heal," Mountain Horse had told Snake Child just the day before, when the girl commented that Pretty Crow hardly answered when someone spoke to her. "Then her mind and spirit. Be patient."

Snake Child held her own bowl and breathed the rich aroma deeply. She hungered, yes, but it was for more than this stew. Everything had gone wrong since last summer when the Black Stone was stolen. After that, Grandmother sat quiet for long periods, brows pinched together. Arguments erupted frequently in the camp. Calf Shield, dead. Running away in the night, angry yelling all around. Now, a new camp where she did not feel at home, could not run to a nearby lodge and enter with ease and welcome, did not know her place when they gathered in another tent. This storm, too early and too fierce, made the poles groan strangely and the walls flap and thump in the wind. Nothing felt right. Pretty Crow bruised, cut, and damaged. White Feather longing for her family.

From the moment they fled to find the Many Children's band, Mountain Horse had tended Pretty Crow, showing Snake Child the plants to gather and chew, how to spread the pulp against swollen and bruised wounds. They had stopped at a narrow, twisting creek and undressed Pretty Crow, helped her sit in the chilly water and gently washed her. In the warm sun, they dried her body with soft buckskin and dressed her in fresh garments. Pretty Crow then slept, curled on the travois, covered in blankets.

Now in camp, one of them stayed near Pretty Crow

constantly, as they took turns gathering wood and chips, searching for the plants that Mountain Horse requested, and placing soaked buckskin on Pretty Crow's forehead.

By the following day, the snow had stopped, and the clouds moved on to harass the land further south. The autumn sun, once it climbed overhead, had warmth enough to melt what lay on the ground, except for patches that clung to shadows.

Snake Child sat on a rock outcrop above the camp, her arms around drawn-up knees. The sandy dog and her pups had followed her, also unsure of their place in camp and cautious around other dogs. The girl gathered red leathery berries, chewed them one by one, sorting seeds from pulp and spitting them out in clusters.

The lake near the camp was more like a catch of spring meltwater, so small it was. From her perch, it reflected bright blue sky and appeared like a hole in the land. I could go to the edge and look through at the sky, she thought, like the woman who married a star and pulled up turnips in order to look down at the earth.

The short cottonwoods clustered in small groups over the grassland, quickly turning gold with the cold, as if in a hurry to age. Closer to the mountains, dark fir and pine stood in a thick mass, quite sure of their decision to be a forest. Eastward, the open prairie permitted trees only in the coulees and along the river. But here, the land was neither forest nor prairie, as if it couldn't make up its mind.

Northward, the grassland rolled in gentle humps all the way to the Black Elks camp. Snake Child was the first to see the rider coming from that direction and recognized him immediately. One Spot had a lanky sorrel with a peculiar gait – a stretched-out neck and arched tail – so he looked about to run even when he walked. Two horses followed on lead ropes. She ran to camp with word of his coming.

They met him just as he reached the edge of the lodges, Mountain Horse breathless. "What news have you, nephew?"

"You were wise to flee, Grandmother. My news is not good." His shoulders slumped as if he carried an invisible weight. Always good-natured, quick to humor and a joke, sorrow now masked him.

Curious dogs and people had joined them, including Spotted Horse, chief of the Many Children. "Come to my lodge. We will smoke and hear your news."

Inside Spotted Horse's Black Bear Lodge, Snake Child sat close between Mountain Horse and White Feather. The lodge was like Calf Shield's, but she did not know the people and felt awkward. With One Spot here, taking the pipe from Spotted Horse, her longing for the Black Elks swelled in her chest.

One Spot began the story of the days after they had fled. "As you know, Calf Shield, chief of the Black Elks, died from a bullet in the chest, shot by a drunk and angry Big Plume, who betrayed the promise to bring no whiskey into the camp as we traded." One Spot paused, breathed deeply, and continued. "I ran with word to the lodges of Calf Shield's family and found them packed to leave. We brought his body and carried it on a travois and rode to the west, away from the anger and sadness in camp."

The young man kept his gaze to the fire, hardly visible in the late afternoon light and nearly burned to nothing but white ash. "I returned to the camp in the morning and found many injured from further fighting during the night. Then, as shame arose, voices blamed the traders to ease their own remorse. Eight warriors rode out and returned with horses, mules, the goods we traded, and four scalps."

Snake Child leaned closer and linked her arm through the old woman's, who had covered her face with her hand. "Whose scalp did not come back?" the girl blurted.

"The one with the green kerchief. The one who broke the promise and deserved to die."

Snake Child's body numbed. She saw the red ribbons at the end of each braid hanging over her chest and with it saw the image of Sings Alone offering the red strands, glistening in the light, as her husband laughed beside her. Why did these two die when the only one who should have, the one responsible for the horror to Pretty Crow and the death of Calf Shield, was spared?

One Spot continued. "Two days later, Shaggy Bull and Prairie Owl returned, disgusted to find what had happened. Prairie Owl rode to find his family's lodges and found that his father had been laid within his own lodge that was set in view of Chief Mountain. The walls had been secured with stones and the entrance stitched shut. Yet Prairie Owl cut the stitches in order to see his father once more, where his war shield and spear, rifles, knives, beaded shirts, and parfleche surrounded him. Prairie Owl then slashed the throat of Calf Shield's big painted horse and stretched it out in front of the lodge while Yellow Star sewed the entrance shut again."

One Spot brushed away the hair that hung over his right eye. Legs shifted, blankets adjusted, throats cleared, while overhead the cry of high geese called farewell and pulled the hearts of those below who ached to follow their freedom.

"There is more sorrow in this tale. The next days were full of tension. Prairie Owl demanded amends from Big Plume as he recovered in his lodge from injuries in the brawl of that night of drunkenness. Big Plume at last sent ten horses, hides for three lodges, and rifles. Prairie Owl accepted. But the question of which direction the Black Elks would go to trade, and who would lead them, remained.

"The Hudson Bay men refused the offer to meet further south. Shaggy Bull then advised that we ride to join our Blackfoot brothers in the north and ride to Fort Edmonton together. That way, both tribes could protect each other, and they would also be together for the war council. Shaggy Bull announced this as if he already was the next leader of the Black Elks.

"This was an insult to Prairie Owl, for Calf Shield had made it clear that his son was his choice to be next chief. But Prairie Owl spent the next days offering meat and smoke, talking of his father's great deeds, his kindness, and his wisdom as a leader. I was there in his lodge at this time, for Calf Shield was like a father to me. I hoped Prairie Owl would take his role."

Snake Child shivered, although the air was mild. A child cried in one of the lodges, and horses crunched grass nearby. The regular breathing of listeners filled the air inside the lodge, warm and thick with the scent of bodies.

"And then a strange thing happened," One Spot continued. "As we sat within, we heard the steps of someone walking close around us. Prairie Owl jumped up to see who spied on our conversation, but Yellow Star said, 'No, my son. Do not go outside. You are hearing the footsteps of a ghost.'"

Snake Child pressed her body against Mountain Horse and held the woman's arm with both her own.

"The dogs whined and barked. Soon the footsteps were so close we could hear breathing. Prairie Owl whispered to his mother, 'How can you know it is a ghost?' Yellow Star answered him." One Spot lowered his voice to a whisper. "She said, 'Do you think after all these years I do not know the sound of my own husband's footsteps?'

"This brought confusion in the lodge. Why had Calf Shield not gone to the Sand Hills? Yellow Star then said, 'I will speak with the ghost.' Outside we could hear her voice but could not understand what she spoke. Then she called to us. 'My people, my children and sisters, my grandchildren – I love you but I must leave and go with Calf Shield on his journey to the Sand Hills. He sends this message. Do not follow Shaggy Bull when he rides north. Stay within the Grandmother's land for the winter. Farewell.'

"We heard the sound of two people walking to the east in that night. We listened without breathing until we could hear no more."

Within the Black Bear lodge, no one dared to breathe.

"We stayed together in the lodge that night," One Spot continued. "In the morning, all the camp packed up. Prairie Owl rode first, to the southeast and Shaggy Bull rode northward. One by one, families chose which man they would have for a leader.

"Shaggy Bull rode only a short distance when he gave a great cry. Before him in the grass, Yellow Star lay dead. Many saw this as a bad omen and decided to follow Prairie Owl, even though they had moved into the line of Shaggy Bull's lead earlier.

"The women set Yellow Star's body in a cottonwood tree near the Wolf Lodge. I saw the Black Elks divided and I rode south alone with a troubled heart, wishing to be far away from this sorrow. With the horses earned in my service to Calf Shield, I rode here to the Many Children, as Grandmother had done."

"Did my father ask about me?" said White Feather.

"Yes, but no one could tell him where you had gone."

"Did he send scouts to find me?"

"If so, I did not know of it." One Spot then sat quietly, his story finished. He nodded assent when Spotted Horse welcomed him to join the young men of his lodges as a herder and scout.

That night, as flames warmed the Otter Lodge and lit it golden, they told One Spot's story to Pretty Crow and lay together in the dark, comforting each other in their sorrow.

CHAPTER 12

SNAKE CHILD LAY on the crest of a ridge, arms crossed, chin on her forearms. Below, dark clusters of buffalo grazed on thick, dried grass of early winter. To her left, at the base of the ridge, four young wolf pups of this spring's litter romped and chased each other. Two grays, a black, and one – a curiosity – white. This one grabbed the tail of a gray, who yelped and turned to attack. The white gamboled away, the gray clumsily chasing on its heels until it caught up, and the two rolled over each other in a confusion of legs and snarls. They tumbled down a narrow incline, scrambled to their feet, and began the play again.

Snake Child had discovered the wolves ten days earlier and had come each day since to watch them from the ridge, a long rocky outcrop that ran north-south and sheltered the lee side where the grasses thickened, protected from the wind.

Dusty green wolf willow and shiny alder bunched along its base and made ideal protection for the pups. In the thickets, close to where they played, Snake Child knew a den was hollowed out where the young ones slept or took refuge from threat of weather or creature. She had not been able to locate its hiding place.

The white pup reminded her of a rabbit in early spring when it is easily spotted, out of place in a snow-free landscape. But in winter, Snake Child thought, that white pup will move as unseen as the rabbit when it leaves footprints from an almost invisible body.

As she watched from the ridge, riders appeared, small dark spots to the southeast, heading in the direction of camp. She squinted but could not tell who they were, visitors or ones from the Many Children band. She stood and turned toward the camp herself.

At the Otter Lodge, the pups greeted her by jumping in the air and running in circles while their mother wagged her tail vigorously. Snake Child left the dogs in camp when she went to watch the wolves. The yellow learned quickly to not follow when the girl turned and stared and stamped her foot. The pups tried longer but eventually gave up and remained with their mother. Only the small black and white one resisted Snake Child's attempts to keep her back and followed the girl farther each time.

"That one's your little shadow," Mountain Horse said and the name stuck. Now Shadow hung at Snake Child's left leg as she entered camp.

The riders were hunters from the Many Children, returning after several days to the east. They came with bad news.

Later, in the Otter Lodge, Snake Child sat motionless with White Feather and Pretty Crow as Mountain Horse leaned against her backrest, a mask of sorrow over her face. "The prophecy comes true. Disease has struck to the north, south, and east in the camps of the Blackfoot, the Piegans, and also the Bloods. It spreads like fire in thick summer grass."

A large fly hummed around Snake Child's head and landed on her left knee. She brushed it away and watched her hand move slow and thick as if it belonged to another body. A horse whinnied, and another answered from the herd that grazed beyond the camp. Everything goes on the same. Why doesn't it stop when news like this comes?

Mountain Horse looked to White Feather with even greater sadness. "They also brought news of those who rode north with Shaggy Bull," she said with a deep, slow breath before continuing. "This group camped near a band of Blackfoot where the sickness had arrived. Within days, all the Black Elks were dead." She lowered her eyes. "I'm so sorry, White Feather."

White Feather sat like a stone. In a voice soft and deep, nearly a whisper, she asked, "And the ones who followed Prairie Owl?"

"No news."

"Will we get the sickness, Grandmother?" asked Snake Child. "Will it come here?" Shadow had followed her into the lodge and lay along the girl's right leg. She rested her hand on the pup's head and scratched behind its ear.

"No one, knows, little one. No one knows how far the prophecy will go."

Pretty Crow leaned her head on Mountain Horse, then

rose and went to White Feather's side, wrapping her arms around her friend. White Feather released her sorrow with low moans and great heaves of her chest.

Snake Child ran from the lodge as if she could escape the impact of the riders' news. The dogs gamboled about her. At the rock outcrop she stopped, out of breath from the upward run, looking down to the small lake and the camp. Then she curled herself against the yellow dog and slept.

The bark of a pup woke her, cold in the dim evening light. By the time she reached the Otter Lodge, the sky was black with night. Pretty Crow and White Feather slept side by side. Grandmother's bed was empty. The fire was nearly gone, but Snake Child had no thought for it and lay in a tight ball to sleep again, the chill she had absorbed from the ground no match for the one in her chest.

In the days that followed the news of the sickness and death of so many Black Elks, Snake Child found respite from despair by roaming the land around the camp. She no longer commanded the dogs to stay behind. The troupe wandered in each direction and, on return, she gathered firewood for the evening's blaze.

She walked this day from the west, a biting wind at her back, blanket full with dried lichen-covered spruce and poplar branches slung over her right shoulder. Whitish clouds clung low over and down the mountains, leaving snow wherever they touched. She walked with her head down and nearly collided with One Spot, who was standing just to the side of the trail. With the wind toward the camp, the dogs had not picked up his scent and had given no warning. Snake

Child gasped her surprise, and Shadow gave two quick barks as embarrassed apology.

"I'm sorry to frighten you. I whistled but the noise of the wind hid it. I wanted to talk with you."

Irritation lingered from being startled. "Why?"

"Do you know why I came to the Many Children band? I came for White Feather."

What did he mean? Did he plan to take her back to Shaggy Bull? It was too late for that. "White Feather belongs with us."

"I love White Feather and have for a long time. I came here hoping to win her affection. While I was in the service of Calf Shield, I could not yet take on the responsibility of a lodge and family. My debt to him was nearly done when..."

Waves of loss washed over him, as it had over her, time after time, since they left the Black Elks.

"So much sadness," he continued. "Will you take a message to White Feather? Tell her my feelings. If I have no hope of winning her, then bring that message to me and I will leave this camp." He looked around where he sat, as if it might be the last time. The poplars now had lost most of their leaves, and the ones remaining were like bits of yellow earth splattered through the air, sticking here and there on the branches. "You should also tell Pretty Crow that Black Eagle watches for her. He does not understand why she does not come out of the Otter Lodge. He wonders if she no longer cares for him."

"Black Eagle?" He was one of Bird Rattler's sons, a nephew of Mountain Horse. Snake Child remembered the shells, Pretty Crow's distress when the raven stole one. "So that's who gave her the ornaments at the Sun Gathering."

They rose from the chilly ground as if having made an agreement to do so just then, the dogs immediately doing the same. One Spot's horse grazed a short distance away and stamped a foot, impatient to move, snorting plumes of mist through the cold air of late afternoon.

Snake Child hoisted her blanket of firewood over her shoulder. "I'll give your message to them both."

At the Otter Lodge, Mountain Horse was gone. Snake Child sat with Pretty Crow and White Feather. "I met One Spot on the trail on my way back," she said. "He asked me to give a message to you both." When Snake Child had finished, the two sat quietly, hands in their laps.

"He asked me to bring him a message in return, White Feather. If he has no hope, One Spot will leave the Many Children's band."

"What can I tell him with all that has happened? My brother betrayed my dearest friend, we had to flee our own people to a camp where we are still strangers, my family is lost to disease, the brothers and sisters of our tribe lay dead and dying on the prairie." White Feather reached her hand to Pretty Crow. "Black Eagle asks after you. This is welcome news, is it not?"

Pretty Crow gave no response, but White Feather replied, "Tell One Spot that he should not leave the Many Children's band. He should remain here where he has found welcome and where, for now, we are safe. But it is too soon for promises. He should tell Black Eagle to be patient while we grieve the loss of our Black Elks family."

Later, when Mountain Horse heard One Spot's message, she sighed a deep, slow exhalation. "He was loyal to Calf Shield, a good hunter, courageous. We can use the help of such a man this winter," she added, "to bring hides that we can tan and bead into parfleche, leggings and moccasins. I have discussed with Weasel and will need a suitable contribution for a Bundle transfer at the next Sun Gathering."

"What must you give, Grandmother?" Snake Child asked.

Mountain Horse knelt before the kettle that bubbled with irregular pops and filled the lodge with rich, inviting smells. "A worthy gift, to honor the Bundle spirits, to show willingness for sacrifice and the hard work needed to care for it." She ladled steaming chunks of meat into Snake Child's shallow horn bowl. "We are a lodge of women. No warrior hunts for us, brings horses back from raids, or hides from the chase for us to use for trade. We have no buffalo ponies. We must do what women have always done: use our skill with tanning, stitching, and beading. When the Bundle comes to live with us, it will be with honor."

Mountain Horse passed bowls to White Feather, then Pretty Crow. "Eat, now, sweet one. You need to grow strong again."

Pretty Crow took the bowl without lifting her head.

Snake Child furrowed her brows and watched the older girl. When will this strange behavior end? What did the green-kerchiefed man do to Pretty Crow that had left her so vacant? Was he a ghost after all? Did he steal Pretty Crow's spirit and wander with it now over the prairie? She heard such things said in the children's camp at the Okan. The spirits of the Real People go to the Sand Hills. Where do the pale-skinned ghosts go? She hoped it was far away from the land of Napi's children.

"Grandmother, why don't we get our own buffalo pony? I could hunt for us. Brown Weasel Woman rode with the men and hunted like they did. Running Eagle fought on the war trail with her husband and became a great warrior. I could learn to ride and shoot." This appealed to Snake Child, to be outside through the days of the long winter instead of hunched over leggings, stitching tiny beads, and getting tired eyes.

Mountain Horse chewed a chunk of steaming meat slowly before she answered. "To hunt buffalo is dangerous. You need a rifle. You need years of riding full gallop until you and your horse move as one, until your horse understands every thought and you understand every hoof beat. It takes much practice, the way the young boys are guided by their uncles now, every day in the fields beyond our camp." She chewed another mouthful before continuing. "I cannot let you do what is so unsafe. It is enough to be born a man and have to do these things. To be born a woman and choose them would be foolish."

But the idea had settled in Snake Child's mind. For the first time since they left the Black Elks, she felt hopeful.

Next morning she carried White Feather's message to One Spot as he prepared his sorrel to ride out hunting. He listened attentively as she told him what was said. "So I can have some hope then. Thank you, Snake Child."

"One Spot, I need your help. I need to learn to shoot a rifle and gain skill with riding. We are a lodge of women. We need our own hides so we can trade and not be poor. We need to hunt for our meat."

He laughed gently. "Have no fear, young Snake Child. I will make sure your lodge has enough to eat." He jumped on his horse and galloped to catch up with the other riders.

Snake Child tightened her brows and stamped her foot. "I'll find my own way to get a horse," she hollered after him. In long strides she headed for the ridge, eager to watch the wolves. The dogs happily bounded alongside and she made no effort to send them back to camp. Shadow stayed close to her left side, the yellow one trotted steadily ahead, and the other two chased this way and that after magpies, gophers, and jays.

At the crest of the ridge she lay on cold, dry grass, looking below for a sign of the wolves. The wind blew chilly across her back, and the dogs readily stayed on the hillside behind her, out of the cold. Shadow squirmed along her side and she wrapped her arm over the dog, glad for the warmth and closeness.

The broad plain below stretched north, east, and south and nowhere could she see either buffalo or wolves. To her right, to the south, she made out the dark specks of One Spot and his hunting companions, smaller to her eye than the brown spider scuttling under a stone by her shoulder. Had the buffalo moved? Did they shelter in smaller, treed valleys cut into the long ridge as it widened to the north? Had they hidden in thick copses of poplar spread here and there along the ridge's base?

With a horse, she could ride out on the grassland and find where the herd fed. Ride along the base of the ridge and find signs of where the wolf pups denned. The white would be easy to spot. On foot it would take too long. She'd never be back by evening. Even with a horse, she would not risk being outside alone, in the dark, with ghosts about.

It occurred to her that she wouldn't need a buffalo pony in order to scout out the prairie. The roan or the little bay they brought from the Black Elks would do. She could begin practicing riding skills. Maybe, by spring, she could steal her own horse.

In her mind rose stories of Brown Weasel Woman, famous to her people. At the age young women began noticing young men, Brown Weasel asked her father to make a bow and arrow for her. "Let me go with you on the hunts, Father. Let me accompany you on the raids." Her father especially loved this daughter and could never refuse what she asked. Before long, she stole her own buffalo pony from a Cree camp and, soon after, brought down her first buffalo. Returning to camp after that kill, she did not skin or clean or cook. Instead, Brown Weasel Woman sat with her father, her brothers, and her uncles; she talked of the hunt while the pipe passed from hunter to hunter, and the women of her family served her choice cuts of the kill.

I do not want to sit with men while being served by women, Snake Child thought. I want to be able to sit without the men and the trouble they bring.

One Spot and the other hunters had veered south and disappeared into a shallow coulee. Yes, the buffalo could hide there. And if not, there would be fat, black-tailed deer. But it was the eastern grassland that drew her eyes again and again as it rolled in front of her. There was something her eyes could not detect, but it called her gaze to keep steady, ready for slight movement, any irregularity that revealed a presence she sensed.

She caught a movement in the corner of her eye. All still again. Her heart raced and breath caught, dry and constricted. What could she not see? So many possibilities out there at such a distance: a hawk jumping on an unsuspecting rabbit; a badger digging to send dirt flying; an antelope lying in grass, flicking a fly from her ear; a red fox pouncing on a mouse. Or a Crow war party moving along the shallow, snaking path of the small stream that curled its green way in the groove worn into the earth in its ages of passing this way.

Snake Child watched a long time, until her body stiffened with cold seeping into it from the ground and her imagination. Even the dogs whined impatiently to move. No other hint of movement appeared.

She had to tell someone. Even if it meant being teased, for letting her mind go wild. She would not risk saying nothing, even if it was nothing that was there.

CHAPTER 13

WHEN SHE TOLD Mountain Horse what she sensed or thought she saw, Snake Child doubted its validity, but her grandmother listened, eyes down, chin against her chest, without interruption. When she finished, the old woman rubbed Snake Child's head, the way she did with the dogs.

"You did right, little one, and I will tell the others." That night, extra guards surrounded the camp, and owners tethered favorite horses outside their lodge, bells tied to manes and tails.

At daylight, six men, One Spot and Black Eagle among them, rode to investigate the area described by Snake Child. She approached One Spot as he saddled a brown and white pinto with a white eye and pink nose. "Let me ride with you," she said. "I can show exactly where the movement was."

"We don't know what we'll find. If a raiding party or enemy warriors are hiding, we might have a skirmish.

Everyone would need a fast horse and a weapon." One Spot slid his rifle into its buckskin case and looped his rawhide-wrapped hatchet and club over the pommel.

"Lend me a horse, then," she persisted, "one that runs quickly. If warriors are there I can ride for help. When we get close to where the water winds and a hiding place could be, I can stay back and watch. If there's trouble, I will race to camp to get support."

One Spot took a breath, as if to explain why this would not do. But he released it silently. Perhaps she sounded reasonable, or perhaps he did not think real danger waited. One Spot liked her, she knew, and wanted Snake Child's goodwill in winning White Feather's affection.

But it was Black Eagle, already mounted on his bay with the white blaze on its face, who spoke aloud on behalf of her idea. "You can ride my horse here. He's fast and reliable. I'll take that gray who's eager to come along anyway."

One Spot shrugged. "Okay, little sister. But you have to stop when I say. I don't want to face your grandmother if harm comes to you. If I give a signal like this," and One Spot raised his hand and pushed it forward and down, "Then turn your horse and gallop as fast as possible back to camp."

Snake Child could hardly contain her excitement. "Of course I will."

She rode behind the group, the dogs beside her. If the men had really expected danger, they would not have risked having the dogs along, where a careless bark could alert an enemy.

The sky was cool, pale gray from one horizon to the other, and the chill air knew how to find an opening in any piece of clothing, twist its way next to skin, and suck the warmth out of it. Snake Child wrapped her blanket closer and watched plumes of breath steam from her horse's nostrils, felt the rhythm of his eager, gentle gait. Feathers adorned his mane, tied with bits of fur and beads, the same as those in Black Eagle's hair. Black Eagle rode to the right of One Spot, while a younger man on a small black horse rode on his other side. Black Eagle and the younger man shared the same broad, squared shoulders and long neck, sat astride their mounts with identical posture. Brothers, surely, she thought, or near relations.

They stopped a short while later while One Spot adjusted his scabbard. The young man on the black turned, smiled, and said, "I'm Little Ear, Black Eagle's brother." He was handsome, but it was his black horse that intrigued her, fine-boned and alert, watching in each direction, eager to keep moving. That's the kind of horse I'd like to have, she noted.

The group rode east to the ridge, then made their way north out of the wind with the ridge on their left. They moved in open ground and kept a slow pace. One Spot brought his rifle from its sheath and laid it in front of him; the others did the same. A strange quiet filled the air. No sign of buffalo, wolves, or any game, except one rabbit that gave a good chase for the dogs until it bounded into a hole on the side of a small knoll. High in the sky, a hawk circled slowly.

One Spot reined in his mare. "I want you to wait here, Snake Child. You have a good view. Keep your eyes on me, and if I signal, go immediately back."

She did not like the feel of the quiet. The unease of the previous day returned. Shadow refused to go on when she stopped. The dog sat next to the bay horse, whining as the other three trotted on with the riders. The bay whinnied long, his chest vibrating with his call as he tried to follow. Snake Child kept a firm hand on his rein until he finally stretched his neck to graze.

She would have liked to walk or sit in the grass, her legs and buttocks numb from the ride. But if One Spot signalled, she wanted to be ready, to show him she could follow the commands of a hunting party, that she could be trusted.

Horses and riders grew smaller as they rode farther. She hunched her shoulders to hold in warmth, glad the chill was at her back. Though the land appeared flat from where she watched, now and then the riders disappeared as they descended a hollow or invisible cut. This was the way throughout Napi's country, his great body never quite as it appeared, full of hidden places.

The horses were visible again, tiny, but she could still distinguish which was which. They stopped. One Spot dismounted and walked ahead, then went down on one knee, examining a track, or spoor, a sign left in the grass. One by one the others also walked, this way and that, examining the ground at intervals.

She strained her eyes to see. Shadow sensed her intentness and whined anew as she watched the dogs, their shapes just discernable, all together in a group. Black Eagle and One Spot stood side by side. The silence was unbearable.

Then it broke. Snake Child heard pitiful yelps and cries of dogs in agony, screaming their pain. What had happened? The men and horses all looked in one direction. She could no longer see any dogs. Why was no one running to help? They were being tortured, and Snake Child could no longer bear it.

She pulled up the bay's head and kicked it to a gallop, straight to the group, Shadow running abreast on her left.

As she neared the others, she slowed to a canter and then pulled up the reins. A shape lay in the grass before her. A bloodied buffalo carcass. She guided the horse closer to examine it. The dogs were silent now. Why did they not run to greet her?

Everything seemed in slow motion, except her thoughts. One Spot shouted, "Call Shadow back. Keep her with you. Do not let her come further."

She yelled to the dog, "Come here, Shadow. Come." At the same time she began to take in the scene. The buffalo was well devoured by wolves and the scavengers who follow them. But all about lay skinned carcasses that were not buffalo. They were wolves.

She slid from her horse, coaxed the whimpering dog to her and slid a thong around its neck to keep it close. The whine of another dog directed her to yellow fur further on. There her yellow friend lay on her side, legs flailing as if she ran, eyes wide and terrified. Froth foamed from her mouth. She showed no recognition of Snake Child. The grass where her paws ran in frenzy back and forth was covered in dark blood, her legs worn raw from the motion she was powerless to stop. Snake Child stood frozen, unable to comprehend what was happening. Shadow whined and tried to nudge her mother, but Snake Child pulled tight on the cord until the dog choked with strain.

She looked for the other dogs. In a small hollow lay the brindled brown, on his back, legs stiff and shaking straight in the air. A short way beyond were two dead magpies and a raven, also on its back, stiff as if dead, yet croaking a faint call every few moments.

She looked in each direction from where the helpless yellow dog wore her paws to bone, driven to run by an incomprehensible demon. Bloodied carcasses of skinned wolves, unskinned coyotes, a badger, more magpies and ravens littered the grass, radiating out from the yellow dog the way the stone markers radiated on the Medicine Wheel. Round and round she stepped as if in a solemn dance. One dog she had not yet seen, the black-and-tan male.

One Spot, Black Eagle and the other four stood by their horses in a world suspended and silent but for the swish of the senselessly running legs and the croaks of the raven. Even Shadow had ceased her whines and sat in quiet stillness, watching her mother.

Then One Spot moved. He walked purposefully to his horse and took the hatchet from the pommel, then walked east to where the land dipped and she could see his body only from the knees up. He raised his arm and brought the hatchet down hard and swiftly. This blow, she knew though could not see, struck the black-and-tan dog.

He walked next to the brindled one and did the same. The hatchet severed the dog's head and its body lolled to the side, the stiff protest of his legs now still. One Spot looked to Snake Child, who knew the dear yellow mother was next. A swell of gratitude for his action rose in her chest. She pointed to the raven who had just uttered another feeble croak. One Spot brought the blunt end of the hatchet swiftly and smashed the black head.

Snake Child knelt at the yellow dog's side, holding

Shadow close with one hand and the other on the mother's shoulder. "Good-bye dear friend. Thank you for your loyalty. I will remember you always." She walked away and, with her back to the dog, heard the smash of One Spot's hatchet. Shadow whined pitiful moans, one after the other as the girl dragged her to the horses.

As she prepared to mount, wanting to be back at camp as quickly as possible, Snake Child remembered the white wolf and her littermates, the playful pair of grays and black brothers. Had they too fallen to this carnage?

She called to the men who had already turned their horses west. "Did you see any sign of a white wolf? Any carcass with white fur?"

They shook their heads. Snake Child jumped astride the bay, who eagerly turned for home. She kept Shadow on the thong a long time before releasing her to walk on her own again.

Mountain Horse waited at the edge of camp. She always knows, thought Snake Child, when something is wrong. Snow mounded on the blanket that wrapped the old woman's shoulders. Snake Child slid from the bay and leaned into her grandmother, burying her face into the familiar chest as blanketed arms wrapped her.

At the Otter Lodge, Shadow curled into a ball beside the robes of Snake Child's bed.

The girl sobbed out the story of the day, then watched the fire, unmoving, hungry, yet without interest in eating, tired, yet avoiding sleep. The four sat in silence until only dim coals remained.

"Has Napi forgotten us, Grandmother?" Snake Child's small voice interrupted the stillness.

Mountain Horse reached for a branch and pushed the charred ends of nearly burnt pieces into the center of the ashes. White flakes, disturbed from their rest, swirled up like small birds, then settled again the way a flock of geese relaxes to resume calm floating. "That Napi – he likes to make life. Likes to get it going. Then leaves it to tend itself once it's here. That's the work he gave the People, to tend his creation."

"What has done this killing of wolves and dogs and birds?"

Her grandmother wrapped her large arms around Snake Child again. "This is what I heard. When Spotted Horse and Shot Twice traded in late summer, they learned from our people to the south and east of men who kill the wolves for their hides. They put poison in a buffalo carcass and leave it where creatures will eat from it. Whatever does eat dies in the terrible anguish that you saw. These men, wolfers, have come far into our land."

Snake Child curled her legs and leaned into Mountain Horse's lap. Her grandmother rubbed her back. "You must have seen them far in the distance when you watched from the ridge, as they skinned the wolves."

"I hope the white wolf is safe. I wish the dogs had stayed behind. I wish I had said nothing." She drew her knees up more and her head inside the blanket.

White Feather pulled her own blanket tighter and rested her head on drawn-up knees. "My father was right, Grandmother. It would be a good thing to destroy these pale-skins once and for all."

Pretty Crow shuddered, stood, and went outside. Shadow whined and followed.

Mountain Horse stirred the fire again. "We cannot destroy them. But we can keep them out of our land. Perhaps. Perhaps it is too late."

The snow had stopped. Pretty Crow's softly crunching footsteps, the snap of fire coals, the snort of a horse gave the illusion that all was in its proper order.

CHAPTER 14

WATCHING, WAITING, and uncertainty followed. The sickness had been troubling enough. Now, wolfers penetrated the People's land. No news had come from camps and lodges to the east, south, or north. What was happening there?

Spotted Horse sent his son, Running Bird, and nephew, Crooked Back, to ride east for news. He sent them with warnings: avoid any band showing signs of sickness, sleep under the sky, shun places with whiskey.

A full moon cycle passed, through winter's darkest time.

Inside the Otter Lodge, the women stitched and beaded the soft hides Mountain Horse had tanned and stored in parfleche. When Snake Child folded over and wept for her dogs, her grandmother hummed and stroked her limbs the way she had comforted Pretty Crow. Shadow, true to her name, clung to the girl's side.

One Spot came often, as he had promised, with game: a

white hare or a grouse, a portion of deer. Black Eagle often accompanied him, and occasionally his younger brother, Little Ear, who had gone with them the day the dogs died.

Day by day White Feather and Pretty Crow emerged from their quiet withdrawal. The two young women began to walk together for water and firewood. On milder days, when sun broke through and turned the snow to a blanket of tiny stars, they took the longest to return. The flash in their eyes like that of the snow, an upright posture, a quick smile – these returned with them.

Snake Child grew restless, irritated at the actions of the two young women, especially Pretty Crow. This one, so beloved, as much a sister as any blood relation, had been distant and out of reach since they fled the Black Elks. Now, when her former self returned, when Snake Child happily anticipated the laughter and easy chatter of her company, she was lost in a conspiracy with White Feather in a secret world that revolved around the intrigue of young warriors.

"This is how it is for Napi's children," Mountain Horse said, as Snake Child scowled, watching the two walk toward the river. "Men and women, pulled and tugged by their nature, the way the geese are sent honking in arrow-shaped flight and buffalo cannot stop themselves from rolling in the wallows that dot all the great grassland." The old woman pulled a length of sinew through the light buckskin on her lap and threaded three green glass beads. "We can take heart that our Pretty Crow is herself again."

On a morning not long after their conversation, a morning bright with sun and the glare of thin new snow, Snake Child

left the Otter Lodge, restless to walk in long strides to the
southeast of the camp. There, the river curled in a wide arc,
and the horses grazed, guarded by herders at each direction.

Shadow trotted ahead, her nose near the ground on the
track of a pair of deer that had cautiously stepped past in the
night. Snake Child copied the gait of the dog, an easy comfortable pace she felt she could keep as long as the day was
light.

This is how the young men train, she thought, until they
run a whole day and night without stopping. Or so she had
heard, for this is never the training of young women. She
had listened when Mountain Horse instructed Pretty Crow,
"Take smaller steps, slower steps, my pretty one. Look how
the graceful whitetail doe steps among the shadows of the
fir and pine. No creature has more beauty than these." How
long would it be before she heard the same from her grandmother? A long time, she hoped. A very long time.

Snake Child nearly ran past Little Ear, who hunkered
in the lee of a large lichen-crusted rock, grazing horses scattered in front of him. She slowed at the same time he called,
"What's the hurry, Snake Child?"

"No hurry," she said, her breath in quick, short gasps. "I
keep warmer this way."

"Where are you going all alone?"

Snake Child pulled her blanket tighter, making the cloth
bunch about her neck. Her breath escaped in white plumes.
Shadow returned, whined and sat beside her. Since the death
of the other dogs, Shadow was at ease only when she was
moving. Whenever Snake Child stopped, she grew restless,
ill at ease without the other dogs, and anxious to be going, as

if she might yet find her lost family. Snake Child knew how she felt, seeking what had been lost. She just wasn't sure what it was.

"I've got Shadow with me. I'm not alone. I'm going to catch the roan mare to ride south to the river." But, she thought, I don't have to account for what I do. She kept her eyes down, intent on the angles that bits of grass created, their frozen, dried shafts in haphazard lines where they broke through the snow.

"Can I ride with you?" Little Ear asked. "I don't have to stay here to herd today. There are plenty of herders. I just wanted to get away from watching my brother and One Spot make accidental meetings with the two from your lodge." Little Ear stood and stretched, then stamped each leg the way a horse will do when it has been long without moving.

The image of the two love-struck men made her laugh, and this made her relax. "I know what you mean. Do they think us so thick-sighted that we do not see their efforts, and the attempts to hide the efforts? The way a duck pretends a broken wing if we step too near her nest. No one is fooled."

"The duck can't help doing what she does and neither can they," Little Ear shrugged. "They only fool themselves. Or in the case of the duck, maybe the coyote." His laughter brought her into the humor of the situation as he walked toward the grazing horses, as if Snake Child had already given assent for him to ride with her.

She hastened her steps until she walked beside him. He was taller than she by a head and wore plain buckskin leggings and shirt, with a fur vest, hair on the inside. Lynx, she thought. Did he hunt it himself? A single black braid hung down the center of his back, one small feather and three blue beads knotted near its end.

Shadow bounded ahead to assume her steady trot, confident they were going somewhere interesting now that two people followed. Snake Child laughed at the dog's enthusiasm and at how good it felt to move over the frozen grass with companions.

The roan nickered a greeting when Snake Child approached and did not resist when she slipped a rope over her head and looped it across her nose. But when she attempted to lead the mare away, the horse stiffened her front legs and refused to move.

"She doesn't want to leave her friends from Calf Shield's herd," said Little Ear. He mounted his small black mustang and rode behind the stubborn mare to gently push his horse against her haunches. Unbalanced, the mare released her locked legs and jolted forward, swishing her tail angrily and laying her ears flat as she turned a sour look to the black horse. "The buffalo ponies never care about leaving the herd. They want only to race in the hunt, like this little fellow loves to do."

"I'm going to get my own buffalo pony," Snake Child blurted. She waited for Little Ear to tell her that women only needed travois ponies, not the fleet sturdy racers that chased all day in the hunt without tiring.

"I'm going to go on my first raid this spring," Little Ear replied. "Crooked Back is my uncle, and I'll go with him, maybe as soon as when he returns. Maybe he'll bring news of Crow camps close by, or a Cree raid that needs an answer."

The two rode side by side, the black with his ears forward and an eager step that said, let's run now. "Even if Crooked Back says, 'No, you aren't old enough yet,' I'm going to follow. If not in the first raid, then in the next. When I've proven myself worthy, I will steal my own horse. Maybe more than one," Little Ear said.

Snake Child still expected a rebuke for wanting her own pony. But none came as she rode and breathed the rich, thick scent of the mare whose winter coat grew thick and soft. The roan gave up her efforts to stay with the other horses and walked contentedly next to the black. Snake Child too relaxed, accepting that Little Ear was not going to dismiss her intent to get her own horse.

This was the first of many days that winter that the two rode together whenever the freezing north wind or biting deep cold did not keep them in their lodges, or when Little Ear was free of herding duties and Snake Child could leave behind the stitches and beads of the buckskin work.

Little Ear and his black horse moved like one body. "I've trained him since he was a yearling colt," he explained, "and he understands what I want of him with just a slight pressure on his shoulder or a touch of a finger."

"How could the roan understand me like that?" Snake Child asked.

"She's too old. But still you could work with her. She gallops more readily than she once did. I'll show you how to guide her with your knees. Then we can start grabbing sticks from the ground as we gallop by."

On Snake Child's first attempt to grab the short pole stuck upright in the grass, she slid right off. The mare galloped a few strides and stopped to look back, curious at this new behavior.

Little Ear showed her how to lean, hold a shank of mane firmly, and keep her balance as she grabbed the stick and righted herself. It took several tries before she managed to pull the stick out and pull herself upright again. She was thrilled and held the stick aloft the way she had seen young men holding their spears in war games.

"And when you get really good, and with another horse I think, you can learn this." With that, he galloped past her hanging on the side of the black, running at full gallop, looking at her from beneath the horse's neck. "This is how we shoot at our enemies," he explained, "and keep ourselves hidden at the same time."

Yes, Snake Child told herself, I'll learn that. I'll have a horse that I train myself. But for now, just grabbing sticks was challenging enough. She turned the mare around, prodded her again to a gallop, and ran toward the pole.

This day, Snake Child and Little Ear rode to the top of a low, rounded hill south of the camp. Little Ear dismounted and knelt with one knee on the ground as his eyes scanned over the prairie, stopping at times to examine the shadows of brush or small cottonwood clumps.

The black horse stood beside him and looked south also, ears pricked forward. He snorted, shifted his weight from one side to another, swished his tail, and exhaled loudly. Little Ear raised his left hand to the black's neck and the animal quieted at once, but his ears were still pushed forward and his eyes intent. "He sees something," Little Ear said, and looked in the same direction as the horse.

Where Little Ear's hand rested on the black's neck, Snake Child saw for the first time that most of his last finger was missing.

"I'm going to go closer and see what it is he sees. Hold his rope and put your hand on his neck like this if he gets restless or tries to follow." He handed the rope end to Snake Child with his other arm and saw her staring at his hand. "My grandmother," he said. "When I was born. She gave my finger to the Sun so I would have protection." He took his hand away and turned so it was hidden. "I won't be long."

"But maybe it's wolfers out there again," Snake Child protested. "We should go back. I have to get firewood anyway before it gets dark." Her stomach tightened and she felt cold.

"More likely a mule deer. Maybe even a lone buffalo. We could use the meat."

Snake Child called Shadow to her side as Little Ear walked to a cluster of low wolf willow and disappeared in the foliage. Though she watched closely, she could not see where he went after that. The black horse watched intently as before, and she strained to see what it was that he saw, more certain with each passing moment that wolfers had returned. Images assailed her of bloodied pulps in the grass, of the dog's first scream, the raven's croak, the helpless frozen eyes and senseless running legs. Little Ear appeared suddenly from behind the hill, trotting in an easy springing gait the way a coyote will do.

"It's Running Bird and Crooked Back," he said. "They've got half a dozen horses with them." Little Ear's eyes sparked excitement. "I'm going to ride out and meet them. They'll have news. Will you come?"

CHAPTER 15

SHE RAN. It was her only relief from the horror of the news that Running Bird and Crooked Back brought, news that evoked the warnings of the Black Stone's loss.

The scabby disease had spread now to the south. From camp to camp, dread and fear crawled into lodges like ColdMaker's winter breath. *Is this the end of Napi's people?* The question hung in round, bewildered eyes.

Also from the south, Sioux, Assiniboine, and Crow pushed further into Blackfoot territory where buffalo still remained. Whispered doubts rustled in cottonwood branches: Have the great beasts forsaken the middle world of their human companions? Have they gone once more below to graze the green pastures of the long-ago time?

From the east and north the same story: the search for buffalo bringing enemies to Napi's land. Eastward, where the broad, slow river winds, a Blackfoot war party, weakened with sickness, had surprised Cree hunters far beyond their usual range. Soon the riverbanks were cluttered with Blackfoot bodies while the water ran red with their blood. Not one survived to hear the Cree's gloating whoops and victory cries.

North, east, and south, whiskey's evil invaded the People's efforts to resist as it infected their spirit, greedy as the scabs for their bodies. In its power, they do not know what they do. When they wake, they drink again to keep from knowing what they have done.

Nowhere could any speak of the Black Elks who followed Prairie Owl. Had they escaped the prophecy's reach, or did their ghosts wander, searching for those who could give proper prayers and smoke so they might find the way to the Sand Hills?

These words from Running Bird and Crooked Back swirled round and round in Snake Child's mind, as if carried by one of the small twister winds of summer. Hoof beats interrupted the turning. Little Ear on his black mustang loped toward her.

They sat side by side watching the narrow river, eager in its swift, swollen flow to make up for the long, frozen winter. Snake Child had exhausted her sorrow for the moment, restlessness given over to heavy stillness.

"Crooked Back prepares for a horse raid. It's owed for ones stolen last fall by Nez Perce. I'm going, too."

"Let me come," Snake Child pleaded. "I need to get my own horse. I need to learn how a raid is done."

At the Otter Lodge, Mountain Horse leaned forward from her backrest as if bitten by a wasp. "Go on a horse raid?

ALANDA GREENE

Ask Crooked Back to take you? I thought this matter was put
to rest. Yes, there have been women who chose the path of
hunter or warrior. But these were not women whose grandmother was visited by Snake Beings and given the task of
keeping you safe. Even if that hadn't happened, I could not
give you leave for such risk. The way of women is different,
Snake Child. Napi gave us a harder way of quiet listening,
watching, understanding. This is how we serve our people. I
do not know your path, little one, but I do not doubt that a
destiny awaits you. If I gambled like the men, I would place a
high stake that it did not lie with hunting buffalo."

The raiding party returned in five days and guided eleven
horses with them. Little Ear rode last, leading a spotted mare
swollen with a coming foal. The successful foray would be
celebrated that evening, every detail described and acknowledged. Snake Child found Little Ear beforehand as he brushed
the mane of the mare, tethered outside Crooked Back's lodge.

"No," he told her. "I didn't capture her myself. She's only
a mare, but ready to foal. Crooked Back rewarded me with
her for noticing a guard coming toward the others as they
were bringing out the last horses. I ran to signal my uncle and
we all escaped."

"What happened to the guard?"

"Running Bird came behind and slit his throat, clean and
silent." Little Ear sliced his hand through the air before his
neck.

"Will they follow you for revenge?"

"Too small a camp. They won't risk coming this far into
our territory."

Snake Child wondered if the legendary fear the People

evoked in their enemies was still alive. Maybe they would come. "It must have been exciting, and she's a beautiful horse. You did a brave thing." Would she be able to act swiftly, quietly? Would she slit a throat if needed? She could slit the throat of a paleskin, she thought. Especially one with a green kerchief.

The spring, which had showed so little interest, at last came alive. Luminous green stained the prairie, and Snake Child ran each day, Shadow at her side, to the river's bend, to the horses and the newborns. Earlier, swallows had hollowed the riverbank for nests and now veered back and forth as the cheeps of hungry young ones filled the air. She lay flat, her head over the edge, as they glided in intricate patterns. And she watched the other direction especially, watching for Little Ear's mare to birth.

This day, the spotted horse had moved away from the others and stood with her head down, shifting her weight back and forth, turning in discomfort. Her legs finally buckled and she rolled on her side. Soon a leg appeared, a slimy head, and suddenly the whole foal slid from its mother, propelled to the grass. The mare turned her head, clambered to her feet, sniffed the newborn tenderly, and began to lick it head to tail.

Engrossed, Snake Child did not hear Little Ear arrive. He lay in the grass beside her without a word, equally absorbed. Having cleaned her young one head to tail, the mare nudged the foal until it began to collect its gangly legs, too long for the tiny body. Black, with white patches scattered over its rump and face. It tried to rise to its feet and collapsed, tried again, wobbled, and collapsed again. Finally all four legs, splayed and shaking, held upright. The mare nickered softly and sidled to her new one. It took little time for the pink nose to nuzzle into the teats and suck noisily.

Little Ear spoke softly, keeping the wonder of the birth present. "It's a filly. She can stand so quickly. She'll be running around by this time tomorrow. It takes us so long to stand and take care of ourselves."

"You were hoping for a colt, yes?"

"There will be time for many colts to come. She's a good mare, still young. You take the filly, Snake Child. It will be a long time before she is ready to ride, but you can train her, become her friend, learn with her."

She held her breath, the pounding of her chest sounding like a drum echoing into the ground. "I have nothing to give in return, Little Ear. A horse is a big gift."

"Friends can give gifts, Snake Child, and in return they have friendship and the pleasure of a friend's gladness. That's enough."

CHAPTER 16

SPOTTED HORSE'S WIVES struck their lodges on a morning of gray sky, signalling the women of the band to do the same, to prepare to move to the place of the Sun Gathering, the Okan. The Many Children had moved in recent weeks, yet already a stale breath saturated the air around the camp, and the urge to wander again over Napi's body was ripe.

Snake Child ran to get the travois horses at the first hint of lodges coming down. The filly's spotted black body had grown more proportioned to her long legs as she filled out, healthy and strong. "Those legs will always be long," she whispered to the young horse, stroking her neck "You'll be a fast runner. little friend, as fine a buffalo horse as any colt."

The herders arrived to collect horses and begin driving them ahead. No time this day to rub the foal's pink nose or stroke the mare's neck, to laugh at the filly's antics as she kicked and gamboled in circles. The roan, bay, and pinto would follow the others if she delayed.

The filly eased Snake Child's restlessness and sorrow. Yet, a somber mood pervaded the spirit of the band and eclipsed the usual excitement of going to the Okan.

"There are camps choosing to keep away this year, in fear of the sickness," Mountain Horse said as she laced a cord around the travois pole and tossed its end to Snake Child to tighten on the opposite side.

"Who isn't coming?"

"We won't know until we get there."

The riders of the Braves Society had the role of leading each arriving band to its place in the great circle. Spotted Horse rode at the front of the Many Children, and in spite of this year's fearsome omens, they arrived to a welcome of excitement and anticipation. Escorts guided their procession, flags fluttered in lively patterns from upright spears, horses whinnied, dogs barked, and young men whooped as the band circled the gathered lodges to their designated spot. Several spaces were empty, and no lodges stood in the Black Elks' place.

They raised the Otter Lodge at the eastern edge of the Many Children's camp, the tawny buttes of the Belly River to the north with shimmering flat grassland arching round to the blue-hazed mountains. Two days later, a sub-band of the All Tall Peoples rode triumphantly and proudly to the entrance of the circle. Bedraggled and haggard, with few horses and clothing thin and dirty from wear and use, they were mostly older men and women, mothers and children, and five warriors.

"Look how they ride upright with shining eyes," Mountain Horse said, "how proudly they come to claim their place. They have suffered much. So many missing. So few warriors." The dust raised in their coming reflected the sun and hung in the air, engulfing the circle's center in a golden-hued cloud, as even the wind stopped to acknowledge the dignity of their arrival.

"Is it sickness that caused such hardship for them?" asked Pretty Crow. The four women stood in a line at the circle's edge to raise their arms in greeting as the band rode by.

"Sickness, or war, or hunger. Our enemies now come far inside our land, and even Napi's people begin to complain of small, scarce herds of buffalo."

"Will a sickness come here? Or attacks?" White Feather was barely audible over the snorts of horses, thrum of drumbeats, and yips of dogs.

"We have strong medicine still. Five women pledged to make the sacrifices to sponsor the Okan this year. Many warriors vowed to offer their flesh and pain in the dance. These renew our strength."

Her grandmother's unsaid words hung in the air around Snake Child's ears as clearly as the jingling of the escorts' harness. We do not know if it will be strong enough.

"Come with me." Mountain Horse beckoned the three others and walked to where the new arrivals stopped to set camp. "We will help these old ones with their lodges and invite them to eat with us tonight."

More bands straggled to the gathering in the next days. In the evening, young men rode their finest horses inside the circle created by the lodges. Where young women watched, the horses stepped slowly, past quick smiles and the glances of bright eyes. Sometimes a horse stopped as a woman gave her hand to be pulled up behind the rider. In this way the whole camp knew, as they rode together in the twilight, they were now betrothed.

Pretty Crow and White Feather swung up behind Black Eagle's pale gray and One Spot's lanky sorrel on the same evening, while buckskin fringes quivered, black braids shone, and eyes glistened.

In these quiet days of arrivals Mountain Horse often looked east, as if her eyes went as far as the Hills and then beyond, where the remaining Black Elks were last seen.

"You long to meet them again, don't you?" said Snake Child. She sat beside her grandmother and rubbed Shadow's swollen belly.

"Prairie Owl is my husband's brother, the only one left of Calf Shield's and Yellow Star's children." She ran her hand over the dog's side. "Shadow will be having babies soon. This is good. Dogs do not sleep in the same lodge as the Bundle. She will have her little ones for company."

"Why can't she still sleep beside me? She has done so since the others died." Snake Child had worked through the winter and spring along with the others in the Otter Lodge to prepare the gifts for her grandmother to offer at the transfer. But she hadn't known her work meant Shadow would be banished.

"The Bundle means sacrifice, Snake Child. Shadow won't

mind. You will see." Mountain Horse sighed and scratched the dog's neck. "Yes, I long to see the Black Elks. Prairie Owl is now head of a family of which we still are part. He could sponsor our two young women in their marriage, so they could have gifts. They cannot enter their husband's lodge bringing nothing, and all the Otter Lodge has will be given in the Bundle transfer."

CHAPTER 17

IN THE LODGE that evening, Mountain Horse called them all to sit within. The walls were raised at the bottom so a breeze, cooled in dim evening light, drifted across the circle. An orange sky blended upward to vivid blue that glowed above the western horizon. Mountain Horse ladled thick soup into their bowls, her gestures slow and tender. "This is the last night we share together like this, four women. Tomorrow, I join Weasel in the Women's Lodge where I will stay until the last day of our ceremonies, learning my responsibilities. When I return, the Bundle will also dwell with us."

They sat without speaking, sipping from the rims of horn bowls held in both hands, savoring the taste and this time. Snake Child tried to imagine the Bundle sharing this space that Shadow no longer did. If Pretty Crow and White Feather resented its coming, they showed it neither in speech nor expression. It's worse for them, she thought. They want to be with husbands and because of the Bundle, they have to wait. Shadow was moved outside the lodge when her three new pups arrived, and as her grandmother said, did not mind her exclusion.

"Tomorrow," Mountain Horse continued, "Sings At Dawn, second wife to Crooked Back, will join you here for the days I am in the Women's Lodge."

This did bring expressions of dismay from the young women, which brought a wide grin to the old woman's face. "At the Sun Gathering, grandmothers have a duty to make sure the young women are within their lodges before the darkness and the young men appear. If the grandmother is busy," she shrugged, "she makes sure she gives the duty to another." A sigh of resignation was the only audible response; shoulders drooped, just a little, the only visible one. Snake Child was indifferent.

This morning, the fourth since Mountain Horse had gone, wind blew strong from the west and pushed against Snake Child's back, whipping strands of black hair across her face. She had woken early, sticky and hot. Outside the lodge, she squatted in the grass and discovered that blood stained her inner thighs and marked the grass below her. Now, her body would move with moon's own cycle. She would leave behind being a girl and enter a new status, like Pretty Crow and White Feather. A woman. Snake Child wiped the blood from her legs and told no one. She would wait, she told herself, until Grandmother returned and the ceremonies of the Women's Lodge were done, when there would be time in the Otter Lodge to acknowledge her transition.

This was the day she would be painted. It comforted her to know that Mountain Horse sat within that lodge as she imagined entering and standing before the one who wore the huge headdress. She wanted to bathe for the ceremony and walked to the river, followed it eastward to where it curved and the south bank steepened. Here, the ground that lined the water was thick with round stones, strewn the way a bucket of giant berries might tumble over the grass. Damp silt covered the ground between the stones and the tracks of birds and animals indented it in clearly defined images. A coyote's prints, pressed that morning, followed the edge of the river eastward.

Usually she came with one of the others of the lodge; one bathed while the other kept watch. But even Shadow was busy, and Snake Child did not feel like waiting until someone was available. The thought of the cool river pulled her mind, how the first splash made her gasp, how her skin tingled when she rose from the water and stood dripping at the shore.

She slipped out of her moccasins and loosed her hair. Soft cool silt oozed between her toes. Her dress she folded and set on rocks where it would keep dry. Willow scrub grew in patches along the shore, and she wound between them to the river's edge, stepping cautiously where the green slime on the stones made them treacherously slippery. She leaned over and moved like a four-legged creature, hands braced apart, stone by stone, until the water deepened to a swirling pool. Its surface glistened as she curled onto her side in the water, her breath catching in the exhilaration and shock of the coolness. Here the water was just deep enough to cover her when she lay on her side. Closer to the middle, it deepened but flowed too quickly. Even here she grasped a stone with each hand to avoid being pushed and tumbled into the rocks. Snake Child rolled on her back, and the current spread her hair out, the water like fingers that pulled the strands. She spread her own fingers and stretched them through the thick tendrils. Her skin had accepted the coolness and now the flow across her body was a caress, like the strokes of a gentle hand, or the feather-light drumming of tiny fingers tickling every part of her. Inhaling deeply, she lowered her face beneath the water and her entire body felt the current, like unending laughter. Her belly contracted into laughter itself, and she sat up quickly to avoid sucking water and to secure her hold in the push-pull of the river. Unbalanced, she rolled to shallows to prevent being jostled against the rocks.

Standing in the sun, Snake Child closed her eyes as its warmth exaggerated the tingling of her skin, cooling as droplets rolled and dripped over it. She wiped the water from her with long strokes, first one hand and then the other. Rivulets ran from the ends of her hair, along the center of her back, across her chest, following the contour of breasts now firm and protruding. She shivered at the intense hum of this body, the awake alert tingle of her skin, the intense pleasure as her hand moved back and forth over her nipples.

Snake Child opened her eyes, suddenly alert to the world around her and the sense that she was watched. Scanning the top of the bluffs across the river revealed nothing, nor the shores opposite. It was behind her. She turned, black eyes flashing, ready to scold whoever dared spy. Just at the rim where the land angled down to river bottom sat a coyote, mouth open in a grin, pink tongue lolling, ears perked up, but eyes relaxed, as if in deep enjoyment. It looked directly into her eyes.

She exhaled, relaxed, and shook her fist. "Rascal, to spy on me when I bathe." The soft buckskin lay dry, and she slid it over her head. When her eyes emerged, the coyote was gone. She glanced about to see if it had come down to the river, but no sign emerged. Carrying her moccasins, she stepped barefoot stone to stone, their smooth rounded surface warm on the soles of her feet. At the top, she could see no evidence of the animal; she shook her loose damp hair and walked toward camp. By the time she reached the Otter Lodge, the black strands shone like the glint of the river.

That afternoon, Snake Child walked to be painted at the Women's Lodge with Pretty Crow and White Feather. Each carried an offering of tobacco and pemmican in a small parfleche. She followed the other two within, her hair gathered on each side, wrapped with a buckskin thong. The thick smoke felt hot, irritated her throat, and hurt her head. Two drummers, the only males ever allowed in this lodge, pounded a steady beat just inside the entrance.

It seemed bigger than she remembered from previous years. The holy women sat in a half circle, headdresses emerging from the smoke and receding back into it like creatures in a swirling mist, demons gathered around the center pole. Snake Child wanted fresh air, wanted cool water to ease her scorched throat. Her eyes stung. The cloud of smoke was too dense to breathe. Her mind was thick, the drums loud, the singing harsh to her ears. A shrill whistle shrieked like the eagle whose bone it came from and pierced her ears painfully. Pounding inside her head matched the drums at the door.

Pretty Crow stepped forward to stand in front of a woman who fanned smoke up and down her body as she sang in low moaning syllables and waved the eagle feathers that sent smoke around the young woman.

Swirling images came in the smoke. Snake Child wanted to leave and get air, but Pretty Crow was done, her hand on Snake Child's shoulder, her voice low and soft. "Now you go." She squinted her eyes against the sting of the smoke and pushed down the urge to cough, to run. Her grandmother's voice rose in memory, the many times she had guided Snake Child in how to show respect, to have courage in the presence of the holy ones, to honor what was given.

Her head still pounded in rhythm with the drums as she stepped before the woman who had smudged and painted Pretty Crow moments earlier. She knew it was a woman, but it did not resemble any woman she knew. Snake Child could not take her eyes from the headdress with its circle of upright feathers and tangle of hair, fur, claws, and beads about its base. The woman dropped a pinch of powder on the coals, sending swirls of smoke into the air. Feathers fanned it over her body, the woman sang as she fanned, the whistle shrieked again, drums, and somewhere a rattle. Smoke drifted in and out of the feathers on the headdress and made it appear to move. The sound of rattles again. Confusing. All around the fur and hide of the headpiece, the smoke curled and twined itself. Bright black, glassy eyes looked out from the swirling mass. A tiny owl's head, the kind that burrowed into the prairie to make its home, rose from the mass of swirls and set its round eyes to hers, shook itself and relaxed down, the way a bird will do that sits on eggs. Again that rattling sound.

What is it that twists around the woman's head? Why does she have a great snake in her hair? The snake writhed and slithered and raised its head as the owl had done to fix its eyes upon Snake Child. The drums were distant now, the woman's voice barely audible. Only the rattle kept its intrusive, jarring noise. She saw now – it was the snake's tail that shook and sent the confusing sound. The snake opened its mouth. "Sing with me." The voice came from inside her own head. Then another sound as the snake sang. This voice soothed her, cleared away the confusing clamor, cleared her mind. She breathed deeply, the air now fresh. Yes, she knew this song, she could sing. She joined her voice with the snake's, rocked back and forth, shifted her weight from one foot to another. Had she closed her eyes? She opened them. The snake closed its mouth, settled again into the tangle of hair. Snake Child had stopped singing, yet the song echoed in her mind. She heard the drums again. They pounded on the inside of her skull. Rattles. Piercing whistle. Black.

SECTION FOUR

Suspicion

CHAPTER 18

ELEANOR CARRIED the coal sack over her left shoulder, holding its end with both hands while she angled up to the coulee's rim. The tipi circles were close, and she was curious to see them again. She walked around each ring of stones, seven in all, then stepped into the center of the most western ring, sitting to look across the coulee. An Indian woman might have sat in the same place, she thought, and watched antelope like that small group on the other side, watched the land go on as if it went forever.

It was a wonderful thing, my girl, the way you could ride the prairie for days and never see a fence or road or house. Then, a wisp of smoke might rise and there they'd be, the lodges of buffalo hide, each painted in a different design.

Near her left shoe, a sharp point protruded. She pushed away dirt and dead grass to pull it from the ground: a black stone, chipped along its outer edges. Arrow? Spear? Her hand held what their hands had held, and a thrill shivered through her. Placing it in her skirt pocket, she headed toward their house, a small bump on the northern horizon.

The sense of being watched made her stop and turn. There, on the far side of the coulee, the hills rising beyond, sat a coyote, its pink tongue lolling and clearly visible, even across the valley. Beside the first lay another on its belly, neck up, huge ears perked high. She knew they looked directly at her, even though she was too far away to make out where their eyes aimed. But I can feel them, she noted, feel them thinking of me.

Eleanor imagined telling this to her mother or father and knew it would be thought silly. "Imagination running away with you," her mother would say. Her father would explain, "Animals don't think, dear. We must not put human characteristics on them."

The coyotes continued watching. The one with its tongue hanging looked like it grinned. But if I could tell Uncle Bernard, she thought, he would not think it silly or imagined.

It was a wonderful thing to see, my girl, how the Indians could communicate with animals. I've seen a young warrior stand near his camp, looking to where the horses grazed, and pretty soon over the grass comes trotting his favorite pinto, ears up and tail swinging. And wouldn't the horse walk right to that brave and put his soft nose against the man's ear and nicker a greeting. The Indians understood that animals have souls too, Eleanor. That they're players also in this big play of life.

But Uncle Bernard was not here. She had to trust in her own experience. She raised her hand in farewell to the two coyotes. When she looked back a few paces further, the spot where they had watched was empty.

CHAPTER 19

"THE TWO FIDDLERS who played at Christmas are coming again. Next Saturday, at the Wagners." Stephen had returned jubilant from Seven Persons and talked non-stop. "You'd hardly believe how the town is growing. A new lumberyard, new hotel, another bank, and the general store stacked floor to ceiling. There'll be a meeting about the new school before the fiddling starts."

On Saturday, the Donaldsons drove Belle and Charlie to the Wagners' homestead where they were greeted by Hattie, who flew out the front door, took the porch steps two at a time, and rushed to seize Eleanor's hands. "I'm so happy to see you. I'm so happy winter's over. Did you hear? We'll have a school and see each other every day." She spoke in breathless excitement, Carl and Adam behind her. Adam grinned directly, Carl gave a soft smile, a quick glance, and a gentle hello.

"Come on." Hattie pulled Eleanor's hand and led her to a group of other young people that included Lydia and a girl with dark brown curls. "This is Elizabeth. She's your age and has three brothers." Hattie completed whirlwind introductions.

"The school meeting is about to start, but the students don't have to go to it," noted Lydia.

"Who would want to?" Adam boomed. "We've got enough here for a ballgame." Two teams were quickly organized in the field west of the house.

They played for the best part of the afternoon before the door opened to spill meeting participants in twos and threes. "All done," called Hattie, and she ran from second base to the house, calling as she did, "Let's find out what's going to happen."

At the same time, four riders approached from the south. They wore large Stetsons, kerchiefs, shirts of heavy cotton, and thick leather vests. Two had rifles in scabbards at the side of their saddles. As other players abandoned the ballfield for a better view of the new arrivals, the riders dismounted at the hitch rails on the east side. "We heard there's fiddle music," the first to dismount said.

Eleanor gasped, taken aback, to see coyote pelts piled behind the saddles on two of the horses. She stood frozen, eyes on the skins as Carl arrived at her right.

"They come from the Ross Ranch, looking for stray cattle after winter." He scuffed his left foot and kept his eyes on the groove of bare earth his action created.

"Why are those skins on their horses?" Eleanor asked.

"'Cause they like to kill. 'Cause they can get a few pennies for a pelt. 'Cause they would have done horrid and cruel things before the coyotes finally died." He spoke in a whisper that startled her with its fierceness.

"Do you know them?" she asked.

"Can't tell from here. I worked on the Ross Ranch for a year before joining Uncle George. Ranching life isn't for me. I don't much care for the company," he said.

Hattie hollered from the porch. "C'mon, it's time to eat."

Carl walked towards the ballfield. "I'm not hungry. I'll walk awhile."

Eleanor couldn't decide whether to join Hattie or follow him. The thought of seeing the coyote skins closer brought a sudden dislike for the ranch hands. She caught up to Carl.

"I saw a pair of coyotes watching me from across the coulee. It was so strange because it felt like they were thinking about me." The words escaped Eleanor's mouth before she realized. They sounded odd, spoken aloud.

"The spring before I left the ranch, I watched a den of pups alongside a dried up creek bed, every day. Their parents let me get really close. They trusted me." They walked on in silence until Carl abruptly said, "You better go. If Hattie sees us walking together there'll be no end to the teasing. And I don't need to give Adam another reason to be annoyed with me."

Eleanor's head was full of questions, but the image of Hattie setting off comments about her and Carl walking together turned her back. Keeping her thoughts and eyes away from the coyote pelts, she walked directly to the house. What did he mean about giving Adam a reason to be annoyed? She reached the porch steps just as Hattie opened the door.

"There you are. Where have you been? Your mother has been asking about you." Without waiting for a reply she reached for Eleanor's hand. "I'll tell you all about the new school while we eat."

As the meal finished, the fiddlers began to make long, mournful tones to warm their instruments, a signal to the others to push furniture to the edges of the room and clear the floor for dancing. The first dances were a slow waltz, a two-step, and a polka. Eleanor, Hattie, and Lydia joined a circle of threesomes in a schottische and then a circle dance in which the fiddlers called out the steps.

When the tempo increased to a lively Irish jig, the tallest of the ranch hands, the one with a thick, black mustache and bushy eyebrows, locked his thumbs in the belt hooks of his black pants while his red kerchief bounced in time with his feet, moving ever faster as the fiddlers bowed with increasing gusto. Onlookers gathered around the dancer and clapped to the lively beat. Another man joined, a huge, thick-chested farmer with dense black hair and dark eyes. He crossed his arms at his chest and kicked his legs high, the floor booming each time he stamped.

When the fiddlers closed the piece at last, the men grinned, foreheads wet with perspiration and, as those surrounding applauded, the ranch hand gave an exaggerated bow, bringing more applause and laughter. He then took up a conversation with Stephen in a voice deep and rich. He sounded like Uncle Bernard. But Uncle Bernard would never kill coyotes to sell their pelts for pennies.

Adam leaned against the opposite wall and talked with Elizabeth, whose dark curls shone in the light of coal oil lanterns hung along the walls. He waved to Eleanor, but she turned away as if she hadn't seen him.

She felt ill at ease in a room where she didn't belong. Coyote pelts, Carl's distress, the ranch hand's vigorous, joyful dancing, Adam's attentiveness to Elizabeth: why did these disturb her? No one else seemed bothered.

When her father announced it was time to leave and said, "There's talk that a blizzard is on its way," she was relieved.

CHAPTER 20

THE STORM UNLOADED thick, dense snow that smoothed every depression and left the land flat, silent, and white. For three days, Eleanor waited indoors while the clouds emptied their burden. On the fourth, a refreshed sun rose in a clear eastern sky and scattered shimmering sparks of itself over the whitened land.

"Feel that west wind." Eleanor's father stood next to her in front of their home as both looked to the wrinkle of mountains on the horizon. A thick, flat bank of cloud promised a chinook. "Most of the snow will be gone by this afternoon."

"It's a good thing," Eleanor added, "though it's beautiful. But we're nearly out of coal, and Mr. Pacey said it will be another week before he's able to deliver again." She raised her hand to shield her eyes from the sun and followed the flight of a bird from west to east. "That's a new one. They're coming back. Spring must really be here." The bird was out of sight, but she kept her hand up and watched, as if it would return any moment. "Maybe I could take Belle to the coulee and put the sacks over her back. I could carry more coal that way, riding her there and leading her home."

Catharine joined them in taking in the brilliance of the morning. "Why not lead her both ways, Eleanor? She's much too big to ride."

"She's gentle as a lamb," Eleanor protested, "and she almost reads my mind, she's so eager to do my bidding. I could ride her easily."

Stephen put his arm across Catharine's shoulder. "You needn't worry, my dear. Riding Belle will not threaten her being a woman with proper graces."

Catharine folded her arms at her chest. "Eleanor should be going to school, learning music, reading literature that uplifts her mind, not riding a Percheron workhorse to haul coal to a house made of dirt." She shook her head and patted her husband's hand on her shoulder.

"It's more important here that I learn to ride and drive a team, Mother. What if I needed to go for help?" The look of distress on Catharine's face made her regret that statement, valid as it was. Their isolation disturbed her mother enough without adding to it with reminders of potential threat.

"It's a good point, you must admit," her father said. "Let's go get the horses their breakfast oats, Eleanor."

In only a week, new green fuzz covered the land as wind and ground drank up the snow. Stephen turned over a rectangle of grass east of their soddie where Catharine and Eleanor now carried rocks from newly exposed dirt that would be their garden.

"Spuds, onions, turnips – food to last through the winter – that's what you want to plant," Ada had advised on hearing Catharine speak of a garden.

Catharine had set her lips tightly but did not reply to Ada. Today, she worked the dirt with resolve. "I want to plant things other than hardy root vegetables, Eleanor. Someday there will be roses here. And inside, a piano." Her mother set another stone along the north edge and pressed her hands into her back. "Here's your father already back for tea, and I've not even started water to boil."

Eleanor looked south to where her father was a dark speck and saw beyond him a red splotch that could only be the bright jacket of Constable Whyte from the Royal North West Mounted Police post. He made regular visits, as he did with all the homesteads, to check on the family's wellbeing, bring news, and ease his own isolation. Catharine's fresh-baked biscuits and tea often encouraged long conversations.

"Constable Whyte is coming too, Mother." Now she could recognize his familiar long-legged horse, Scalliwag. Beside him, dust rose up, but she could not tell what made it. "Someone else is with him."

By the time steam wafted from the kettle and Eleanor's father had finished washing away the dirt from ploughing, the Constable had stopped at the house along with a black buggy pulled by a fine-boned gray horse. "I'd like you to meet Miss Lily Hamilton," the policeman announced, and he offered his hand to help the well-dressed woman step down.

"So delighted to meet you all. Constable Whyte has been full of praises about you and your hard work. For the last three miles he has talked of nothing but your excellent biscuits, Mrs. Donaldson."

Eleanor could not take her eyes from this woman, who was elegantly dressed in a brown skirt and jacket with a white, high-collared blouse. Her hair hung loose in thick curls beneath a wide-brimmed hat.

Everyone gathered inside at the plank table as the rich aroma of biscuits that had just been put in the oven filled the room. Eleanor's mother poured tea from the blue-and-gold china pot that she had retrieved, with its matching cups, from the trunk.

"Constable Whyte is kindly guiding me to various homesteads. We'll be staying in Altorado this evening." Lily Hamilton sipped her tea and glanced around the room. "You've accomplished so much already. There'll soon be fields of waving grain where the Indians once hunted buffalo."

Eleanor thought she could listen to that voice all day, its rich, musical tone. Lily Hamilton sounded so at ease with herself, so comfortable in their small home.

She spoke further. "You're part of a time of rapid change, which relates to what brings me here. I represent the Royal Ontario Museum, which has a great interest in collecting evidence, artifacts of the Plains Indian way of life, a life that so rapidly disappeared."

"But first," Constable Whyte interrupted, as Catharine set a plate of golden-topped biscuits between them, "You must try the new treasures of the west."

Miss Hamilton laughed and broke off a corner to savor with thoughtful chewing. "Your reputation is well-deserved. Delicious."

"Please, tell us more about your work," Catharine prompted, obviously flattered.

"What I request is that, if you uncover arrowheads, scrapers, spear points, or any other Indian tools as you turn the soil and wander over the prairie, please save them. In another three months, I'll be back this way and may be able to offer a small recompense for objects the museum could use."

Eleanor thought of the pointed black rock she found at the tipi circles. She had placed it between the folds of her shawl and was about to offer it to Miss Hamilton. She hesitated.

"Before I take more of your time, there is one more thing." Miss Hamilton opened a small pouch on the belt of her skirt and took a card from it. "Here is my name and address at the museum. Sometimes Indians offer to sell items from their ceremonies or special clothing and so forth. If anyone approaches with such an offer, would you ask them to return in a couple of weeks and write to me immediately with details and price? I can send money for the purchase. You would be helping to preserve valuable knowledge of a vanishing people." She turned to look directly at Eleanor.

"Eleanor, the Constable tells me you like to walk to the coulee and regularly gather coal. That's a wonderful place to find artifacts. I hope you'll watch for some."

"Yes, I will," she answered hesitantly. She would. The next time Miss Hamilton visited, she would have found more. But the black stone was her first. She wanted to keep it.

Catharine had paused with her cup mid-way to her mouth. "Are we likely to have Indians coming around to our door with things to sell?"

Constable Whyte popped a last bit of biscuit into his

mouth, swallowed rapidly and leaned forward. "You have nothing to worry about, Mrs. Donaldson, unless word about your biscuits reaches the reserve."

Catharine smiled, but concern had not left her face.

He leaned further. "One of my jobs is to take back Indians who haven't a good reason to be away from the reserve. It happens now and then, but it's usually in Fort MacLeod or Lethbridge. Nothing to worry about out here."

"Is there a reason, Miss Hamilton, that you wouldn't go directly to the Indians on the reserve to purchase items?" her father asked.

"Unscrupulous buyers have tarred us all with the same brush in the eyes of many Indians, I fear. We meet suspicion and resentment on the reserve. Instead of direct purchase, we'd prefer to buy from those who willingly offer a sale. Our objective is to preserve and safeguard these things."

"I'm afraid we must be on our way," Constable Whyte said, "if we're to be at Altorado by evening."

Stephen continued. "I just wouldn't want to take advantage of their sad plight,"

"We are not responsible for their sad state, Mr. Donaldson. But the fact is, their way of life is done. These items from their past are often sold just for whiskey. They're disappearing rapidly. Much better to have them valued and preserved with the museum's efforts than lost entirely."

Miss Hamilton picked up her gloves from the table and turned to Catharine and Eleanor as she pulled the soft leather over her hands. "Thank you so much for your time and hospitality. I look forward to my next visit, and to what you find in your walks, Eleanor."

With that, she stepped into her buggy with ease and gave a slight flick of the reins that sent the gray into a steady trot. Beside her, Constable Whyte waved an enthusiastic good-bye.

"You see," Eleanor noted, "She drives a horse and is obviously a well-mannered woman."

"She doesn't drive a workhorse and a wagon. Neither does she ride." Her mother returned inside to clear the table.

"Eleanor," her father called, gathering his hat and jacket, "walk with me back to where I'm ploughing, and then you can go on to the coulee for coal."

The sun warmed their faces as they walked. Eleanor scanned from east to west, the hills dark gray before them. "Do you think we'll ever visit the hills, Father?"

"I'm not supposed to mention anything yet, my dear, but Uncle Bernard is planning a visit. If he comes, he'll very likely take you to those hills. But not a word until we know for sure."

CHAPTER 21

ELEANOR SAT OUTSIDE the door, the cream-colored envelope addressed in Uncle Bernard's flowing script in her lap. Would he come this spring or not?

With a deep breath, she opened it.

"There's no sense going on and on, wearing my fingers to the bone, when I'll be talking face to face with you very soon. Yes, my dear Eleanor, I am coming. I do long to see you and your parents. It will be a joy to visit the west again, but I confess to being a little nervous as well. It's a bit like going to see an old sweetheart after many years."

That was all she needed to know. Of all that was left behind in Ontario, he was what she missed. But I miss him here, she noted, not there. He belongs here with us.

She read further, hardly taking in the words until his closing.

"I cut this from the newspaper for you since it connects to the Indians of your area."

A black headline on carefully clipped newsprint announced:

Indian Medicine Bundle Stolen From Museum
On Friday, March 3, a piece of Plains Indian history, a Medicine Bundle, was stolen from the Royal Ontario Museum. A woman who claimed to be researching decorative patterns of ceremonial items requested a viewing. 'She seemed knowledgeable and respectable,' said a museum staff member. 'I had no reason for suspicion. I displayed several pieces, and she examined the beadwork and stitching. Then, she suddenly seemed about to faint and requested a glass of water. When I returned with it, she and the Medicine Bundle were gone.' The whereabouts or identity of the woman is unknown. Anyone with information is asked to contact police.

Eleanor tucked the clipping into the envelope. How odd, she thought, to steal such a thing.

The next day, Hattie leaped from the Wagner's wagon before it had even stopped. "The school is nearly done and everything's arranged. You're going to ride with us, Eleanor. You can meet us near the coulee, and we'll ride all together straight north to school. On bad weather days, we'll come all the way here to get you. Isn't that marvelous?"

The Wagners had come again to help Eleanor's father cut sod. As the wagon and men headed for the south corner, Ada expanded on Hattie's exclamation as she carried two baskets inside.

"The route is flat and safe," she said. "And we've a light wagon that just needs its axle fixed."

Catharine stoked the stove and filled the blue enamel kettle. "This is truly generous, Ada. We've been stumped as to how Eleanor would get to school. It's too far to walk, and we can't spare Stephen's time to drive her."

"I needed a plan to get the whole bunch to school. George said he couldn't spare the boys. But I set him straight." She waved her hands to the girls. "Away you go, get a good bunch of coal, and leave us to catch up on news and have our tea."

They sat in the grass at the tipi rings, Lydia on the western edge, Hattie and Eleanor inside the nearest circle. A mild and sweetly scented breeze carried smells of cottonwood buds and melted water. "It's going to be hard to be indoors at school now, as the good weather comes," Eleanor said. "I'd like to be riding all over like Miss Hamilton. Isn't she terrific?"

"I bet we could find things right here that she would want," suggested Hattie. She began scraping dirt with a stone, sending dust clouds around her.

Eleanor sucked in her breath. Though Hattie first showed her the circles, she had come to consider them her own special place. Hers and the people who once camped at this spot. "But if there are things here, shouldn't they just stay, along with the stones? So much is gone already."

Lydia leaned back on her arms, legs outstretched, ankles crossed. "That way of life is all done. It's the old west. We're the new west. The Best West."

Hattie stopped her digging. "Still, it was Indian land for hundreds of years. Maybe we should leave things be."

Lydia shrugged. "It will all be ploughed under and seeded to wheat. If you want to see Indian tools in the future, you'll have to go to Miss Hamilton's museum. Let's go get the coal."

Eleanor walked last, unsettled by the image of the entire prairie gone, nothing but fields of rippling wheat all the way to the mountains, just like the poster had shown. Where would the antelope go? The coyotes?

Two days following, Constable Whyte visited. "I'm just checking in to all the homesteads. Lily, Miss Hamilton, will be returning earlier than planned as there's been a theft from her museum, and we have reason to believe the person who did it might end up in this area. We're asking everyone to keep a look out for anything unusual." He stood beside Scalliwag and declined, regretfully, Catharine's invitation for tea and biscuits. "I thank you. That's a difficult offer to refuse, but I've quite a distance to cover today."

"Eleanor," Catharine asked, "Didn't Uncle Bernard send a clipping about an item stolen from the same museum? Run and get it and show Constable Whyte."

"That is indeed the same story," he affirmed. "If you see any strangers moving through, I'd much appreciate your letting me know. You can tell Miss Jensen, the new school teacher and she'll get word to me."

"Is there anything to fear, Constable?" Catharine asked. "Eleanor will be walking alone each day to meet the Wagner children to ride to school. I don't like the idea of her walking alone when there's a thief about."

"Mother, it's so flat. No one could get within five miles without being seen."

"All the same, I don't like it."

"We have no reason to suspect danger, Mrs. Donaldson. The woman who took the Medicine Bundle seemed very peaceable," Constable Whyte assured her. "But if you see anything, please let me know right away."

The walk to and from the meeting place each day emerged as Eleanor's favorite time. This day, the sky arched from every horizon in pale blue. The wind was quiet, and a herd of antelope grazed on new grass along the opposite side of the coulee. Two young ones gamboled between the elders, who were intent on the serious business of morning feeding. The calves' hide-and-seek antics made her laugh aloud.

A meadowlark called, melodic and haunting. At the coulee bottom, soft gray-green willow leaves and glistening cottonwood colored the borders. Eleanor was just about to turn north and walk the few minutes to meet the wagon when what looked like a thin column of smoke rose from a cleft in the far side. It can't be smoke, she thought. Can it? Mist? One thin blue strand? She walked to the coulee's edge but could see nothing that gave a clue to the origin.

The sound of the wagon's rattle alerted her, and she ran, her satchel flapping against her hip. "Sorry I'm late," she gasped. "I got distracted with young antelope."

At school, the day stretched long, and Eleanor could not concentrate. She wanted the day to end, wanted to be at the coulee rim with thoughts that twisted up on a curl of misty blue. What was in the coulee? Was it smoke? From what? From whom?

SECTION FIVE
Dissolution

CHAPTER 22

SNAKE WOMAN OPENED her eyes. She lay on her back, her forehead felt cool and something dabbed it. Who was leaning over her?

"So you have come back to us, little one."

Her grandmother, that's who it was. She could not make out any features on the form above her, silhouetted against the pale gold of the lodge hide. Warm, rich scents filled her nostrils – sage, sweetgrass, smoke – and that particular, pleasant fragrance of the old woman's breath.

Mountain Horse laid the cool cloth on the young woman's forehead again. Snake Woman's throat felt swollen and dry. Another cloth, sopping and cool, touched her lips. They were cracked, stuck together. Water dribbled from the cloth into the crevice of her mouth and loosened the hold. It ran down her face on each side as her lips opened and drops found their way through to moisten her thick tongue. She swallowed. Her throat ached. Why did Mountain Horse say she had come back? Had she gone somewhere? She tried to make her tongue, mouth, and lips work to ask, "What has happened?" But none of them moved.

"Soon you will have your strength back, little Snake Woman. Suck on the cloth. Then rest again. I'm here with you."

Her grandmother's deep, resonant voice washed over her like warm water. She sighed deeply and slept.

The next time she woke it was dark. A weight pressed on her body. She tried to throw it off, but could not make her arms move. She heard breathing beside her, a slow rhythm with a soft sigh on the outbreath. Mountain Horse.

The walls of the Otter Lodge glowed pinkish gold when she next woke. Her grandmother leaned against her willow backrest and angled her body so she could look closely into Snake Woman's face. "So, you look much like yourself now. Would you like water?" The woman daubed her lips with a soaked cloth.

This time, her mouth and tongue and lips responded to her efforts to speak. "What happened, Grandmother?" Her voice came from far away, pale, like it was another person's and not her own.

"You have been sick for many days. Now you are better, still weak. You must get strong again. Can you take this?" Mountain Horse dipped a finger into a shallow bowl and then to Snake Woman's mouth where a dribble of broth drained between her lips. She licked them and swallowed. The old woman repeated her action. "That will help. Have a little more. Then wait. You did not eat a long time, little Snake Woman. You must take food slowly."

"Am I not Snake Child?" Questions crawled about in her mind as if they moved in mud.

Her grandmother smiled her broad grin and brushed her fingers lightly over Snake Woman's forehead. "You have left behind the child, little one. Now you have begun the woman."

When she next woke, Snake Woman sensed something different in the lodge. Mountain Horse sat before a cookfire and dropped pieces of chopped root into the pot that bubbled over it. Was another person in the lodge? She moved carefully to avoid sending sharp spears of pain through her head and looked behind on the west side. A red blanket draped a long, cylindrical shape that hung on a tripod of poles. "The Bundle has come. Was there no ceremony?" The effort to turn her head and speak tired her.

"You slept through it all. Sun rose and set five times while you did not open your eyes."

"What happened, Grandmother? I went to be painted and did not feel well inside the lodge." Images flitted through her mind: swirls of smoke, drums, an owl, golden eyes, a snake's head, a rattle. A song. Confusion swirled like the memory of the smoke. Had she dreamed this?

"You collapsed when you stood before the Holy Woman. We feared we had lost you." Mountain Horse pushed herself to standing and wiped her hands on the blanket that hung over her shoulders. "When you are stronger, we will talk more."

Three more days passed. The old woman sat beside Snake Woman in the shade of the lodge, passed a tin cup half-filled with water to her, and nodded. "Tell me about when you went to get painted. Everything that happened that day."

Snake Woman recounted all she remembered: her bleeding time, her restlessness, the bath in the river. Sometimes Mountain Horse prompted her for details. Which direction did you walk? Where did you lay your clothes? Who did you see? With this question, the memory of the coyote arose, which brought more questions. How did coyote stand? What did she do? Which direction did she leave?

"I don't even know if it was a she," Snake Woman replied. "I didn't get that close."

Mountain Horse grunted. "On the day you are to be painted in the Women's Lodge, the day you begin your woman time? It was a she, you can be sure."

Snake Woman's memory of events inside the Women's Lodge were vague and confused. The old woman's questions prodded gently and became specific. Yes, the girl thought, her grandmother had been there, had witnessed it.

"What did you see when the smudge started?"

"I don't remember. My head hurt. The smoke stung. I felt sick. You were there. You must have seen." The strain of searching her memory brought beads of sweat to Snake Woman's face. She clenched her hands and knotted her eyebrows.

"Stay calm, little one. Have a sip of water." Mountain Horse ran a finger across Snake Woman's forehead, as if to smooth a winkled cloth. "When you were smudged, you began to sing. You sang an ancient song that belongs to the

Bundle of the Holy Woman who fanned the smoke. The song stays inside the Women's Lodge. No one understands how you could have learned it. That's why I ask you like this. Trying to find the meaning. Old Man Snake has visited you again. But what does he want? Why has he given you his song?"

Snake Woman shuddered. As soon as Mountain Horse spoke of the singing, she saw vividly the headdress of the Holy Woman before her and the snake that rose swaying from it to invite her to sing. She told her grandmother what she remembered, then crawled into the lodge and slept.

The last days of the Sun Gathering arrived, and drums pounded for the men who danced, sunrise to dark, round and round the sacred pole. Those who did not dance sat to watch, to support the dancers with prayers and their presence as they circled in rhythmic steps without food or water, day after day. A wall of meshed poplar branches sheltered those who needed refuge from the sun's heat and glare, the old and young and sick. Snake Woman tried to sit in the shade, but shafts of light pierced her head and made her dizzy and weak. Throughout the dancing she remained in the lodge, mostly alone, troubled by the sense of something she had forgotten to tell her grandmother, the way a dream will haunt daylight with vague images, yet never reveal the details.

Pretty Crow and White Feather remained at the circle as long as Black Eagle and One Spot danced, watching their future husbands turn and step in the relentless heat to the drumbeat and shriek of bone whistles, circling until they tore the skewers that pierced their chests and backs free of the flesh that held them.

All the time she listened to the drums and whistles, Snake Woman felt the presence of the Bundle. The lodge felt fuller, as if others had come to dwell there also.

Every morning, Mountain Horse sang prayers and burned powder before the Bundle, then lovingly carried it outside to hang from its tripod on the west side, covered in the red blanket. Each evening, she carried it within, again offering prayers and smoke.

Some nights Snake Woman woke in the blackness and heard a hum, as of distant singing, coming from where the Bundle hung. She did not know if the sound was comfort or if it disturbed.

CHAPTER 23

THE OKAN DISPERSED in the days following the men's Sun Dance. The morning the Many Children prepared to depart, Little Ear rode to the Otter Lodge on his freckled mare, the spotted filly trotting at her side, eyes wide in anxious curiosity in the camp bustle. "She's grown so much, you needed to see her, to remember how she looks. I'm glad you're getting well."

"She's tall, Little Ear, like her mother, and getting long. Her spots have faded; they look like clouds on her back. I'm going to call her that. Cloud." A surge of gladness filled her in seeing the filly and in Little Ear's kindness.

This made lying on the travois as the band traveled north more bearable. She had not ridden this way since her grandmother introduced her to Old Man Buffalo Stone. The hum of his song on her hand had delighted her then as the filly – and Little Ear's friendship – did now. The weakness that kept her from riding a horse was not delight, as it hadn't been those many years ago.

Next to her, Shadow's pups squirmed, whined, and slept in a fur-lined basket while the dog trotted beside, sniffing them from time to time. The horses they rode from the Black Elks were gone, offered as part of the Bundle transfer. Snake Woman regretted the roan's leaving and that she hadn't said farewell. The sturdy mare's nicker of welcome when she walked to find her, the rides alongside Little Ear and his black mustang, these were pleasures gone. "Shadow, being pulled on a travois and seeing from behind is not so agreeable as looking ahead." The center pole of the great camp grew smaller; the offerings tied to it flapped in the wind until they were as tiny ribbons on a stick, and then gone.

Scouts had reported buffalo in large numbers grazing the thick, rolling grasslands to the north, near the huge pile of rocks known as Okotoks, the Big Rock. This is where the Many Children chose to camp for their fall hunt. All the tribes knew the stories of how Okotoks came to be here, far from the mountains of his earlier home.

Mountain Horse again told Snake Woman the story as they approached the camp. "That Napi gave his coat to Okotoks as a present. Then he wanted it back, and when the rock said 'No,' Napi grabbed it and ran. Big Rock chased him and chased him, all the way to here, trying to get that coat back. Then that trickster Napi scooted around and ran uphill to the mountains. Big Rock couldn't run uphill so he had to stay here."

Each day in the new camp, Snake Woman's strength increased, and the pain from sunlight lessened until she scraped and soaked and stretched hides alongside the other women. She could not yet walk far, but worked close to the lodges and rested when needed.

This day, Snake Woman and Mountain Horse knelt side by side, scraping the hide of a young cow. Clouds that were thick that morning parted like torn cloth, exposing irregular scraps of blue, letting shafts of sun illumine the hills in a golden sheen. Excited barks stopped their work, and they squinted to see what had set off the noise, walking toward camp for a closer look.

Five horses, three with riders, approached through the space between the rock and the lodges. The riders wore the broad hats of paleskins. When close to the camp, they reined in their horses and dismounted. WindMaker ruffled the grass before them, and it shimmered like the winter waves of light in the night sky.

Spotted Horse, Shot Twice, and Crooked Back walked toward the three, whose rifles remained in scabbards beside their saddles. The dogs kept up their barks, trotting back and forth along the edge of camp, noses in the air.

Snake Woman stared. She wanted to run to the safety of the Otter Lodge, or beyond the camp where these paleskins were not. But she did not move. Her heart pounded, and she scarcely breathed. Did they come to trade? With what? From where? Why had they come here in the middle of the day?

Women and children collected at the eastern edge of the lodges and looked in curiosity. Most of the men were out with the hunt. The women, Pretty Crow and White Feather with them, gone to skin the slain carcasses, drag them back on sagging travois, not returning until Sun sank close to the mountains. Spotted Horse walked toward the Bear Lodge and the three paleskins followed, leading their horses, with Shot Twice and Crooked Back behind them.

Layers of wolf hides mounded the packhorses. As they passed by Snake Woman, she saw them: gray, black, brindled. And on top of the second load – an all-white pelt.

Waves of horror crashed through her. She ran to the Otter Lodge and threw herself on the robes. Her eyes burned, and she choked on the urge to scream. There could not be more than one white wolf. It had to be the same one. She buried her face in the brown, matted hair of the buffalo hide, breathing rapid gasps to keep her tears back, keep the dread that welled up from her heart from escaping, from swallowing her up. "No, no, no," she panted. "This can not be." Not this, not the pelt of the beautiful white wolf thrown on the back of a paleskin's horse.

She sat up. It has to be a mistake; the sun breaking through the clouds made the pelt seem brighter. It was not a white one but another color, pale gray. She saw the image in her mind again, knew that it was not the sun that made the fur white. She leaned her forehead on her knees. The white wolf dead. Killed by a paleskin. A ball of hatred burned in the center of her belly. She felt its heat radiate through her body, rise through her chest. The urge to scream she felt was rage, rage for all the paleskins who had come to their land, for the ones who traded at the Black Elks camp, the ones who stole the Black Stone, who brought whiskey into Napi's country, for the cruelty she heard in so many tales, for their pride and scorn and greed and lies. She hated them all, and she hated most the three men in the camp right now.

Her breath had become deeper and slower, though still strained. She lifted her head and looked about the lodge, the familiar surroundings there: the willow backrest, the fire pit, the space the Bundle occupied each night, the top of the lodge wall stained dark from smoke. The threat of being engulfed in horror had passed, driven away by the fierceness of her anger.

The flap opened and Mountain Horse entered. "Are you ill?"

"No, I am angry. Did you see the wolf hides on their horses? Did you see the white one? They've killed the white wolf. They've killed all those wolves. I hate them. They are the ones who should be killed, made to eat poison and have their skin stripped off. All of them."

Her grandmother sat, leaned against the backrest and stretched her legs. "Maybe. But you've heard the stories. For every paleskin killed, a hundred Real People are killed in return. They say the paleskins are numerous like the leaves of the aspen in summer."

Snake Woman leaned her forehead into the palms of her hand. "Why have they come here? They have to be stopped, Grandmother. For the life of us all, the People, the wolves, the buffalo, the dogs. Shaggy Bull was right when he called for war."

The old woman nodded. "They are a mystery and a problem, yes. They do not have the ways Napi gave to us that teach us balance and harmony. We have our Bundles, our ceremonies and medicines to do this work. Here in the Otter Lodge too, we have our Bundle, standing just there outside." Mountain Horse waved her hand to the west.

Snake Woman nodded. She knew that outbursts of anger

in the presence of the Bundle showed disrespect. "I understand." She understood what was expected of her, that she not display anger this way, but she wanted to shout: Why does the Bundle not send these paleskins away, give disease to them, kill their friends, let them writhe from the agony of poison? Make them suffer?

Her grandmother answered as if she had spoken aloud. "The paleskins are not without suffering. The wife, a sister, two children in the family of those who took the Black Stone died from the sickness. The man whose wife gave you red ribbons. He had kindness."

Her words evoked the memory of that man's brother, of Pretty Crow bloodied and swollen with months of sorrow that followed, of Calf Shield in his new red shirt dead, of Yellow Star cold on the grass. Had the paleskins not come, none of these hurts would have happened. Now paleskins again in their camp, and the white wolf dead because of them. They did not belong here.

Mountain Horse pushed herself to stand. "We can go learn why they come."

They sat in Spotted Horse's Lodge, Snake Woman next to her grandmother on the women's side, near the wall. She hunched over and from time to time glanced at the strangers. The one next to Spotted Horse, tall with pale brown hair that hung in waves almost to his shoulders, spoke clearly in the language of the People.

"We thank you, Spotted Horse and all your band, for your hospitality and generosity that you invite us to stay in your camp."

Stay? She could hardly believe she heard this. Why would Spotted Horse let them stay?

His name was Alexander Sterling, and he came from far to the east. "I was fortunate to hire these most able men," he pointed to the pair with him, "as my guides through Blackfoot country. I wish to visit camps and learn the ways of the tribes." He paused and looked at the faces watching him. "I work for what is called a museum." The faces showed no understanding. They looked to Spotted Horse and Shot Twice to see if these more traveled elders knew what this meant. "It is a great lodge made of stone and wood," he continued. "The people of this lodge want to better understand your ways. They asked me to bring tools, clothing, and knowledge of how you make and use these." Several men and women lowered their faces to hide chuckles, murmured and shook their heads at this funny story. They looked to each other with incredulity. How would seeing a tool or a shirt be of any purpose?

The two who accompanied Sterling kept their eyes down and made no effort to interact. They drank the tea offered by Spotted Horse's wife, smoked the pipe when it came to them, but kept silent and still. The man next to Sterling sat cross-legged, his black hat resting on one knee. The other kept his brown hat on, brim pulled low, face hidden. He sat further back than the other two and stroked the finger of his right hand with his thumb, as if to rub something off.

"My guides," Sterling went on, "have made this a hunting journey also. You have seen the furs that show their hunting was good." Heads nodded acknowledgement. Who could have failed to notice?

"Many wolves," said Spotted Horse. "Did you see other game?"

At the mention of the wolves, Snake Woman could not get enough air to breathe, although she breathed deeply and rapidly. But the air had no life. She felt empty, gasping. A memory darted through her mind of the afternoon in the Women's Lodge when she stood to be painted, when her lungs could not find what they sought. She slid toward the wall, reached behind her, and lifted the hide where it met the earth. She turned to breathe the cool air that slipped into the dim light.

The brown-hatted man watched her, then immediately lowered his head when she saw him. But Snake Woman had seen the opening at his shirt, had seen the small bit of cloth exposed, the small bit of green kerchief. She had seen also the same look on his face during the afternoon of trading while he watched Pretty Crow. She felt nauseous. Had he recognized her? Of course not. Why would he? Why would anyone from the Black Elks be in the Many Children's camp?

With the shock of recognizing the man, Snake Woman hadn't taken in the conversation. Sterling was talking about the wolves. "She gave a fight to see, that one did." He shook his head as if a fly buzzed around his ear. "Conrad there didn't want her hide spoiled with a bullet. Figured a white pelt unmarked would bring a good price." The lodge was quiet as all ears tuned to the details of the hunt.

Snake Woman wanted out, looked for a way to pass between sitting bodies without drawing attention. But she could not stand, could not take her ears away from the story, no matter how much the words burned into her heart.

"She was running like the wind, and he was after her full gallop. Got a rope around her neck. Pulled her up. And didn't she leap around and cut that rope with one bite. So the same thing again, and she snaps it once more. This time he shot her in the leg, got a rope around her again, and she turned and ran right at him, leapt up and bit into his leg."

Snake Woman felt her grandmother's hand on her shoulder. *Do not scream. Do not wail. Do not sob. Do not show what is felt.* This passed to her thoughts from the hand.

"She bit him high enough to get above his boot. He's got quite a slash on that leg and had to douse it with whiskey and bind it tight. Then he shot her right in the chest. Spoiled that big, thick, white coat, but she wasn't going easy. A magnificent fight she gave, that's for sure."

In the silence that continued after he finished, Snake Woman stood and walked calmly between the sitting people and left the lodge. The ones who were hunting and skinning would return soon. She had to warn Pretty Crow to keep clear of the strangers. She needed also a plan for how to deal with the green-kerchiefed man. For Pretty Crow, Calf-Shield, Yellow Star, and the white wolf, she needed to talk with One Spot.

CHAPTER 24

SNAKE WOMAN WALKED in long strides in the direction the hunters had ridden that morning, where the skinners would be dressing the kills of the day. The travois ponies trudged with heavy loads, poles sagging with the weight of meat and skins. Pretty Crow and White Feather walked side by side in the slow, contented way of easy friends after a hard day's work.

She told them about the paleskins in camp and about Conrad, about the white wolf. "I'm sorry to bring such news. But you needed to be warned of his presence, to avoid him. I'm going to walk awhile and clear my anger before Grandmother scolds me for my behavior in front of the Bundle." She had to find One Spot before he got back, and she had to keep it to herself.

Snake Woman had not walked this far since her illness, and she found it hard to climb the hill west of camp to gain enough view to see the hunters returning. She sat and planned how she could call One Spot without raising curiosity, how they could avenge what had been done.

For One Spot, the death of Calf Shield because of the trader's betrayal had left a grievous harm unanswered. If he was given the opportunity to avenge Calf Shield's death and did not take it, it would insult the spirit of the chief, insult One Spot's debt to the man who took him in like a son. But the paleskins were guests of Spotted Horse and under his protection. Spotted Horse had taken them all into the Many Children's camp, and they owed allegiance to him. A twisted, crooked path wound its way through obligations and debts, but she knew there was a way to follow it to right action.

The lanky sorrel's gait alerted her in plenty of time to meet One Spot as he neared the camp, Black Eagle and Little Ear riding with him. Both the older men rode bare-chested, though the afternoon air was cool, for the wounds from their flesh sacrifice were still red and swollen. A shirt would chafe and aggravate further. "One Spot," she called. "Can I speak with you? A message from White Feather."

The others rode on, and the two sat while she told him the plan she had made. "There will be feasting tonight, tales of the day's hunt, strangers in camp. Pretty Crow and White Feather will not go. I will say I am going to see Cloud, be away from the horrible Conrad. I know how to get him to follow me. You must say your wounds are painful and the day's hunt has made you too tired for feasting and stories. The man Conrad sits apart from the others. He will sneak away unseen." One Spot listened as she recounted the details of her scheme. They separated to return to their lodges.

With the hunters returned, the fires burning, strips of fresh meat roasting over the fire, the Many Children were soon gathered. Sterling and the man with the black hat, Davis, already sat in the fire's circle in the center of the camp. Snake Woman had walked past Conrad where he leaned against a stump. She walked back again, seeing his eyes follow her, seeing the look she remembered so well. She walked again, more slowly. Now, the words of Mountain Horse given to Pretty Crow, to walk in the slow, graceful steps of the black-tail deer, guided her, restrained her impulse to run far from his vile face. She looked sideways, coyly, swayed her hips, and headed toward the Big Rock. If she wanted to be like the warrior women, wanted to face the dangers and demands of raids and hunts, then she had to show courage and control. She was disgusted, her stomach was a hard ball, and she knew his eyes were on her. She knew he would follow.

Once on the other side of the rock, she squeezed between clefts and clambered up, her moccasins grasping the rough footholds. One Spot was hidden between the huge boulders. She hoped. She lay flat on the top. When Conrad's horse appeared, she descended and as he rode into the stone's shadow, she stood some distance beyond it. Wind fluttered her buckskin tunic and blew wisps of loose hair around her face. She turned to face him, his back to the rock. She thought of Pretty Crow and the harm he had done, of Calf Shield, and of the white wolf, dead from his gun.

Conrad dropped his reins and lurched toward her like a crazed bull, a twisted leer distorting his face in a grotesque grin. His hands unbuckled his pants as he approached and he had no warning or chance to raise his arms and stop One

Spot, who grasped him with one arm and gave a deep, quick slice across Conrad's throat with the other. So fast he could not scream or call. He only gurgled as blood spurted from the wound. His eyes were round and unbelieving.

"He does not understand the tongue of the Real People," Snake Woman said, "so there is nothing to say. But he sees, in those eyes where the light has not yet dimmed, that I have lured him to his death. Stand here where he sees you, One Spot, that he also remembers Calf Shield."

It took both of them to hoist the dead body onto his horse, each of them weakened from illness or injury. "I'll take his body to the river cliffs and drop it between the rocks there. He'll never be found." The effort of lifting the body had broken One Spot's wounds open, and blood seeped down his chest.

"I'll clear this area of any signs. With hunting, skinning, and travois, it would be hard to detect anything. Will you drop the saddle and bridle into the rocks too, One Spot? Let his horse go without anything to catch or hinder it."

The fire gleamed bright in the darkened early night when Snake Woman returned to the Otter Lodge. Mountain Horse had not come back. Pretty Crow and White Feather were too absorbed in sorrowful memories to ask her why she was so late.

Conrad's absence was not noticed until morning. "Someone must have seen him." Sterling spoke with Spotted Horse and Bird Rattler. "He would not leave without saying something. His horse is gone." Sterling looked beyond the lodges to the green hills around the camp, as if Conrad might be on a leisurely morning ride and appear at any moment.

"He wouldn't leave without his furs," added Davis.

Snake Woman was startled to hear Davis also speak in their tongue. What right do they have to use these words? How dare they use the language given to us by Napi that we may work together in harmony.

"He didn't join the feasting, or I never saw him. We will have to wait until he returns."

One Spot stood beside Black Eagle and Little Ear, relaxed and laughing at something Little Ear said. That is how he looked in the days we lived with the Black Elks, Snake Woman remembered. In all this time, One Spot has not looked so happy, even with White Feather.

Davis rode to search for tracks or signs of where Conrad might be. Spotted Horse sent riders to scout the area around the camp. Hunters and skinners left in the routine of the fall days.

At the Otter Lodge, Snake Woman again worked beside Mountain Horse, scraping a large hide pegged to the south of the entrance. Her grandmother had spoken little that morning beyond the brief directives that concerned their work. Did her grandmother know? She always knows. If she does not know the details, she knows I have a secret. But Snake Woman had given her word to One Spot and he to her; they could not compromise their place in the Many Children's camp by revealing their betrayal of Spotted Horse's hospitality. She had no easy way to deal with what was done. These paleskins threaten all of us: people, dogs, wolves, all of Napi's world.

"When the responsibility of the Bundle is given and received, it requires great sacrifice from all involved."

Snake Woman started in surprise.

Her grandmother set her scraping blade on the grass in front of her and sat back. "The greatest sacrifice is that a person must live true in every way in the presence of the Bundle. They must live in truth, serve one's people in generosity, honor the ceremonies. Not always easy. Not always a clear path." Mountain Horse pushed herself to standing and Snake Woman did the same.

She stood eye to eye with the old woman and wondered again that she stood as tall as her grandmother. What did she mean with those words? Did she know? Did she want Snake Woman to tell what had been done? In the dark eyes of the old woman – eyes more familiar than those of any other, beloved eyes large, wide, knowing – Snake Woman saw only love. No judgment. No anger. No disappointment.

"You will be worthy of that responsibility, my Snake Woman. The Bundle has not come only for me. Sometimes I think it has come to meet you. Now go on scraping while I talk with Weasel and find out what's been learned about that man."

Snake Woman knelt and resumed scraping the hide, pushing the scraper evenly with both hands, all her weight behind them. Shadow lay in the shade of the lodge, her pups lolling about her, worrying a strip of hide that Mountain Horse had earlier tossed their way.

"You are very skilled, the way you clean that hide." His words were slow and awkward, though she understood them clearly. It was the Englishman, Sterling. "What will you do next with it?"

His voice was unexpectedly soft, more gentle than how he spoke in the Bear Lodge. It reminded her of poplar trees, or a duck who gathers her young ones when they stray at the edge of the water. She did not want to speak to him.

"My name is Alexander. Alexander Sterling. I also am called the Englishman. What is your name?"

She stood and turned to face him. Shadow approached cautiously as he held his hand for her to sniff. The all-black pup smelled his boot and tugged on a bootlace. When the lace slipped from its mouth and he fell back on his haunches, she laughed and wished she hadn't. But her hatred for these paleskins was softened right now. They did not seem so terrifying and unstoppable.

"I am called Snake Woman. The hide will be rubbed with brain and soaked. How is it you speak our language?"

"I was born far from here, across huge water. Stories of your land made me hunger to see it." He crouched on one knee and wiggled a finger in front of the pup, who seized it between his jaws and rolled on his back. "I was hired to come west to gather the items of your way of living and to gather facts about the people of the plains. Before it is too late." The other two pups, curious as to what the black had discovered, joined in assaulting the Englishman's hand. "I hired someone to teach me the languages of the prairie people and began my travels."

She tried to imagine what he talked about. Sun Woman traveled far to the homes of the Earth Mound People. She went for a purpose, because the Dream Spirit woman asked her to do so. Why did this man journey? Why did he want the things of their camp?

"What is the Bundle that hangs by your lodge?"

The question took her by surprise. How was it these

paleskins had such strong medicine and knew so little? How could he speak about the Bundle, he a stranger, in its presence? Did he understand nothing? They are to be pitied more than hated, she thought.

"At the place where I work there are Bundles from tribes to the south and east. But so far we have none from your people and would very much like to have one." Sterling walked closer to the tripod. The edges of the red blanket fluttered in the wind.

Surely he will not touch it. He must know at least that much. "My grandmother keeps it." The words came loud, fierce.

"Where is your grandmother?"

"She comes soon. It would be better to ask Spotted Horse or Bird Rattler about such things."

He touched the brim of his hat and nodded. "I will do that. Thank you. Snake Woman, is it? Thank you, Snake Woman, for your conversation. Perhaps we can speak again." Sterling walked to the Bear Lodge where he looked closely at the designs painted on it and took out his small book to scribble marks on the pages.

Davis returned in mid-afternoon. "No trail. Riders and horses and people been all over in every direction." He loosened his saddle and set it down, leaving his horse, a small bay with a black mane, to graze, the reins dragging beside him. "But no way would Conrad leave without his skins. Don't make sense."

Spotted Horse invited Sterling and Davis to stay as long as they needed. "Perhaps your friend had a dream that sent him to hunt. He will return when done."

Davis sat on the ground and leaned his elbows on bent knees while he chewed a stalk of grass and poked its hard end in the spaces of his front teeth. "Conrad isn't much for dreamin'. Unless it's nightmares."

Sterling continued to explore the camp, observing cutting, drying, pounding, scraping, stretching skins, and boiling bones. All the while he made notes and drawings.

When Snake Woman told Mountain Horse of the Englishman's interest in the Bundle, her grandmother shrugged and said nothing. After this, however, one of the men of the camp not busy with the hunt kept Sterling company. "To answer his questions," explained Mountain Horse.

On the third day, Sterling said they might as well leave. "Conrad must have gone back, that's all."

Spotted Horse gave Sterling gifts that the Englishman had shown interest in: a scraper, a horn, moccasins beaded in green, red, and yellow designs. And a buffalo robe.

"Spotted Horse was generous," Snake Woman said to Mountain Horse, as once again they worked side by side. The paleskins had left in the morning and she had stayed inside the lodge to avoid seeing the painful sight of the wolf hides.

With their leaving, she wished she could celebrate like the men did when returning successful from a hunt or raid. She wanted to holler and shout how an enemy was dead. She wished One Spot could tell a friend of his victory, how he bravely slayed the man who caused Calf Shield's death. Wished she could shout for Pretty Crow, to let everyone know her dishonor was avenged. She didn't need to shout aloud for the white wolf. It was enough to know.

CHAPTER 25

NIGHTLIGHT SHOWED half her face, hid to darkness, and came once more to half while nights grew cooler and thin morning frost coated blades of grass. Above, geese flew against the bright blue of autumn sky, stretched out in their flight like the ragged tip of a huge arrow. The cries pulled to all who heard them, calling to follow, to move across the land and feel the wind, the joy and beauty of this great expanse, this body given to them to know. In answer to the plaintive call, the Many Children packed lodges and robes on a morning when the frost spread out from the shrubs like the hairs on a young coyote.

Hunting had been good; parfleche swelled with dried meat, and new hides replaced the worn walls of their lodges. Robes for trade, stacked thick on travois, promised blankets, tobacco, knives, rifles, and ammunition. They had worked hard in the last weeks and now looked ahead with pleasure to the winter camp to follow trading.

Would they return, Snake Woman wondered, to the camp of last winter near the small lake, close to the mountains? In spring, when long days brought yearning to move across the land, the urge to be gone filled her. Now, as days shortened and brought memories of long, dark nights, images of that place rose, welcome and pleasing.

One Spot came that morning with horses for the move, frequent in his acts of kindness to the Otter Lodge. Little Ear surprised Snake Woman by bringing the spotted mare for her to ride. "So Cloud will travel close to you," he explained.

Mountain Horse rode to her right on a sorrel, stocky and sure-footed, the red-blanketed Bundle carefully tied on the travois dragging behind the horse. The old woman was often silent these last weeks, since the paleskins' visit. Snake Woman several times looked up to meet her grandmother's watching face, an expression on it as if she examined a track in the dust and sought to decipher its clues. Once she had questioned, "Any more head pain?"

"No. None at all. I'm well again." She was. Her secret of the green-kerchiefed one's disappearance both burdened and elated her. She feared it caused Mountain Horse's distance. No, not distance so much as being inaccessible. Snake Woman missed the loving attention that her grandmother now devoted to the Bundle.

This day, the old woman's eyes moved back and forth along the horizon. From time to time she gave a satisfied grunt, pleased to recognize a particular clump of trees, a certain rock, a hill. "This was a good hunt, Snake Woman. We have hides to work again. Those girls will become wives by the winter ceremonies."

"Will we have winter camp at the small lake, Grandmother?" Even if Pretty Crow and White Feather had their own separate lodges, the thought of them together in one camp, near the mountains, was comforting. They would be close. She and Little Ear could ride again. He would help her train Cloud.

"I don't know what Spotted Horse plans. First we trade near Old Man's River. Learn what has become of the rumors swirling like those pesky winds of late summer." She spoke slowly, as if tired. Yet the day was new, and they were well rested. Did something distress her?

"You sound tired, Grandmother. Are you well?"

They had come to the top of a gentle rise and Mountain Horse pulled up the sorrel, who leaned her neck to crunch thick mouths of still-rich grass. Snake Woman stopped beside her. The land sloped gently down before them, the horses and riders of the Many Children stretched in a scattered line like the flight of geese. Patrols rode casually along the sides, confident in knowing they were far within the safety of Blackfoot territory where a raid or attack was a remote possibility.

Gentle hills rolled to the west, one after the other, rising to the mountains that stretched deep blue along the skyline on their right, their tops already white. Dense, dark green covered the hills along their base with the thin straight pine that gave lodge poles and where the rich-furred creatures dwelled, whose pelts gave winter warmth.

"All this beauty given us, to move through across Napi's great body, to know the stories that guide us on a true path. We will fiercely fight to keep this." Mountain Horse swung her gaze almost full circle as she spoke.

"Napi gave us this. The People have kept true," Snake Woman said. "Is it for always, Grandmother? Was it an always promise?"

"How can we know with Napi, that great trickster? He might be playing another of his terrible tricks."

Pretty Crow and White Feather stopped near. "Is all well?" Pretty Crow asked and nudged her gelding closer to the spotted mare. Cloud shyly sniffed the gelding's nose, then bolted playfully, short tail high, flaring like a pennant on a shield. She stopped a few lengths ahead, snorted, and stamped her foot, bringing laughter to all the women.

"We are well," Snake Woman answered. "We stopped to enjoy the beauty." As the two young women rode on, the black filly ran in circles about the mare, as if to alert them that there was no time to linger when the day's adventure lay ahead.

"You were just like that filly," Mountain Horse said, pulling up the sorrel's head to urge her forward. "You could never be in one place for long. I was busy just keeping my eye on you, to keep you safe, make sure you didn't wander too far. Even now, you aren't content to stay in the camp. What path does this reveal, I wonder?"

Was she hinting at something? Snake Woman resolved to tell Mountain Horse that night what had happened to Conrad.

It was a night of clear autumn sky, and stars flickered like distant fires in the deep blue-black. Snake Woman invited Mountain Horse to walk, to sit and view the heavens. "When I was little, you took me out at night often, to look at the trail of the Wolf Children and tell of the Seven Brothers. We have not done this for a long time. Come," she coaxed, "let's do it this night."

"In your little days, when I tried to get a restless girl tired for sleep, my bones did not feel the cold so much," Mountain Horse answered, but she readily wrapped her blanket about her and pushed open the flap covering their exit.

"I'll bring a robe to sit on," Snake Woman added.

They sat on an open hillside that faced south and west. She told her grandmother what she had done and, when finished, leaned her crossed arms on drawn-up knees to relax into the pull of the sky and stars, meeting the friends who peopled Napi's sky as surely as his human children walked on the ground. "I did not want to keep this secret from you," she concluded.

Mountain Horse reached her arm around Snake Woman, who rested her head on her grandmother's shoulder. When the old woman's arms enveloped her and she was absorbed into Mountain Horse's strength and warmth, her grandmother's body seemed smaller than she remembered. Was she growing smaller or had Snake Woman grown larger?

"Sometimes," Mountain Horse said, "a secret is a necessary choice. Sometimes the best thing is when others do not know. It keeps a secret safe."

"You are not bothered that I did not tell you? That One Spot and I did this thing?"

"Little one, although I call you that, you are not such a little one anymore, and you have been following your own path as long as you have been with me." Mountain Horse straightened her body and put a hand on each of Snake

Woman's shoulders to look directly at her. In the dark, Snake Woman could just make out the old woman's face, a hand-width from her own. Yet the light of her grandmother's eyes shone. "What matters, Snake Woman, is why you choose a certain path. I know you have a good heart, so your secret did not worry me. You had good reason for your choice." Mountain Horse released Snake Woman's shoulders, and leaned back to look at the stars. "When horses are taken in a raid or a warrior killed in attack, our men go out and steal horses or kill someone of the offending band. In this way we keep balance. Now, you and One Spot have avenged a wrong. This is the way given us."

Snake Woman leaned against her knees again. A shooting star arced across the sky in the south, looking as if it landed on one of the distant hills. "You have seemed quiet these last days. Even sad. I thought you were displeased."

Mountain Horse rubbed Snake Woman's shoulder. "I have been quiet and even sad these days. You are a part of that, but not for these actions you tell. I am not displeased, but I have concern. I have concern for you and the path ahead."

"Because I was sick at the Sun Gathering? I am fine now." A movement in the grass below distracted her. "Look. An animal walks below us, toward those poplar." She pointed west where a dark shape, just slightly darker than the night world about them, lumbered in a slow, rhythmic gait.

"A bear," said Mountain Horse. "No sound at all does it make."

"Do you think it is a real bear, or is it a person with strong medicine who takes the appearance of a bear? Do you think there are still such people with the power to do that?"

"Perhaps," Mountain Horse answered. "I know for sure there are young women with the power to steer the talk away from what they don't want to discuss."

Snake Woman laughed. Her grandmother always saw behind her words, even on a grassy hillside on a dark night. "I will listen then. Why do you worry for me?"

"The strange thing is," her grandmother continued, "that bear has not come out of those cottonwoods. It could be that I worry about you getting eaten by a bear."

"Now you are trying to frighten me. It's too dark to see that far."

"Maybe it is the same for the path ahead. Too dark to see. Maybe nothing to fear. But I am old, granddaughter. No, no, that does not worry me. I do not worry about my death." She waved her hand as if to brush away a fly, "Pretty Crow and White Feather will soon leave our lodge. Then only you, me, and the Bundle. A darkness clouds my mind when this thought arrives."

Snake Woman slid closer to lean against her grandmother. The cold air chilled her nose as she breathed, and cold from the ground seeped through the robe where they sat. "I will take care of us. I will take care of you. Cloud will be my buffalo pony. I will get horses for our lodge, hides, and meat to keep us strong."

"A lodge with two women, one of them old with a Bundle to tend, is much work. But the Otter Lodge has been a women's lodge for a long time with no man to dwell within it. Now, the thought of a man to share our lodge is not agreeable." She took Snake Woman's hand. "If…when…the time comes that you are called to leave – a young man calls your heart, another call pulls you away – you must go."

"I would not leave you. You would come with me. But this is far away, Grandmother. If you did not want this man in your lodge, you would live beside us. Then, I could have my Shadow inside again. Now, let's go back. If you aren't frozen, I surely am." She stood and kept her hold on Mountain Horse, to help her up.

"When you have your own lodge you might find you don't want a dog in it, anyway."

"That could never be," Snake Woman grinned and hooked her arm through her grandmother's. "Besides," she added, "soon you'll have all the children of Pretty Crow and White Feather to fill up the Otter Lodge."

Snake Woman woke and pushed the robes away from her body. She was sticky and wet with sweat. Her heart pounded. The lodge was dense with night, fire embers cooled to invisible, yet something was present. Not the sleeping women, Mountain Horse beside her, Pretty Crow and White Feather across the floor. Had someone entered without waking them? Why didn't Shadow, sleeping outside the entrance, bark? Had a ghost come? Shadow would still bark; dogs always recognized a ghost. But strong medicine knows how to silence dogs.

She breathed slowly and carefully to make no sound. Her body had cooled with the robes thrown off, but she did not want to move to cover herself again. She listened. Night sounds, the expected sounds, emerged into her awareness, suddenly clear and audible where she had not noticed them earlier: a screech owl far away; rattling aspen leaves in the soft wind; faint burbling of the stream winding alongside the camp. The ringing, comforting hum of the night, Napi's hum. Nothing unusual. But she could feel it, this presence, and that it felt familiar disturbed her. Where had she met this before? She did not want to remember, did not want to know, and pulled the robes over her to slide into their warmth. It prodded her, would not let her sink back to sleep. The hum of the night and stars and the vast land rang louder, as if from inside her head. The sound drew her in, relaxed her, and the sense of a presence in the lodge no longer bothered her. Was that another sound that blended with the hum? A song? She had heard this before. Yes, at the Sun Gathering, in the Women's Lodge. It was the snake's song. That was the presence in the lodge this night.

Snake Woman felt a blast of cold shoot through her body. The singing stopped. She sat up, heart drumming, mouth dry. Her chest heaved as if she had been running. Her eyes looked through the dark, seeing nothing, but hunting for a source for what she sensed. There. On the west side, near the lodge wall. An echo of the singing vibrated in the air, or was it in her mind? Did she dream this? Her eyes rested where the Bundle hung. This was the presence she felt. Was the snake at the Women's Lodge now inside the Bundle? Was this what it held? She tried to swallow but couldn't, couldn't stop the quick, loud beat of her heart.

She laid down once more and pulled the robes over her. This has been a dream, she told herself. One of the dreams that bring fear, hard breathing, and a pounding chest. What is true in the dream world is not always true in the waking one. She told herself this again and again until, finally, she slept.

CHAPTER 26

THE MANY CHILDREN moved at a leisurely pace, a day or two or three stopped, then a day's travel to another camp. Snake Woman rode peacefully, relieved of the burden of secrecy, the concerns of past and future suspended in the beauty, as if belonging to a long-ago story. The spotted mare kept a steady, easy rhythm as she swayed over undulating grasslands, the ridge of mountains, golden aspen, and cold wind to the right. Cloud gamboled, galloped, or walked close to the mare's flank. Each evening, or during pauses in the day, Snake Woman stroked the soft nose that was softer than spring willow buds, ran her hand over the filly's haunches, neck, legs, and belly. Cloud often followed her, nudging like a dog that seeks affection, once pushing Snake Woman to the ground in the strength of her thrust.

In the quiet ease of these days, the changes of the last year cycled through her memory: the dogs gone, along with the roan mare, the white wolf, her childhood time. The harm to Pretty Crow, Calf Shield, and the wolf avenged. The Many Children were untouched by the scab disease or attack, and their parfleche were thick with abundance.

WindMaker rippled the grass that rolled on and on. The backbone of the world rose to the west. How huge was this great spine, the western boundary of the land Napi gave his people. She looked up in each direction and felt beneath her the circle of earth, truly a great lodge floor whose walls were the sky that met in the center where she looked above. She understood it now, felt it in her body as when she was a child, felt all this move through her, felt her own self move through it. The People and the land – Napi's body – moving through each other.

They had traveled for half of Nightlight's cycle when the Many Children set their lodges in a narrow valley bounded by low hills, their tops covered in the deep green of fir, spruce, and pine. Spotted Horse called a feast, and all ate well around the fire. A clear night covered them, and in the north, ripples of light waved from west to east and back again, pale green shafts, a distant sky dance whose faint crackle filled the air.

Pretty Crow and White Feather walked casually beyond the fire's circle of light, gone, Snake Woman knew, to meet with Black Eagle and One Spot. Little Ear startled her, suddenly standing near.

"Come and walk with me," he offered. "Nightlight is near to showing herself above that hill."

His presence gladdened her. "Your spotted mare is a smooth, agreeable horse, Little Ear. Thank you. Cloud and I have already become close friends." She walked with him while they talked of horses, hunting, and the filly's antics.

A narrow arc of moon rose over the eastern hill where a line of fir at the crest made a jagged border across Nightlight's face. She grew quickly, her soft, pale circle lighting the land in silvery hue. Shadow trotted up behind and nudged between them to take the lead.

"So much has happened this year. It seems a longer time. I am hoping we return to last winter's camp." Snake Woman spoke with a longing that surprised even her. These days, she hardly recognized herself. After confessing to her grandmother, she had been buoyant, relieved of a burden, like a hawk must feel, she thought, as it floats in circles on WindMaker's breath. Now, walking with Little Ear, she was overcome with a sense of loss, with the feeling that joyful days of riding with her friend were gone forever.

Little Ear walked noiselessly beside her.

"You move skillfully without sound, Little Ear. You'll be out on raids with Crooked Back when trading finishes, getting more horses."

"I expect this to be so. I no longer have to follow as a helper, or a carrier, or to cook. I have earned my place. When we trade, I get my own rifle."

She looked back at the camp where the orange-gold fire illumined shapes of those standing near it, the moon's light enough to outline the lodges scattered over the pale-lit grass. "Mountain Horse will be concerned if I am away too long." She felt awkward again, like the time they first met.

"We will ride again this winter," he said, "no matter where we camp. You can ride the mare any time until Cloud is grown strong enough to hold you. That's going to be two or three years. But we don't need to wait for winter. We can walk together in the evenings now."

They turned back, and Shadow bounded between them again to assume lead. What was this awkwardness? She could laugh, or joke, or talk about something else. "Yes, we could," she offered. "Shadow, come here. She's after a rabbit. The pups must be sleeping. Grandmother makes sure we all gather in the lodge. Tonight was different, with the feast. I might not be able to walk in the evenings."

"We can find other times like this in the next days and at the post. If you want."

"Mountain Horse will be cautious near the post. She fears whiskey. It was whiskey that led to Calf Shield's death when we fled from the Black Elks."

"Crooked Back and Spotted Horse are also against whiskey. There are some of the Many Children who want it." He walked silently some distance, then added, "These things don't need to concern us, Snake Woman."

What did he mean? What concerned her grandmother was Snake Woman's concern, was the concern of the Otter Lodge. Whisky needed to be the concern of the whole camp, of all the People.

They neared the lodges, the fire no longer burned brightly, its coals dull, and Little Ear stopped. "Will you meet me again tomorrow?"

"I cannot promise." She walked briskly in long strides to the Otter Lodge. "I will try," she called over her shoulder.

The Many Children left the small valley next day, riding through a cleft with grassy hills on each side, emerging to a wide expanse. Chief Mountain rose distinctly on the southern horizon. Snake Woman gazed to the shores of the western peaks and the longed-for refuge. If we could just turn west to the small lake, we would have all we need for winter.

They did not turn west. Spotted Horse led the band across layers of grassland that flattened into the horizon. By mid-afternoon, the sun shone white and cold through a pale gray sky. Wind struck from the north, exhaled from a dark bank of cloud. They set camp as heavy pellets of snow fell thick and hard.

Inside the Otter Lodge, the poles hummed in the storm. The women sat close to the fire, blankets snugged tightly around necks and shoulders, robes pulled over legs and feet. The round pot of stew bubbled.

How many stormy nights have the four of us sat like this together? Snake Woman wondered. She wanted time to stop, a rope thrown around it and tied to the trunk of the great earth tree, their days and nights together secured.

She woke in the dark again. Had she dreamed? She had the feeling of having done so, yet could not now recall the images. Had someone called to her? Yes, it was a woman. Who was she? Arms and legs bruised and cut, red scrapes on her face, hair matted and short in the manner of a grieving woman. What did she grieve?

Snake Woman rolled to her side and pulled the robes over her shoulders. Her nose and lips were cold. The darkness was so dense that eyes open or closed made no difference. She listened to soft breathing of sleeping women. The poles had quieted. WindMaker, too, settled for the night.

Nothing stays the same. She thought of Little Ear. The

storm meant no chance to walk together. Would they ride together as he said? Little Ear's place as a young warrior meant his days in all seasons would move to horses, to war and raids, to the skills these required. Did he, too, long for life to stand in one place?

Why had the dream woman called? How could she help if she could not reach her? What warning could she heed if she did not understand its meaning?

"Why are we going south to trade, Grandmother? Why does Spotted Horse choose this new post?" Snake Woman had just returned from outside and leaned close to the fire to face her palms to the flames.

Pretty Crow answered. "Black Eagle says that the pale-skins came to camps over the north and east with word that the Hudson Bay no longer has its claim to trade in this land. All has been transferred to something called the Dominion."

"I don't understand why this means we trade in the south," Snake Woman said.

Pretty Crow continued. "The talk at the Sun Gathering was about this Dominion. We do not know this thing. Our agreements have been with the Hudson Bay. Spotted Horse is reluctant to go all the way north to find poor trading or none. In the south, we have choice with our trading. If it is not good at this fort, we can go to another, or cross the Medicine Line." She picked up the pair of moccasins she had been beading and resumed stitching.

"In the north, the sickness is still strong, and the Cree cross into our land too often." White Feather picked up the conversation. "In the south, we are stronger."

"What about whiskey at the fort?" Snake Woman asked.

Her grandmother replied now. "Spotted Horse is cautious. He sent Crooked Back and Black Eagle to scout the post, make sure they have trade, that no other bands camp nearby while we come, and to ask for no whiskey to be available. The conditions must be met, or we will go elsewhere. Now, I must keep stitching or I won't have moccasins to send for these young women's marriage." She rummaged in the parfleche near the door and pushed the flap open to peer out. "Still snow. We'll need firewood soon, while it's light."

"It might stop soon," Snake Woman offered, hopeful that a better weather condition might appear. Four days passed before clouds broke into ribbons to fade thin and finally disappear, leaving pale, quiet blue.

CHAPTER 27

THE MANY CHILDREN set camp near the post in late afternoon, when the river shone pale in the season's weak light. A great ring of soft colors glistened around the sun, like a hint of summer rainbow.

"There will be more snow," noted Mountain Horse, "and it will be cold. We will need fuel."

Snake Woman had led the spotted mare, dragging a travois, Cloud trotting beside, to gather the chips and dried alder she had noticed as they'd neared the post. Now, she turned back and had nearly reached the camp with enough dung and wood for several days, when three riders approached. One was Alexander Sterling. He urged his horse to a canter when he saw her.

"Greetings. You are Snake Woman, are you not?" He dismounted and walked beside her as she led the mare. "Have you come to trade?"

She walked without speaking. This man was a curiosity. Friendly and courteous, he reminded her of the trader and his Piegan wife, Sings Alone. Yes, he also had been friendly, yet he had brought a brother to their camp who betrayed a promise to bring no whiskey. This Sterling came to the Many Children's camp with that same man.

"We never found Conrad, the man with us at your camp," Sterling went on, "but his horse was here when we got back to the post. Without saddle or bridle. Most strange."

"Yes, a mystery," Snake Woman affirmed.

"Davis suspects foul play," he added, "but I think the man met with some accident out riding. Thrown from his horse, I expect. Perhaps someone took the gear and let the horse go, or it got free. We gave a good search. Nothing more we could have done."

Sterling stepped into his stirrup and swung up on his sorrel. "I rode out with two of the post's traders to welcome Spotted Horse. I'll go pay my respects. Glad to see you again, Snake Woman."

Pale cloud covered the sky now, and the sun faded more than set. Its feeble warmth, too, faded and Snake Woman was glad for abundant fuel. Already the north wind's bite chilled her face and hands. The imagined comfort of the lodge gave relief. Tomorrow trading would occur and the next day, or – at the latest – the one after that, the Many Children would depart for winter camp. This thought also brought comfort.

That night, snow dropped, thick and steady.

In the morning, Spotted Horse, Shot Twice, Bird Rattler, and their families were first to trade and rode with laden travois to the gates. Snow and wind continued through the day as groups went and returned from the fort.

In mid-afternoon, several unknown riders arrived in camp, huddled over their horses and wrapped in robes and blankets, snow dusting their shoulders. From the Lone Fighters band, they had arrived in mid-day and set camp downstream, a short distance beyond the fort. Spotted Horse invited them for smoke and food.

"They didn't stay long, even with this storm," Mountain Horse related on her return. "That means they've got whiskey in their own camp. Nothing else would send them back on such a night, with warmth and food here for them."

"What happened with trading, Grandmother?" asked Pretty Crow. "What was the fort like inside?"

"Trading is nearly done. But we won't leave until the storm settles." Mountain Horse wrapped her blanket tightly. "That Sterling man was inside. Davis too. Asking about the other one, Conrad. Sterling asked about a Bundle, if we had one for trade." She shook her head, the way a mare will shake away flies at her ears.

"Why would he want a Bundle?" Snake Woman sat close to Mountain Horse near the fire. She leaned her head on the old woman's shoulder. "What would he do with it?"

"Who can know? Let's just pray ColdMaker changes his mind soon and stops this storm, so we can leave."

Evening darkness had just settled when two riders who had visited in the afternoon returned. The snow muffled the sound of their approach as they galloped over the white ground, appearing all of a sudden. Startled dogs barked, the two men hooted and hollered. "Come on you timid sleepers.

Come and enjoy this night together in the Lone Fighters' camp." One shot a rifle into the air, and the crack startled the dogs further. They howled and yelped with renewed vigor while horses picketed close to the camp pulled on their ropes and snorted in alarm.

Snake Woman could not see who came out to speak with the riders. Several gathered, collected horses, and rode away with the invitations. The dogs settled again, curled into the snow, and the silence returned.

"They are not bringing whiskey here. Of this we can be thankful," Mountain Horse said as Snake Woman returned inside.

Hoots and hollers woke her from deep sleep. Someone called right outside the Otter Lodge.

"Hey, Snake Woman. I want to talk with you."

Was that Little Ear? It sounded like his voice, but it was loud and rough. Snake Woman pushed the flap open. The snow had stopped but cloud remained. She could just make out Little Ear's black horse, the wide blaze down the middle of his face. "Little Ear," she whispered, "Have you been at the Lone Fighters' camp?"

"And why wouldn't I? All these moons we hunted and followed the herds. Now, we come to trade. And celebrate."

"Go away, Little Ear. You disturb my grandmother."

"Snake Woman." Little Ear slid from his horse and stood to face her. He wore only a light shirt and breeches. "Look. I don't feel cold. I don't feel like sleeping. It's wonderful. Whiskey is strong medicine. I want to sing. Come on. Ride with me. I want to sing loud and have you with me."

She stepped back. What was he saying? Why was he here now? This is not how young men of the People behave – to disregard her grandmother and a lodge where a Bundle dwelled. This was not the Little Ear she knew. "What has happened to you? Have you forgotten how to show respect, Little Ear? Go away from here."

She lifted the flap and entered the lodge. Orange coals still glowed. Snake Woman lay down and pulled up the robes. Thoughts galloped about like the filly in the spring. She wanted to forget this and wake at morning to find it a dream. "I'm sorry, Grandmother," she whispered.

"You spoke well, Snake Woman. You have nothing to be sorry for."

Little Ear hooted a wild call and galloped out of camp toward the east, toward the Lone Fighters.

When light returned, the flat, wide valley lay white and still. Napi's river cut a dark, winding path through it. The fort's upright, straight walls appeared even more strange than when standing on grass. Riders who went to the Lone Fighters in the night had not returned. Spotted Horse's wives gave no sign of packing.

Snake Woman blew bits of coal beneath the ash to life and added chips, twigs, and bark. Mountain Horse chanted prayers, dropped powdered pine and sage on her altar, fanning pungent smoke over the Bundle. She signalled Snake Woman to carry the poles for the tripod. This meant no snow today. The old woman had a nose for weather that matched Shadow's for a prairie chicken, and since the Bundle had come, she divined the elements even more accurately.

At first light, Pretty Crow and White Feather went to Crooked Back's lodge seeking news of their men. They returned as Mountain Horse set the Bundle to the west of the lodge. "There's hardly a young man in camp. They've stayed at the Lone Fighters. Black Eagle and One Spot also." White Feather walked back and forth in front of the lodge entrance as Pretty Crow crouched to go inside.

"Come within," Mountain Horse beckoned and followed Pretty Crow, who sat against the backrest and pulled a blanket tight. "Spotted Horse knows how it is at the forts," the old woman began. "He had his whiskey days. He came to know its problems. The young ones have to learn it for themselves. By tomorrow the snow will melt enough for us to move. Until then, we keep safe. You are not yet any man's wife. You have no duty beyond the Otter Lodge. You do not have to go where the men are." Her voice filled the lodge with words strong and firm, their warning clearly understood.

They sat chewing dried and pounded strips of meat, berries, and fat, strips layered into parfleche at the end of the hunt. But Snake Woman was restless with sitting, as if waiting for something to happen. "I will collect fuel for the night, and water."

She walked away from the fort, toward the west, imagining their travel this way the next day. Shadow and the young ones, nearly as tall as their mother, trotted ahead. She followed a game trail that angled on the hillside to a pile of boulders at the summit, tossed in a haphazard mass. She perched on the rocks with a view of the flats below: the Many Children's camp, the trading post, and farther along the valley, the lodges of the Lone Fighters.

Strands of smoke rose from the Many Children's lodges and flowed on the wind to the east, blending into a sky river of mist to join the smoke of the fort and of the Lone Fighters, flowing like the river below. River, wind: what is it that calls them east? Her own yearning was all to the west, to the ridge of mountains, close to the backbone of Napi and the refuge it gave. A pair of ravens floated above, spiraling in wide circles on updrafts from the valley rim, then pulling their wings in to plummet and begin the upward glide again.

By late afternoon, the sound of revelry in the east carried to the Many Children. "They begin again," noted Mountain Horse. She had just brought the Bundle inside and finished her prayers and offerings.

While Snake Woman gathered fuel, the two young women had walked with Running Bird's family to the fort. They now compared observations and impressions as they stitched beads to the moccasins each decorated. They talked of a trader's horse that had enchanted Running Bird while they traded.

"It was the color of a new-born buffalo calf with the evening sun turning its coat to gold," Pretty Crow described. "But his mane and tail are white. As soon as Running Bird saw it, he wanted it."

"The man didn't want to trade it," White Feather continued. "But then he began to reconsider. Can you believe he said if Running Bird got a Bundle for him, he'd do it."

Mountain Horse froze in her movements. "What happened then? Tell me all the details." An unexpected sharpness accompanied the words.

"Grandmother, Running Bird was angry. He said he had

no Bundle, and even if he did, this is not something to trade like a horse, or guns, or robes."

Mountain Horse relaxed, picked up two flakes of dried dung and laid them on the fire where they quietly caught and glowed with a smokeless flame.

Pretty Crow continued with descriptions of the post. "The man named Sterling spoke kindly and said no disrespect had been meant, that tribes to the east traded Bundles, so the trader thought perhaps they did this here also. Now he understands and apologizes.

"The man with the horse and Running Bird bargained again. Now, Running Bird will give three of his best buffalo ponies loaded with robes and parfleche. In return he'll bring that golden horse to his lodge." Pretty Crow finished the story and stood at the end of it. "I'm going to see if he's back with that horse yet."

But Snake Woman knew it was Black Eagle she wondered about. Maybe the men would spend the night in the gambling games; lose a horse, a gun, blankets, a shirt, and win them back. Play Napi's game of chance that was ever dear to the trickster's heart, who taught the men to toss the stones and sticks and rings, to risk what is most precious in divining the spirit's favor in the back and forth, win and lose of each moment.

"No matter what the men trade, or drink, or gamble," said Mountain Horse, drawing Snake Woman out of the cycle of her thought, "we still have to eat." She stirred the pot that hung over the fire, the dried meat strips swelled and softened, thickened the water. Rich scent filled the lodge, and Snake Woman felt hungry, glad for the meal and the company of these women.

CHAPTER 28

SHE WOKE in the dark to sounds of distant revelry: gunshots, hollers, drums, laughter. All far away.

She woke again to see Mountain Horse sitting near the fire. She had built it up and flames danced a silent, orange pattern, lighting the old woman's face a deep bronze. "Are you troubled, Grandmother?" Snake Woman asked.

"I woke from a dream. Someone called me. I sat up to consider it, to let the voice speak again, let its meaning come clear. Perhaps it is nothing, for nothing more has come."

"What part of the night is it? Are we near to dawn?" Snake Woman sat with her. The blaze lit the space enough to show that Pretty Crow's and White Feather's places were empty. "Where are they?"

"Called by the lure of festivities and their soon-to-be husbands. They are at the Lone Fighters' camp with Running Bird and his lodge."

"Does this worry you?"

"Yes. Yet it has been the way of visits to traders since traders first brought whiskey to this land. Spotted Horse tried to prevent whiskey and has kept it from the Many Children's camp. We will move soon enough. Pretty Crow and White Feather will have many times to learn about trading posts."

A renewed volley of rifle shots split the air, closer than before. "Are they coming here, Grandmother?"

"They have gone to the post," she answered. "They may need more whiskey. Or seek to engage the paleskins in a challenge."

They sat with the fire between them. For a time, the sounds disappeared and the women heard only familiar noises as a horse snorted, a night hawk screeched, coyotes yipped and howled across the river. Once again the babble of revellers erupted. Quiet again. The night felt suspended. Snake Woman looked outside. Stars glistened. Nightlight, in her shape as a bowl, lay on the eastern horizon. A large fire glowed outside the walls of the fort. She clasped her blanket at her neck and went inside just as the sound of horses galloping into camp broke the quiet. How many? Three or four perhaps. Who? Why?

Dogs barked. Shadow and the pups joined the ruckus. The horses stopped at the north end of the camp where Spotted Horse's lodge stood. Loud voices. Was that Shot Twice, Weasel's quiet husband, devoted to ceremonies and sacred ways? Snake Woman could not make out what they said. More voices joined the talking as people emerged from lodges. "Grandmother, should we go to learn what is happening?"

Mountain Horse said nothing, did not move. Snake

Woman left the lodge for the confusion of voices. A loose cluster of shadow figures shuffled between the lodges of Shot Twice and Spotted Horse. She recognized people of the Many Children, blankets hanging across shoulders, and men she did not know from the Lone Fighters. What had brought them here in the night? She stood beside Weasel to listen.

When she returned to the Otter Lodge, Mountain Horse sat just as she had been when the young woman left. "Lone Fighters came to warn Spotted Horse of trouble at the fort," she explained. "The paleskin traders drank and raced all afternoon with men from both camps, then returned to the post at nightfall. The man Davis accused the Many Children of Conrad's death. This angered our men. They threaten to go to the fort and demand he take back his words. The Lone Fighters came in hope that our older men could restrain these young ones. Spotted Horse, Shot Twice, Crooked Back, and Bird Rattler have gone to try."

Snake Woman had hardly finished when sounds from the fort erupted: hollers, shouts, a rifle shot.

"These men," her grandmother sighed. "The whiskey feeds their pride, their anger. One moment they sing and dance. The next, they rage and fight. They forget how to hold their power."

The lodge walls grew lighter as they spoke, dawn closer than Snake Woman had realized. "Grandmother, I need to go to the fort and find out what is happening." The old woman said nothing. When Shadow rose to follow, Snake Woman stamped and stared, and the dog curled against the lodge with the sleeping pups. Most of the snow had melted the previous day, but thick frost coated the brittle grass. Tracks of those who left the camp made a woven, winding pattern like loosely braided thongs.

Nine men faced the fort's closed gates. They wore no blankets and three had no shirts. Snake Woman shivered, glad for the wool wrapped snug around her. She recognized Black Eagle, his broad shoulders bare, and next to him, One Spot. Men from the Lone Fighters stood with them. To one side stood the elders from the Many Children. A murmur of voices drifted through the chill air, indistinct as if the wind brought lodge poles to humming, or the narrow branches of cottonwood whispered in WindMaker's breath.

Toward the river stood a cluster of blanketed women. Snake Child tried to identify Pretty Crow or White Feather, but could not. A man's voice – was it Running Bird? – hollered to the gate. "Sterling. Speak with us," he called. No response came.

Beyond the fort, the sky grew orange-gold along the horizon and blended to blue that deepened as it rose higher. Snake Woman walked slowly closer until she stood the same distance from the men as they were from the gates. She felt exposed, alone and sat down, pulled her blanket over her bent knees, and waited.

A narrow slot in the fort gates, at the height of a person's face, opened with a sharp crack. A voice, a paleskin language she could not understand, came from the black opening. One of the Lone Fighters moved closer and answered in the same tongue.

At each corner of the fort stood men with rifles ready. Did they fear the growing anger of the People who did not want them on Napi's land? Did they fear what happened to the People when whiskey made them wild and unpredictable, when even their own camps did not recognize them in their madness? Why did they bring that poison at all? The People traded willingly for rifles, blankets, powder and shot, knives, and pots, and tobacco. The robes and furs that the traders wanted were given in exchange. What need did they have to bring whiskey?

A crack opened at the large gate. The Englishman stepped out. The men at each corner of the fort raised rifle butts to their shoulders. Sterling walked half the distance to the waiting men and stopped. Running Bird stepped forward and the two spoke, but she could not hear what was said. Spotted Horse joined them, then Shot Twice.

Snake Woman wasn't sure what happened next, for the quiet scene suddenly burst into noise. One of the Lone Fighters picked his rifle from the ground in one hand and let out a chilling war cry. The rifle was not aimed, and he did not hold it as if to shoot. But a trader fired at him. His shoulder exploded in blood, and bits of flesh splattered the men beside him. Confusion followed. The man screamed in agony. Spotted Horse and One Spot tried to calm the crowd, another Lone Fighter raised his rifle and this time did aim at the fort. Before he could fire, gunshot cracked from the opposite corner, and the Lone Fighter crumpled, hands at his chest, blood streaming between his fingers.

Sterling called to the fort, both his hands raised. He turned to face the group outside the gates and spoke loudly. "Please leave here, my friends, and return to your camps before more blood is shed. Let calm prevail. Do not let anyone else be injured."

Shot Twice and Spotted Horse joined their voices in asking for calm. But one of the Lone Fighters, a short, wide man with hair bunched on top of his head, grabbed Sterling with one arm and put a knife blade at his neck with the other. "You come with us," he growled.

The Lone Fighter whose shoulder was hit lay moaning on the ground, legs stretched out and then contracted, his head rolling side to side. Women who watched now came forward, and two of them eased him onto a blanket. Four others took a corner each and gently carried him.

The other man lay still on his back where he had fallen. A woman knelt beside him and rocked back and forth. Others came to roll him onto a blanket. His limbs moved with the clumsiness of something dead.

Mountain Horse stood beside her. Snake Woman did not remember her arrival. "We will go to the Lone Fighter's camp," the old woman said. Side by side they walked behind the ragged line of those exhausted, drunk, confused, and tired, numb with shock.

The man shot in the chest was dead. The woman who rocked beside him was a wife. Now, all three wives keened and moaned their grief, kneeling beside his body carried to lie at his lodge.

The man whose shoulder was now a gaping hole still groaned his pain. Someone pushed a stick of cottonwood between his teeth, to bite and contain his screams as whiskey was poured into the bloodied hole and a dried powder packed into the wound. His cries stopped suddenly, his pain driving him from consciousness.

The angry, stocky warrior still held his knife to Sterling's throat. Men from both camps milled about where the two stood. The group moved the way a swarm of wasps will hum around a disturbed nest. At some point, the wasps will settle, or they will attack.

The old woman moved close to her. "Snake Woman, you practiced your courage with Conrad. Let's see what we can do."

"Listen, all you people," Mountain Horse shouted to the crowd. "Now we have to collect ourselves. Come on, one of you must still have something to drink."

What was she doing? Snake Woman asked herself. Had the madness of the morning's events pushed her grandmother beyond sanity? Suddenly, she grasped the ruse. She had played one herself recently enough. Now, she must play again.

"Who has some whiskey? Come on." Snake Woman staggered to Mountain Horse and leaned on her shoulder. "Who's going to get this old grandmother something to drink so we can have a proper ceremony for these Lone Fighters?" The teeming, buzzing swarm settled to a focus. Why not have another drink?

Most of those present had been up all night. They were tired and worn with grief and anger.

"I've got whiskey here." It was the tall Lone Fighter, the one who spoke the paleskin's language. He carried a wooden keg in one arm and a tin cup in the other hand. He filled the cup and passed it to all who stood in the midst of the lodges. The sun already sat high in the eastern sky, but the air held on to the chill of night. A faint wisp of vapor clouded each person's breath.

"Here you two," the Lone Fighter said and handed the mug to Mountain Horse, who drank and passed it on to Snake Woman. She tipped the cup and gulped a mouthful, shuddered as her throat burned. She fought her impulse to spit in disgust, grinned in mock intoxication, and reeled close to the stocky man who held Sterling. "Here my friend, have a drink to warm yourself. One Spot, come and hold this pale-skin so our friend here can have a drink."

One Spot wove through the group and grabbed Sterling's arm roughly, placing his own knife to the other side of the Englishman's neck. "Go ahead," he nodded. "I'll watch him. Go and see your comrade."

The man released his hold and lowered his knife, took the nearly full cup of whiskey and emptied it down his tilted throat. He lurched to the dead man's lodge and entered.

"The dead one is his brother," One Spot said.

The Lone Fighter who brought the whiskey sat down, keg between his knees. Others sat one by one on each side of him, forming a loose arc, and the cup passed sloppily from hand to hand. Now and then, One Spot shoved Sterling so he was forced to step backward to keep his balance. His face was fearful and confused.

Snake Woman and her grandmother moved in front of Sterling. She saw Black Eagle at the edges of a cluster. "Hey, nearly brother, where's that Pretty Crow sister? Did you leave her at camp? Come and join us," she called. One by one she and Mountain Horse called to this or that member of the Many Children to join the group. Mountain Horse's loud voice and poor balance encouraged her own exaggerated speech and actions.

The Lone Fighters were exhausted from earlier carousing, their night of no sleep, and the shock of events. The renewed drinking subdued them further. Three already stretched on the ground asleep. The wounded man, from herbs and pain, remained unconscious. A woman with a long, thick braid over each shoulder, wrapped in a red striped blanket, sat beside him and rocked gently. A sleeping baby's head rested on the back of the woman's neck, its body under the blanket.

"We'll go to our camp for more whiskey and bring it for our friends here. Come on you Many Children, we will help them." Snake Woman and Mountain Horse continued their babble and staggered and fell into each other in a seemingly drunken muddle. All the time, Sterling was pushed along in the middle, out of view.

Once beyond hearing range, Mountain Horse stopped her pretense to speak low and quickly. "Snake Woman, stay near, and when we get close to the fort, get him to the gate."

Sterling grasped the deceit, muttering, "Thank you, thank you," over and over.

When they were close enough, Snake Woman grabbed his hand and pulled him from the muddle, left him against the walls of the fort, and returned to the swarm of blankets.

At the Many Children's camp, Spotted Horse had already signalled his wives to strike their lodges and pack.

Pretty Crow and White Feather stood outside the Otter Lodge. Shadow and the pups bounded to Snake Woman, leaping about with tails wagging. She felt the heady relief of getting Sterling to the fort, and carrying out the plan, realizing no Lone Fighters pursued them. Now, the camp would move, and the Many Children would be safe.

But Snake Woman's relief drained as she saw the faces of Pretty Crow and White Feather. Fearful eyes, swollen and red, an expression of confusion. What could this mean? Black Eagle and One Spot were safe.

"Grandmother." Pretty Crow's voice was tense and strained. She pointed to the lodge entrance, her brows pushed together as if she was in pain. "Grandmother, the Bundle is gone."

CHAPTER 29

MOUNTAIN HORSE LOOKED in the lodge and left immediately to find Weasel. "Perhaps it was moved to keep it safe."

Snake Woman froze where she stood, and as Pretty Crow and White Feather came to stand with her, she recounted the events at the fort and the Lone Fighter's camp.

The young women had returned to the Many Children's camp when the talk turned to confronting the traders at the fort. "We came to find you both gone and many of the camp gone," explained Pretty Crow. "We stayed at Crooked Back's lodge, and when we returned here, there was no Bundle."

Snake Woman could not make sense of what happened. "Who could take the Bundle? How could anyone come into camp and do this?" She ran her teeth back and forth over her bottom lip. To stand and wait was impossible. She released her paralysis and walked to Shot Twice's lodge to speak with her grandmother.

Inside, she sat behind the old woman, anguished in Mountain Horse's grief. Spotted Horse sent riders to check the horses. In the revelry, the camp was without guards. Had a raiding party come and found the prize?

"Our enemies have been bold these last months," Shot Twice said. "Perhaps they came this far."

Those in the lodge listened, murmured, adjusted blankets or hands as they pondered how it could be true. "The trader at the post wanted to trade for a Bundle. Has a paleskin stolen it?" Crooked Back spoke in slow, deliberate words, his forearms resting on his knees, a blanket around his shoulders, and his face marked with thoughtfulness, as if he listened for a clue that might explain where the Bundle had gone.

Mountain Horse, too, listened and waited, for a sound, a clue, a sign, the way she waited for Pretty Crow and White Feather to return to the lodge on warm summer evenings.

Bird Rattler, sitting the same way as Crooked Back, snorted at the suggestion of a paleskin. "What paleskin could sneak up on our camp? They're loud and clumsy, they'd set the dogs barking, they can't see at night, and they smell strange. They'd only be able to get the Bundle if they got a Real Person to steal it for them."

"There are half-bloods, those from other camps who hang around the fort. Maybe one of them," added Crooked Back. "For whiskey or a score against us."

Voices of conjecture went back and forth. No one could find a plausible story to explain the disappearance.

Snake Woman felt tired, her body heavy and eyes gritty from lack of sleep. She returned to the Otter Lodge and collapsed on the robes.

She woke to darkness, surprised to have slept so long. Had Mountain Horse returned? Had a discovery been made about the Bundle? She listened but could not hear Mountain Horse's regular, familiar breathing. The whole camp was silent. No dog barked or whined, no horse snorted or swished its tail. WindMaker slept also. One sound emerged, at first distant, then closer. It was a woman, crying. Soft sobbing.

Snake Woman wanted to call out, to ask: Who is it? What has happened? But the silence of the camp and lodge was dense and dark. It pressed down upon her and she could not move her mouth, could not take the breath she needed to call out to the woman, to guide her to the lodge. A terror seeped into her, the way cold will seep from the ground, and she knew the woman needed help, needed to be called through the darkness, guided to refuge. And she, Snake Woman, could do nothing, could not push through the weight of this black night to call and rescue the lost one.

In panic, she gave another effort and pushed herself to sitting to cry out, "Here, this way."

"Snake Woman, what is wrong? Are you ill?" Pretty Crow knelt beside her. The lodge was not dark. It was bright with the light of day. The echo of the woman's sobs hung in her ears.

"I heard a woman crying," Snake Woman answered.

"You dreamed, little sister," Pretty Crow said, and sat beside Snake Woman, putting an arm about her shoulders. "Tell me your dream."

Snake Woman repeated what she remembered, and her heart still pounded as the cold, lost feeling saturated her body. Was it the Bundle calling her?

She was hot and thirsty, and the lodge felt thick and sti-fling. Snake Woman stood and shook her head as if to shake away the fog that clouded her memory of the dream. "I am going to the river, to wash and drink," she said.

Shadow and the pups were not near the lodge when she left, and she walked alone north to where Old Man's River twisted along the side of the valley. The shoreline was fine, damp sand, cool, with half-submerged rocks throughout it. The sand was gummy and soft in places. Snake Woman walked with care, knowing that there were places in the river-bank where creatures were grabbed and sucked beneath, never to be seen above ground again.

She knelt and cupped water to her mouth, watched the drops sparkle from her skin to the ground. She splashed her face with both hands and then sat on a flat rock to watch the ripples of clear water glint in the sun. Snake Woman sat absorbed in the glinting, rippling tones of the water, the flow of color as it moved over sand and stone beneath.

She was brought out of her reflection by the sound of footsteps behind her. Just as she turned, Little Ear called.

"Snake Woman, I have been wanting to find you."

It was the first meeting since he had come in the night, full of whiskey, loud and disagreeable. Snake Woman felt awkward, as if the person that was Little Ear, her friend, was someone she did not know, as if her friend had gone and a stranger entered the familiar body.

He sat beside her, drew up his knees, and rested his arms on them. They sat side by side a long time. Snake Woman watched the patterns in the water, watched a gopher on the other side of the river rise to its haunches, whistle, flick its tail, then drop and run along the bank. The shadow of a crow as it passed overhead sent the gopher scrambling into the ground beneath a thick, smooth rock that jutted from the far bank. All the time Snake Woman watched, she listened and waited for Little Ear to speak. She waited to know which Little Ear sat beside her.

"Crooked Back warned me about whiskey." Little Ear spoke at last. "It's a wild fire that it brings. I felt alive, powerful, full of joy and song." He stopped again.

Does he expect me to speak? she wondered. I have nothing to say.

"The whiskey turned against me. Now, I understand how it is called a demon. It drummed inside my head, put fire in my belly. I threw out everything in my stomach. Finally I slept. All through yesterday, all through the night. I woke in the Lone Fighters' camp this morning and came back here. One Spot told me all that happened."

Snake Woman looked at him. His eyes were puffed and red, his upper lip was swollen with a bruise above it, and he smelled sour.

"We were racing with the paleskins yesterday," Little Ear continued. "I lost a bet. I had bet my little black mustang. Now, the paleskin has him."

Snake Woman heard the sorrow in his voice, felt it enter her own body as she thought of the fine buffalo pony and his eager, bright eyes and step. A wave of anger swelled in her. Why would the paleskin have that horse? He was the horse that Little Ear could calm with a touch, call with a single word, guide with silent commands. The paleskins did not know how to be with their horses, how to speak with them, listen to their wisdom, move as one with them. The little black would have a hard, cold piece of metal in his mouth, would have his sides kicked with barbed spurs from the boots of the traders.

"I was sure I could win him back, Snake Woman. I gambled the spotted mare and I gambled your filly, Cloud. They are all gone."

She exploded in anger. How could Little Ear bet her Cloud? How could he betray the trust and closeness of the little black, betray their friendship? "He was your friend. I was your friend. How could you? You don't deserve friends."

His head hung low and regret permeated the air around him.

Snake Woman stood and walked in purposeful strides away from the river and Little Ear. She did not look back once. Her thoughts were ahead, ahead to the night. She would not leave Cloud to the paleskins. She would go to the fort and get her back.

SECTION SIX

Restoration

CHAPTER 30

MISS HAMILTON'S BUGGY waited outside the door, Scalliwag hitched behind it, as Eleanor neared home and ran to greet the visitors.

They sat with her parents around the table. "How nice to see you." Miss Hamilton rose and extended her hand. "Come and sit. Have you found any Indian tools?" She smelled like flowers and spoke with the rich voice that made Eleanor wish she had something to present. Have you seen anyone as you're walking to meet the others, or on your way home?"

Eleanor's belly tightened. She wanted to tell about the smoke, but the tightening held her tongue.

"As the Constable has mentioned, an item of considerable value that came from the tribe to the west of here was stolen several weeks ago. It's likely being brought back."

"Why would someone bring it here?" Eleanor asked. She dunked a corner of her biscuit in the tea, ignoring Catharine's scowls.

"Wouldn't it make sense to sell it in the east, to a collector or another museum?" her father added.

"In this case, no. The Royal Ontario Museum once employed a young Englishman," she said. "Very good with languages. Bit of a romantic when it came to the west. This was long before my time, but his story became one of our legends." Lily paused and turned her eyes slightly upward, looking back in time. "Mr. Sterling ended up marrying a young woman of the Blood Indian tribe and brought her back to the east. Sometimes this sort of thing happened. They never fit in, though in this case them woman learned English well and, when dressed in civilized clothes, passed for a dark-skinned European. He left the museum after a couple of years, and I don't know what became of them, except that he died about six months ago. Some people at the museum think it was Sterling's widow who took the bundle. Poor thing may have recognized it. They can be quite sentimental about these ceremonial objects."

Catharine poured more tea into Lily Hamilton's cup. "Wouldn't it be easy to locate an Indian woman coming west?" Catharine asked. "She must be using the train or else we would not expect her for several months."

"This woman lived in decent society for a long time, Catharine. I hope you don't mind if I call you that. She may be able to conceal her heritage quite well."

Constable Whyte stood. "It's always a sorrow to leave your hospitality, Mr. and Mrs. Donaldson, but we must be going. There's two more households, new settlers both, to the south, where I will escort Miss Hamilton. I'll bring these new arrivals by soon to meet you. Again, in the meantime, if you see or hear of anything out of the ordinary, do please contact me. If this woman gets back to the reserve, we'll have little chance of retrieving either her or the bundle."

As Eleanor listened to the conversation, she felt her heart beat faster, certain that what she had seen at the coulee was indeed smoke. It was essential that she quickly investigate, before anyone else did. As soon as Constable Whyte and Miss Hamilton were gone, she blurted her intentions for the next day. "Tomorrow's Saturday and I'd like to go to the coulee, after we finish chores. With the spring here, there are new flowers coming everyday. And Mr. Pacey hasn't been by. We have to keep the coal scuttle stocked, Mother, so you can make those biscuits on a moment's notice when Constable Whyte comes by. He does love them. I'll go fill the water pails."

"Goodness, Eleanor, you're quite the chatterbox today." Catharine carried the tea china carefully to the wash water that simmered on top of the stove. "I'd love to walk with you, but Ada is coming in the afternoon. Could you wait until Sunday and we could go together?"

Eleanor did not reply and carried the pails outside. Better her mother think she did not hear, for she was determined to go alone.

The next morning, as her mother prepared for Ada's visit, Eleanor walked to the coulee rim where she had seen the smoke rising. The wall on the opposite side was a series of mounded hills reaching into the coulee like the toes of a giant cat. Where the blue spiral had risen was a sheltered cleft with willow and cottonwood on the sides and bottom and, at its entrance, a pile of large stones in a haphazard pile.

Water has to be there, she reasoned, with that thick grass and so many trees, trees that give shelter and don't let me see what's behind them.

I'm not thinking about this anymore, she said to herself. I'm just walking to that gully and I'm going to see what's there.

The rocks lying in a rubble at the entrance were patterned with lichen. They leaned against each other like drunks about to topple, much larger than they appeared from above and three times Eleanor's height, at least. At their base the grass was thick and vibrant green.

She clambered up their rough surface, the dry lichen scraping her hands. At the top she stood to peer at the willow and cottonwood thicket at the entrance to the gully.

A small pool of water shone like a mirror to the east of the rocks.

She sat on the rock and studied the area. The sides rose steeply, covered in willow brush halfway before thinning to tough prairie grass. The small poplar, leaves budding along gnarled twisted branches, shielded her view to the end of the crevasse.

I could wait and ask someone to come with me, she mused, carefully stepping from stone to stone down to the thick grass. But who? I'll just have to do it myself. Walk in between those trunks and see what's there. It's the only way to find out.

But it wasn't the only way. Just beyond the outer trees, in their shadow so that Eleanor had to strain to be sure of what she saw, stood a woman.

Eleanor stared, gradually making sense of the lines, the

light and dark. The woman leaned with both hands on a tall staff and looked directly to her. A bird called a long trill from somewhere behind Eleanor and a ruffle of warm air passed over her cheek. A fly landed on her hand that still touched one of the stones. She stared. The woman stared back.

Eleanor wanted to say something but could not find words. The woman stepped forward. Using the pole to support her weight, she moved awkwardly out of the shadows to stand beside a tree. She winced with the movement.

"You have hurt your leg," Eleanor blurted.

"That I have," the woman replied. She was obviously Indian, dark-skinned, a brown blanket wrapped over her shoulders. She wore a cotton print dress, high leather moccasins, and two long braids of gray-streaked hair that hung half way to her waist. Blood-stained cotton wrapped her left ankle.

"Do you need help?" Eleanor asked.

"It seems so."

"I'll go and get my father and our wagon. We can help you get to a doctor. Your leg might be broken."

"You must not do that." Her voice was clear and smooth. "You must tell no one. But if you could bring me a bit of food, perhaps some tea, while I wait for my foot to heal, I would be very grateful."

"I saw smoke on Wednesday. Have you been here all this time? With that injured foot?"

The woman nodded.

"With nothing to eat or drink?"

She nodded her chin at the small pool without taking her eyes from Eleanor.

"But where do you sleep?" asked Eleanor. "It's still so cold at night." This time the woman pointed her chin over her right shoulder, which Eleanor understood to mean further back in the canyon. Laced at her wrist was a chipped mug of the same blue enamel used in their kitchen. Eleanor pointed to it. "Can I get you some water?"

With one hand the woman untied the thong holding the mug and crooked her arm around the pole. Eleanor walked closer and took the mug to the pool where she knelt and dipped it. The water smelled of melted snow and of the wind that blew cool from the mountains.

"My name is Eleanor," she said, handing the woman the mug. Close up, her face was finely wrinkled, except for deep lines at her eyes and mouth like patterns left in mud by flowing water. Her eyes were large and black like a deer's.

"I expected someone else," the woman finally said. "My name is Snake Woman."

"Pleased to meet you," Eleanor replied and heard the mannered words she had been taught to say sound out of place. She felt awkward and unsure, not pleased. What was the correct thing to say in an entirely new situation?

Snake Woman handed the cup back. "Perhaps you would carry a cup just back in here to save me having to walk out later." She supported herself with both hands on the staff and turned to limp clumsily through the brush. Eleanor refilled the mug and followed.

"How did you hurt your leg?"

Snake Woman sat on a thin blanket folded on the ground, her wrapped leg outstretched. The cleft in the coulee where she hid did not go more than twenty yards back before its wall angled sharply up. A circle of rocks surrounded the place where the blanket was spread, and a large canvas satchel rested against one of them. Eleanor set the mug on a rock and wondered if Snake Woman was going to answer.

Finally the woman gestured to one of the large rocks at the corner of the half circle that framed her resting place. Eleanor understood it was an invitation to sit, and she did. The rock was high enough that she half leaned, half sat. It was cool and rough against her hands, and she moved them to her lap.

"Those very rocks that you climbed when you wanted to investigate this gully," Snake Woman began. "I did that same thing. The sun was high enough to warm the rocks. I never noticed it, but then nearly stepped on it. A thick, long snake sunning itself." She clasped her hands on the bent knee of the uninjured leg. "Never thought to watch for a snake this early in the year. Startled me. I jumped, lost my footing, caught my leg as I fell."

Eleanor winced imagining what Snake Woman described. Then shivered as she realized the snake had been where she stood.

"Not sure how I even got it out – my leg. Crawled in here. Took a chance on lighting a small fire that next morning. Cold in the night. I needed to heat some herbs for the wound."

"Are you meeting someone? You said you expected someone else." Maybe another person will help her.

"I dreamed," Snake Woman answered. "My old grandmother talked with me. She's long dead, of course."

How could she be expecting someone who was dead?

Was she deranged as a result of the fall? Should she just go and get help? And was this the woman who took the bundle? "You speak English very well," was all she managed to say.

Snake Woman leaned against the satchel and drew the blanket close to her neck. The sun no longer reached them, and the air chilled quickly. "Will you give me your word you won't tell anyone about me being here, about meeting me?"

"You have a badly injured foot. You need to have it tended. How can I just leave you out here alone?"

A twitch at the corners of Snake Woman's mouth hinted at a smile. "I've managed this far," she said.

"But you weren't injured before."

"That is so. Sometimes we are asked to carry burdens more difficult than we expected."

What is she talking about? thought Eleanor. "I just have to have a good reason not to tell anyone."

"Maybe I can't give you a reason." The old woman spoke slowly, as if she chose her words with great care. "Maybe it would take a lifetime to explain how I came to be here. Maybe even a whole lifetime wouldn't be enough to give a reason that would satisfy you."

"Have you stolen something? Something from the Royal Ontario Museum?"

This time Snake Woman's eyes crinkled into the waterway patterns as her mouth gave a definite but brief smile. "No," she said. A long pause followed, while a brown iridescent beetle walked along the length of the woman's outstretched leg. When it reached the big toe it flew. "I am returning to its rightful place of belonging something that had been stolen," she added.

Eleanor looked questioningly at her.

"It is a trust given to me. This was once in the care of my grandmother, in the lodge we shared." She nodded her chin to the satchel. "It was stolen. Now it is time to return it. It wants to go home." Snake Woman clasped her hands in her lap and looked at them in a gesture suggesting she had nothing more to say.

Eleanor had one question after another rise in her mind. Hadn't the woman said that her grandmother was long dead? So how could this thing be returned to her? If you stole back something, was it really stealing? Was this woman even telling the truth? Was she sane?

But as the questions rose, she heard something behind the questions, some part of her mind that watched the old woman and listened. That part said, *"You must do as she asks."* Eleanor knew it as the same part that recognized the stars on her first night, that knew the coyotes thought of her. It was the part that knew this land was home.

Eleanor removed her dark blue sweater and placed it beside Snake Woman. "I give you my word. I will tell no one. I must go home, or someone will worry and come looking. I will return with food as soon as I can. The sweater isn't much, but it will give some warmth."

"There you are, dear. I was beginning to worry with the sun getting low. Your father just arrived as well. He's still with the horses." Catharine opened the oven door, and the scent of new bread filled the kitchen. "Whatever were you doing so long? Wash up now, the water's warm." A metal basin steamed on the stovetop. "Ada was sorry to miss you. She brought the mail and lots of news, but I'll wait until your father is inside to hear. There's a letter for all of us from Bernard."

Eleanor scooped water into a cream enamel basin with a thin green trim at its edge and set the bowl on the planks that made a long counter on the east wall. "Have you opened his letter? Does he say when he's coming?"

Catharine lifted the lid of the pot at the back of the stove. "Your father's going to read it aloud after dinner." She brought the bread from the oven, tapped the loaf from the pan, and set it on the warming rack to cool. "We're all ready to eat."

The scent of bread and stew called Eleanor's hunger to surface clear and eager. At the same time, the image of Snake Woman in the coulee crevasse rose up as strong as her hunger. These were nights that still left thick, hard frost each morning. Would Snake Woman risk a fire at night, she wondered. Did she have wood? Why hadn't she thought to collect some for her? She must have matches, for she had a small fire on Wednesday. But how many? Eleanor wanted to grab the warm loaf of bread and run, run while light remained to find her way. I could take a blanket as well, a coat, and just go.

"What is it, Eleanor? You're far away in your thoughts." The door opened just then and accentuated the soft golden light of the oil lamps her mother had just lit. The yellow curtains glowed and made the room even warmer, while the doorframe outlined a rectangle of blue, cold and empty with her father standing in its center. "Here you are Stephen. Now we can eat. I've loads of news from Ada."

"Tell us about your afternoon, dear," Catharine asked again. "You do seem distracted."

Eleanor realized she must be careful in how she handled

this situation. "Sorry," she said and straightened herself, brushing a strand of hair behind her ear. "I expect I'm tired. I walked a long ways along the coulee. There are signs of spring everywhere. But I did a foolish thing and left my sweater. I'll have to go out first thing and get it."

Stephen laughed. "The spring air is distracting you. I have difficulty keeping my own thoughts organized."

"But there's a minister coming to Altorado tomorrow. This is one of Ada's bits of news. It will be the first Sunday to have anything resembling a church service since we came." Catharine stood and put the kettle over the hot box.

"We'll pick your sweater up on the way, Eleanor," her father said, "or on the way back. Now, let's have some tea and hear what Bernard has to say."

"I could just," began Eleanor and then paused. "When is the minister coming?"

"Around noon. We'll have a lunch at the Lynes'. It will do you good, Stephen, to have a day away from the plough." Catharine set the enamelled pot between them and a mug for each. "Bring the sugar, won't you Eleanor?"

Now what? she asked herself while she retrieved the sugar bowl. How would she get a blanket and food to Snake Woman? And how would she get her sweater? Every plan that arose in her mind was full of lies, based on deceit, and carried a risk of revealing the old woman. Even if Uncle Bernard was here, I couldn't tell him. I gave my word.

"Are you bringing that sugar?" Stephen called from the table. "I'm dying for tea, and besides, I thought you were keen to hear what Bernard writes."

"And I still am," Eleanor lied. "Let's hear that letter, Father."

CHAPTER 31

ELEANOR WOKE JUST as the night began to pale. Her father snored softly, and she hoped her mother slept as soundly. Outside, frost glittered cold and haunting while a crescent moon lay casually in her deep blue bed above the dark mounds of the hills. She wanted to ride Belle but Charlie would whinny and stamp if left behind, waking her parents. Instead, she scribbled a hasty note and left it on the kitchen table, clutching a blanket from her bed to her chest. Inside its folds were four thick slices of bread, tea wrapped in a square of green gingham, two slices of salt pork, a few matches, and sugar. Not much, but a start, and not so much as to be noticed. She ran at a slow jog and alternated with brisk walking while she caught her breath, her plan to be back for breakfast.

Snake Woman met her at the crevasse entrance, leaning on her stick, as if expecting her.

"I'm sorry I can't stay long," Eleanor panted. "You must be so cold. Here's another blanket. I'll gather dead wood to heat water. I had to tell my parents I left my sweater. Sorry, it will have to come back with me. But I've got another." Eleanor talked quickly as she removed a thick brown pull-over. "How is your leg?"

Snake Woman nodded, smiled, and sat. "This is very good. Thank you."

"I'll come again as soon as I can, when it is safe." Eleanor turned and walked briskly to the main coulee, then stopped and went back. "Do you want some pieces of coal? It's much warmer than wood."

"Too smelly and smoky," said Snake Woman. "The best fire is from buffalo chips. Hot. No smoke. No smell."

"Right," nodded Eleanor. "I'll bring some next time."

She walked east on the coulee bottom, but it was still dark there though the sky had lightened quickly. It would be brighter along the ridge. She angled up just below the tipi circles and emerged a few yards from their western edge. She stopped in mid-step. Before her, in the center of the closest circle, stood a coyote. Behind it, the first arc of the rising sun glowed brilliant. Standing casually as if her appearance there was a normal event, its eyes locked on hers. The hairs along its neck and back turned bright gold as new rays touched them, setting them to fire.

Eleanor held her breath. Then it was gone. In a leap that defied the possible, it jumped from the circle's center to the coulee edge and sprang again to disappear over its side. She exhaled a slow sigh and shifted her weight, suspended on her left leg as she was just setting her right foot down. Did her heart pound from her effort at climbing from the bottom or from the encounter?

She shivered, put on the blue sweater that she had carried until now, and resumed her quick walk, glancing over her shoulder a few times. The flat land that bordered the coulee lay dusty brown and empty in the morning light.

As Eleanor expected, her mother was perturbed that she had gone so early alone and did not understand why the sweater's retrieval could not wait. "After all, we'll be driving in that direction."

School resumed the following day, and Eleanor was relieved to walk to Snake Woman without having to explain her actions. She ate only a small bit of the bread and salt pork she carried for lunch. Holding the hem of her thick gray skirt with her left hand, she gathered pale buffalo chips along the dry windswept edges of the coulee.

This time, Snake Woman did not stand waiting for her but sat in her small sheltered space, her injured leg stretched out. Eleanor released the dried chips in a pile near the woman's feet. Snake Woman's eyes were sunken, as if she was tired, and her voice had no strength when she gave a weak smile and a thank you. Eleanor filled the mug and re-filled it when Snake Woman finished drinking.

"Your leg is very bad. Can I do anything?"

The old woman was slow to answer, and Eleanor had to move in close to hear her when she did speak. "The small, pink flowers that grow along the coulee sides. A handful of their leaves would help." Eleanor found them easily and brought more the next day.

On the day after that, Snake Woman's eyes were larger and her voice stronger, but she still seemed weak.

"The weekend is nearing when I may not be able to come," Eleanor apologized. "Will you not let me get help for you?"

"Your help is very good," Snake Woman replied. "Wait until a school day to come again. I saw that red-coat policeman riding along the coulee edge this morning. Don't want him following you."

The next visit, Eleanor brought extra bread, tea, and buffalo chips. Her mother had not yet noticed one of Eleanor's blankets was gone. How long until she did? She had, however, noticed her daughter's appetite. "It must be all that walking in the spring air that's giving you such hunger. You and your father are keeping the oven and me rather busy."

When Eleanor came home that Friday, Scalliwag stood tethered at the door, and Constable Whyte sat inside. "We've more evidence that the woman who took the bundle came this way," he explained. He had the usual biscuit in his hand. "A woman who matched her description was seen on the train when it arrived in Medicine Hat. No one saw her leave, but she wasn't on it when it got to Lethbridge."

"You look tired, Eleanor," her mother interrupted. "Give Constable Whyte a proper hello, and come have some tea. Besides," she added while she filled Eleanor's mug and refilled the Constable's, "Mr. Whyte has brought exciting news for us. I was going to wait until your father came back. Go ahead, Constable, have another biscuit. Uncle Bernard has arrived in Seven Persons. Mr. Barton is driving him out tomorrow."

CHAPTER 32

"BUT IF YOU'RE GOING to stay out west, why can't you just live with us instead of in Seven Persons?" Eleanor asked. She and Uncle Bernard sat in the grass near the tipi circles. Just as she had imagined so many times, she had given him a day to adjust and rest and then brought him here. As she had known he would be, Uncle Bernard was delighted. He grew quiet, and they sat side by side where the land began to drop. In Eleanor's plans, Uncle Bernard stayed to live with them.

"No, no, my girl. You've got your school on the weekdays. I'm too old to be out with your father helping him break land." He leaned over closer and said softly. "Truth be told, my girl, and just between you and me, I wouldn't have the inclination to be tearing up that land anyway, seeding it to anything other than the prairie grass that's always been here." He sat up straight again and breathed deeply. "I'd only be underfoot." He leaned back on his hands, wearing the same cream-colored suit and brown hat he wore so often in Aurora. His hair and neatly trimmed beard were soft gray, his eyes the same smoky blue as her father's. His stomach and chest were rounder than ever. "But I won't be far. Your mother already extracted a promise that – weather permitting – I come out at least every second Saturday and stay overnight. So there you are. Much like it was in Aurora except you'll have to be giving up your bed every couple of weeks."

Eleanor looked west to the thick brush and tree growth of the small cleft where Snake Woman hid. She ached to tell him, to link the newspaper clipping to Snake Woman. "You remember the clipping you sent?" she began. "Constable Whyte thinks the woman came this way. He and Miss Hamilton are asking everyone if they've seen any sign of her."

"Have they now? "Uncle Bernard answered. "Well if she is around here, let's hope they don't find her."

"Wouldn't you want whatever was stolen to be returned to the museum?"

"Well, that would depend, now wouldn't it, on how the museum got hold of it in the first place."

Eleanor sensed a story and waited, as she had learned to do, hoping to coax it out with silence.

"Should we be heading back, then, my girl? We don't want to keep your mother waiting, and I can't walk as fast as I once could."

"What were you remembering, Uncle Bernard? You could tell me while we walk. I've missed your stories."

He pushed himself to standing and brushed the dust and bits of grass from his pants. "Have you, now? Some of the memories are sad ones, my girl. Now that I'm back here for a last visit, there's things I remember that I'm not so glad to recall."

Eleanor stood and brushed her skirt. The action sent a group of antelope running on the other side of the coulee. The two watched in silence as they scattered. She hooked her right arm around his left and they walked slowly back.

"My first time west, that rascal Tom Barton was with me then. Do you know the Mounties weren't even here yet?" A gopher sat up ahead of them, whistled its warning and disappeared down its hole. "And one thing hasn't changed – there are just as many of those cheeky fellows as ever. Tom and I were trying our hand at being traders, but finding it not to our liking. Whiskey had been a terrible thing for the Indians. We were on our way back to Fort Benton and staying in a fort along the Old Man's River to the west of here." He turned to point behind and looked beyond his hand, at a memory Eleanor could not see. "There were two camps pitched near the fort to trade. I'm not going into details of what the whiskey led to, so don't even ask." Bernard turned and resumed his slow walk eastward.

"But that night," he continued, "after shooting and fighting between the camps, didn't this one young woman come sneaking into the corral of the fort trying to steal a horse." Bernard grew silent again, his head tilted forward. He shook it lightly as if the memory still made no sense. "There'd been a young man at the fort who worked for a museum. He'd gotten himself in quite a mess with one of the camps. Nearly lost his scalp in all the fracas that day. Men up from Fort Benton working for the I.G. Baker Company ran the fort and they were a rough bunch, not to my liking. Well, she managed to let a fine black, a spotted mare, and a lovely spotted filly out of the corral before they caught her. I can tell you it didn't look good. She was only, maybe, fifteen."

Uncle Bernard stopped again and this time looked at Eleanor. "Just your age, my girl. It was the fellow from the museum who stepped in and said the girl had helped save his life that day, and he wasn't going to let them hurt her. Well, didn't they ask him how he expected to stop them doing whatever they pleased. He'd been collecting things for some months, and he knew one of the men at the fort had been trying to get hold of a medicine bundle. Who knows why. Not like they showed any interest in Indian ways. The man said he'd trade a couple of pipe bundles in exchange for the girl. 'Oh, would you now? And what else have you got,' the chief factor sneered. 'Because I already managed to get hold of a medicine bundle.' And he reaches under the ledge and pulls out something wrapped in a red blanket. At the sight of it, that girl went berserk, hollering and kicking. She got a whack across the face that sent her crashing against the wall and knocked out cold. That museum fellow traded every-thing he'd collected in exchange for the girl. He left the fort and took her with him right that night. She was hardly awake and had to be tied onto him on his horse as they headed out."

Eleanor clutched his arm tighter. "What happened to them? Did you ever find out?"

"I heard later he'd taken her to Fort Benton and got a doc-tor. Then brought her east and married her." Bernard stopped yet again and set his right hand against the one that held his arm. "And what I have shame for, when I tell this story, my girl, is that I didn't do anything to help that young woman.

Didn't step up like that fellow from the museum. The look in her eyes when she saw that red blanket was enough to tear my heart from my chest. Later, I figured out it must have come from her tribe, was one of their sacred bundles. And here it was in some white traders' fort where it had no business."

They were nearly back to the small sod hut, the wind blowing against their backs. Uncle Bernard held his hat in place with his right hand. He stopped and moved his hat out of the wind to rest against his chest, as if at a graveside. "The story I just told you, girl, is not one I have ever repeated. Don't want that young woman's grief and pain to be the fodder for one of my tales about the days in the west."

Eleanor understood. He didn't want it repeated or referred to. She nodded agreement, pleased in his trust.

"Tom and I left the fort that night ourselves. We could feel trouble brewing between the camps and the fort, and the camps with each other. Heard later that it was a terrible ruckus that followed." He put his hat on again and resumed walking, loosing his arm from Eleanor's to lay it gently across her shoulder.

What she remembered was how she could nestle her head against his chest when he did this. Now, her head was above his shoulder and, though he was large, he was no longer the tall man of her memories.

"When I read that piece in the newspaper, Eleanor, the memory of that time rose up strong. And I said to myself, now wouldn't it be just a fine thing if that woman who took the bundle was the one who went off with that museum fellow? And wouldn't it just be the perfect thing if she'd found that bundle in the museum and vowed she'd get it back and take it home where it belonged? It filled my heart when I imagined that could be true. Then some voice in me spoke up and said, 'Send that along to Eleanor, now she's out in the west.' So, that's what I did."

They were just at the west of the house, the side lit golden brown in the low sun. Eleanor took slow, small steps, the way she had when they walked in Aurora and she wanted to keep a story going. "Why would it be so important to bring it back after all these years? Most of the people the young Indian woman knew would be dead now, or living on the reserve."

"What I came to understand, my girl, though it took me years, was that these sacred things like the bundles – well, it's more like the people belong to them than they belong to the people. They take care of them, serve them, you might say. There's some that say these things have a life and a will of their own. They belong to the land. The Indians belong to the land. So, even if the woman's family were gone, she'd want to bring that bundle home where it belonged, as a duty. That's what I like to think, and it does my heart good to imagine it."

"What does it do your heart good to imagine, Bernard?" Catharine came out the door to shake out a baking cloth just in front of them.

"Why, to imagine the fine cooking that I have whenever I'm in your home, of course," he answered, and kissed her on each cheek. "I've had nothing to compare with it since you left Aurora, my dear Catharine."

"You'll find my cooking much changed, Bernard, but it does my own heart good to have you at our table again, no matter how simple the fare." Catharine's eyes shone, and she took Bernard's hand. "Now, come inside and give me news of home, Bernard. I'm aching for it. You're our only visitor from there since we arrived. Eleanor will have to share your story-telling."

Her mother's face surprised Eleanor, for she recognized it as the face her mother had worn when they lived in the east, eyes bright and full of interest, a ready smile, playful talk. She realized her mother had become quieter, less enthused, with more concern, even worry. "You sit with Uncle Bernard. I'll get tea for once." Catharine looked up expectantly. "Yes, Mother," Eleanor said, laughing, "with the special china."

She was glad to have a few moments, as she filled the kettle and retrieved the china from the trunk, to think over what Uncle Bernard had said. As soon as he had told of his own thoughts when he read the newspaper clipping, Eleanor was sure he was right. Snake Woman was taking the stolen bundle back to its home. And just as surely as she knew this to be true, she knew what she had to do to help her.

CHAPTER 33

A DARK BANK of cloud dominated the northern sky, and a biting cold wind pierced to her skin as Eleanor waved good-bye to the Wagners' wagon.

"Let's drive Eleanor all the way home, Adam," Carl had suggested shortly before they reached the usual drop-off point. "That wind is getting colder by the minute."

"No, really, it's fine," she replied vigorously. "The walk is just what I need at the end of the day."

"How come you hardly ate any of your lunch?" asked Hattie. "Are you feeling ill?" Eleanor pretended not to hear, wished Hattie didn't talk so much.

"C'mon, Adam. It's not far out of our way," prodded Carl.

"What do you want to do, Eleanor?" Adam asked.

Eleanor knew Adam would like to drive her, for he had offered on other days, even ones that were warm and pleasant.

But then it was his own suggestion, while today it was Carl's. For once, she was glad Adam had this trait. "Thanks, Adam, but no. I'll be well home before it gets any worse."

Carl persisted. "There's snow coming for sure. These spring storms move in fast, Eleanor. I've seen whole herds of young calves wiped out in them. And there's plenty of stories of people who paid no attention and were found frozen out on the prairie."

Lydia was impatient. "Leave her be, Carl."

"That's right," Adam nodded. "It's not that bad. See you in the morning, Eleanor. If it snows I'll drive right to your door."

Eleanor picked her way down the now-familiar angling trail of the coulee side, hoping Carl was wrong. The cold nights had been bad enough. A spring storm would be insufferable for Snake Woman.

But Snake Woman showed little concern. "This is a good blanket you brought," she replied with a shrug after Eleanor told of the coming storm. "And the storm's not coming yet. Few days until that happens."

The Indians can tell weather like it was written out in a book, my girl. Now she was learning this for herself. If Snake Woman was right.

"I know what you're doing," Eleanor blurted, "and why you're doing it. You're taking that back aren't you." She pointed to the satchel that Snake Woman leaned against.

The old woman sat with her injured leg outstretched and looked quizzically at Eleanor, her head tilted to one side. "Am I?"

"How much further do you have to go? If I came with a wagon and helped you out of the coulee, could I get you where you need to go and be back by nightfall?"

"Even if you could, where would you get a horse and wagon without someone being suspicious?" Snake Woman asked. "Without someone finding out?"

"I don't know." Enthusiasm drained from Eleanor. When the idea had flashed into her mind to help Snake Woman get where she was going, it felt clear and certain. Details had not been part of the certainty. Now it seemed impossible, the obstacles too many. Despair rushed in to replace her depleted optimism. "I'm worried about you. Your leg must be broken. Constable Whyte is watching for you. Lily Hamilton is asking everyone if they've seen anything unusual." Eleanor leaned back on the rock and folded her arms on her chest. "And now a storm is coming."

She turned her hands up in a gesture of resignation, then removed from her school bag what was left of her lunch, plus more tea and sugar. She filled the mug, and while Snake Woman drank, walked out to the main coulee to gather buffalo chips scattered to the west of the cleft entrance. At least she'll have some warmth, she told herself.

Eleanor released her gatherings from the pouch of her held-up skirt, close to where Snake Woman sat. "The storm looks close. If snow comes, I won't be able to visit. It would leave tracks."

"Tomorrow," Snake Woman said, "I will say more. No snow will come tonight." She smiled a broad grin that crinkled her brown face.

For a moment, Eleanor forgot all the concerns, the

unusualness of the situation. She felt a rush of affection rise up and was surprised to realize how fond she had grown of the old woman. "I hope you'll be warm."

To keep out of the wind, she walked in the coulee bottom, but it all too soon angled southeast and away from her destination. The climb to the rim gave warmth, but the wind soon sucked it from her, replaced it with icy prickles that poked through to her skin. She shivered, drew her shawl over her head, held it firm at her chin, and walked with her head turned away from the cold north blast.

She did not hear the hoofbeats until the horse was nearly beside her.

"Eleanor, where have you been?" Carl called. He rode a large chestnut gelding. "I came back to give you a ride, but you had disappeared. Here, take my hand and get up behind me."

"Carl, did you go all the way to my house yet?" Eleanor stepped into the stirrup, pulled against his hand and swung up behind him.

"No, I figured you couldn't have got that far, so I tried to find you. Thought you might be in the coulee out of the wind, but you weren't there." He sat half-turned in the saddle and had not signalled the horse to move. "You frightened me."

Eleanor was flustered and felt anger rising that it was such a close call. What if he had seen her gathering buffalo chips? He would have ridden down and everything would be discovered.

"Are you all right? Hattie thought you might be ill. Are you?"

Carl was usually shy and quiet, his speech soft. Suddenly he was pestering her for explanations. She couldn't find words.

Then a sudden insight let her relax. Carl was sweet on her and had been truly worried. It all made sense. Relief flooded her. "Sorry, Carl. You startled me coming up fast like that. I did go into the coulee to get out of the wind and found a place on the hillside to just sit, in a thicket of willows. I love willows, don't you? There were mule deer across the valley. I guess they distracted me. I lost track of time and never saw you at all." It wasn't a total lie. It had been another day that she'd sat and watched mule deer, not this day. "It's very kind of you to come and give a ride. But honestly, it's not that cold. I really do enjoy these walks."

Carl flicked the reins and the gelding headed toward the sod hut. He said nothing more.

Stephen and Catharine emerged from their home as Eleanor slid from the horse. "Carl rode back to give me a ride with it being so cold," she said quickly, and hoped Carl would say nothing more.

"How thoughtful," Catharine said. "Do come and have tea before you ride back. Such a cold wind. Stephen came back early."

Carl touched his hand to the brim of his hat. "Thanks, but I need to get back. See you in the morning, Eleanor. Unless it snows heavy." He rode away in a slow canter.

Dark came early, the dense black clouds gliding relentlessly from the north to claim the whole sky. Cold wind circled the sod walls in low, persistent moans.

"I'm grateful for our coal supply right now. You've built it up quite well with what you bring each day, Eleanor." Stephen sat at the table, an oil lamp just to his right that turned the papers he leafed through a dull, warm gold. "We're warm and dry in here. I know, I keep saying it," he raised his hands like a man under arrest in response to Catharine's hands-on-hip sigh, "but this dirt house has been very liveable."

"I still look forward to a real house," Catharine replied. "You've made such good progress with the clearing and seeding. We'll be in good shape to build by late summer. Eleanor can have a proper bedroom. You look tired dear," Catharine added when she looked to where Eleanor sat at the other end of the table.

"Yes, I'm going to bed. The noise of this wind makes me want to sleep. Good night, Mother, Father."

In the night she woke. The wind had stopped. She had heard another sound. Had she dreamed it? Like singing, but not a song. More than one voice. A discordant harmony that left a hollow, tingling sensation in her throat. The high-pitched ring of silence emerged, but Eleanor knew it had been a different sound from that. Not entirely comfortable.

Had it snowed? She did not want to get up to check, did not want to disturb the stillness and the lingering presence of the singing. A warm, heavy drowsiness returned as she sank toward sleep. The singing began again. Haunting, high voices. Behind them, the drone of deep, low sounds. Disturbing, yet comforting. I remember now, she told herself. Isn't it funny that I had forgotten that I knew this.

This was the thought that still hung in her mind when she woke in the morning. She could hear her mother and father talking softly, the soft clunk of coal dropped into the firebox, water poured into basin and kettle, the nicker of Belle as she anticipated morning oats. Bit by bit, the remnants of the singing faded, but Eleanor remained still and listened a long while before finally giving up the hope that it would return.

No snow. The wind had carried the clouds to hover like black shadows in the southern sky. The last stars gleamed in the sky, now uncovered, timid and shy to leave the dark blanket of night behind.

Eleanor sighed in relief. No snow meant no tracks. Meant she would have a chance to get food and more fuel to Snake Woman without drawing suspicion. What was it Snake Woman had said? That she could say more tomorrow? Which was today.

She walked briskly west to the usual meeting place with the Wagners. The morning was chilly, but the absence of wind made it seem warmer and more spring like. A meadowlark trilled behind her, a startled rabbit leaped up to her right, and two large birds circled in slow arcs above the coulee.

The scent of morning and spring air filled her lungs. Snake Woman's plight and the worry of finding a way to help did not seem as onerous or heavy. "Nothing could be hopeless on a day like this," she said aloud.

But at school that morning, Constable Whyte brought Lily Hamilton to speak with all the students. In a white high-collared lace shirt, her thick hair curled and shiny, she was handsome and gracious, as usual. She encouraged the students to contact her by letter if they found any artifacts and wrote her address on the blackboard in a flowing, even script. "You will be doing your part in the great work of history," she said, "and making a valuable contribution to the knowledge of the past." She then gave an encouraging talk about the work museums do so that the bygone days were preserved. She inspired everyone to be part of it. When she next told of the theft of a valued museum piece and her desire for its return, the thieving seemed a dark and heinous deed.

Constable Whyte asked everyone to be on the lookout for an unusual person, any stranger. "Just report it if you see something suspicious. Don't try to talk or investigate yourself. We have reason to believe the thief has come this way and want everyone to be watchful."

"Eleanor, how good to see you again." Miss Hamilton shook her hand warmly. "How have you been? Have you found any items of interest at those tipi circles? You really must take me there one day, so I can look around myself."

"I haven't found anything. Sorry." Eleanor felt awkward. She wished she could say to Miss Hamilton, 'I know where the stolen item is. I'll bring it to you.' Eleanor didn't want secrets and lies. She could get help for Snake Woman. Except Snake Woman would be arrested. Put in jail as a thief.

"Well, I must be off, Eleanor. See you again soon, I hope."

Eleanor wanted to take her by the shoulders and explain. 'But she's not a thief, not in the regular way. This once belonged to her family and was stolen from them. She's just bringing it back.' And what would Miss Hamilton say? What would her parents or Constable Whyte say? 'How do you know this, Eleanor?' they would say. 'What nonsense you are talking.' Uncle Bernard would know the truth. Eleanor had to convince Snake Woman to let her tell Uncle Bernard. Then they could take her where she was going. That would solve the problem of getting a horse and buggy. They would use Uncle Bernard's.

Through lunch and the wagon ride from the school, the talk was all about Miss Hamilton and the intrigue that the museum thief was suspected to be in the area.

"If it's an Indian, I bet they never find him," said Hattie. "They can see in the dark and walk without leaving a trail." She scanned the prairie on each side of the wagon, her brows squinted.

"Never find *her*, Hattie. The thief is a woman. And don't be silly. The Mounties catch Indians and put them in jail all the time. Women as well as men." Lydia balanced herself against the rolling motion in the back of the wagon, a hand flat on each side of the boxboards.

"What does it matter, anyway?" Adam, alone on the wagon seat, looked over his shoulder. "Who cares about some old Indian stuff? It's not worth all the fuss."

"The Indians care about it. It's theirs, after all," Eleanor blurted.

"It was theirs," Adam corrected, with emphasis on the word *was*. "They're finished. They can't adapt. You heard what we learned in science. Survival of the fittest. That's us."

Eleanor looked away from Adam's self-assured face that grinned at her over his shoulder. What would be the point in hollering at him the way she felt like doing. 'You're wrong, Adam Wagner, all wrong,' she wanted to say. 'You're arrogant and sure of yourself and you think you're right about everything. But you're wrong.'

"Maybe they're not finished, Adam," Hattie voiced. "We don't know everything."

"Oh, Hattie," Lydia said and rolled her eyes. "Of course they're finished. But it's still important, Adam, to keep a record of their life."

Adam shrugged. Eleanor tightened her lips. Carl said nothing, but she caught him looking at her with a curious expression, as if she had said something strange.

I have to be careful, she thought. I cannot risk Snake Woman being discovered.

At the entrance to the gully, where Eleanor first had seen her, the old woman leaned on her pole.

"Did you keep warm last night?" Eleanor asked. "The wind was dreadful."

Snake Woman did not answer. She stepped into the cover of the willow. When Eleanor offered to let the old woman lean on her to walk back, she used her own pole. "I'm used to this now," she said.

Eleanor recounted the Constable and Lily Hamilton's visit at school, how Carl had come back looking for her, how she needed to be extra careful, and finally, as they reached Snake Woman's small camp, Eleanor told her idea of enlisting Uncle Bernard's help. She poured out to Snake Woman all that Bernard had told her about long ago at the fort, and about the newspaper clipping. The old woman nodded, eyes inward and distant.

"When he comes, maybe this weekend, I can tell him you've come back. We'll take you to safety." Eleanor sighed in relief, happy to finally have got all she knew out, confident that Snake Woman would agree to her idea.

"Now you sit." Snake Woman lowered herself to the ground and waved her hand for Eleanor to do the same. "That's a good plan you have. But there's not enough time."

"What do you mean?" Eleanor began a protest, but the woman signalled with her hand to stop.

"Just listen," she said. "Lots of snow is coming. Not for long, but lots. Hard for travel. Last night I asked about you."

Eleanor looked puzzled. Asked who?

"I asked the Bundle," Snake Woman continued, as if Eleanor had questioned aloud. She put her hand behind her and patted the satchel.

Quick thoughts ruffled through Eleanor's mind, like those when she first met Snake Woman. Is she, in fact, a crazy old woman? What am I doing imagining that she could be the one who stole the satchel, the one that Uncle Bernard saw forty years ago? Like a patch of ripples on the surface of a lake, her thoughts rose and ceased, the breeze of doubt suspended again.

"Never mind if you don't understand," Snake Woman continued. "It isn't to understand. It's to do what has to be done. The Bundle is close to home. There is danger. I cannot move quickly. You can take the Bundle to safety. She has given permission."

Eleanor did not want to hear what Snake Woman said. She reviewed the words in her mind, seeking the place where she had misheard, where something else was meant. She couldn't find it. The doubt breeze picked up again.

Snake Woman went on. "There is a place, less than half a day's ride, where you can leave her, hide her safely. I will tell you how to get there. You need a horse. Snow comes in three days. Before that time, it must be done." The old woman sighed, crossed her arms, and smiled.

Eleanor could find no words. She wanted to say that this was not possible, that she would have to wait for Uncle Bernard. In her mind, she heard the counter argument. If it snows, he will not come this weekend. He will not come until another week has passed. She wanted to say that she could not get a horse, but already thoughts arose that gave a possibility. For every contradiction that her mind presented, a bit of hope offered itself. Finally she asked, "But what will you do? You still need a doctor."

Snake Woman smiled. "I need time to heal. That's all. When the Bundle is safe, the Constable will find a simple old Indian woman with a hurt leg, leaning on a pole. Her horse ran away. She can't speak much English. She needs to get back to the reserve. He will take her there. He is a kind man. She will be safe. The Bundle will be safe. When her leg is healed, she will go and get the Bundle and bring it to where it wants to be. The woman's young friend can tell her Uncle Bernard the whole story after the Bundle is safe."

She makes it sound so simple, Eleanor thought as she walked back, reviewing the possibilities of how to do what Snake Woman asked. Every idea had a flaw. Which one had the best chance of success?

CHAPTER 34

THE NEXT MORNING when Eleanor climbed onto the wagon, Adam slid over to give room for her to sit on the wagon seat. She pretended to not notice and stepped into the box where Lydia, Hattie, and Carl sat on burlap sacks. Eleanor sat beside Carl, opposite the girls.

At school, Carl unharnessed the horse and tethered him to graze until school was done. "I do the driving, Carl does the harnessing," Adam had explained on their first ride. This day, Eleanor lingered, pretending to fiddle with the straps on her school satchel while Lydia and Hattie went quickly to join in conversation and games before Miss Jensen rang the school bell.

Once they were gone, she moved close as Carl released the straps on the wagon poles. She had thought through what she needed to say, but no amount of rehearsal could make it sound reasonable when the time came to speak.

She took a deep breath. Carl is the best, maybe only possibility, she thought. "I have a favor to ask you, Carl. But it has to be secret."

He crinkled his brow. "What favor do you need?" He continued undoing the harness.

"Could you bring the saddle horse you rode a couple of days ago to school tomorrow? I need to borrow a horse for the day, one that is strong, but that I can handle. I'll have it back, I think, by the time school ends. I can't tell you any more than that."

Carl rubbed the shoulders of the small horse where the harness had chafed the hair. "How will you explain being gone from school all day?"

"I'll say something. I don't want to deceive anyone. I don't want you to have to lie. But there is a reason I ask this."

"I can bring Smokey," he said matter of factly, and led the horse to the tether stake in the field east of the schoolhouse.

Eleanor hardly slept that night. All the possibilities for mishap rose in her mind, one after the other. Why not just get up early and take Belle? No, Father needs the team to plough. If I disappear on Belle, Father will be after me on Charlie, who would follow like a bloodhound. Why not take the wagon horse? Too small. Not broke to riding. Wouldn't be able to do such a long day. Why not wait and check the weather? Maybe Uncle Bernard will come. But a stronger voice from within told her, *'You just have to do this, Eleanor.'*

Only Lydia and Hattie sat in the back when the wagon arrived. "Where's Carl today?" Eleanor asked.

"He went early and rode Smokey. He thought there

might be stray cattle to the north and went to check before coming to school."

"Carl likes to get out and ride sometimes," said Lydia. "He hated ranching, but he loves the riding."

Smokey stood at the hitch rail outside the school. Carl leaned against it, one leg crossed over the other, a grass stem between his lips. Eleanor patted Smokey's neck and combed his black mane with her fingers.

"I pretended to loosen the cinch," Carl said, as his eyes followed a skylark that rose and dipped to the west of the school, "but he's ready to go." With that he went inside.

Miss Jensen opened the front door to ring the bell and announce the start of school. A press of bodies moved through the door. Eleanor usually dashed inside before or as soon as the bell sounded, while Hattie lingered to come near the last. Today, Eleanor waited behind and called as Hattie started up the steps. "Hattie. Can you take a message? I've gone and forgotten my schoolbag at the coulee rim. I'm going to take Smokey and go get it. Carl said I could ride him anytime. But Hattie – it's so great a day – I might spend a bit of time riding before coming back. Wait till I'm off before you say anything."

For once, Hattie was lost for words. Eleanor loosed the reins quickly, climbed on Smokey, and turned him toward the coulee. She did not look back as Smokey broke into an easy canter. So far so good.

Snake Woman leaned on her pole, the satchel beside her, just inside the crevasse opening. She always expects me, but how does she know? Eleanor prepared to dismount, but Snake

Woman raised her hand in a signal to stop. She hoisted the satchel over her shoulder and limped to Smokey's side. "Hold this in front of you. Like a child," she said and lifted it as if she handed her a sleeping baby.

"Smokey is a strong horse," Eleanor said. "You can ride behind and tell me where to go. Then I'll take you to safety."

Snake Woman shook her head and smiled. "I thought you were worried about me. Are you wanting to kill me, bouncing around on the back of a horse with this leg? You need to ride fast, not gentle walking. Now listen carefully." She pointed to the southern side of the coulee, west of the gully where she had been camped. "You go up there. You hold your eyes on the highest peak of the Sweetgrass Hills, on the west. Ride straight toward it. After a couple of hours, the sun will be there." She pointed above to a spot in the sky. "You'll see a large rock. Ride toward it to the edge of a small coulee. Near the bottom there will be more rocks, like these." Snake Woman pointed to the pile of boulders where she had injured her leg.

"At the very bottom," she continued, "it's like a small cave. Lay the satchel in there. Do not open it. Say a prayer. Then ride back." The effort of bringing the satchel out to Eleanor had tired the woman. Her face was creased by lines of pain.

Eleanor began her plea once again for Snake Woman to ride with her, but stopped when she realized the old one was right. "I'll come back here when it's done," she said. "Then it will be safe to get help for you."

"No," the old woman said. "You mustn't come this way. In a while I'll build a fire. A smoky one. That Constable will be here in no time. Then he can get this old woman back to the reserve."

"But when will I see you again?"

Snake Woman shrugged. "Don't know. Didn't know I'd see you in the first place." She smiled again. "But now we're both friends of the Bundle. She likes her friends to see each other."

Eleanor knew Snake Woman wanted her to leave, but she couldn't accept this might be the last time she saw her. How would they ever meet? How could she bring Uncle Bernard to her, to finish the story begun in the fort so many years ago?

"Go on now," Snake Woman said, waved her hand, turned her back, and began to limp toward the willow thicket.

Eleanor leaned the satchel against her body and supported it with her left arm, like she would a sleeping child. Nudging her legs against Smokey's sides, she sent him eagerly forward, angling to the south coulee wall and up the side. At the top she wanted to stop and look back, to wave, but kept the reins slack instead, and put her eyes on the highest peak of the hills. Smokey felt the angle of where she looked and aligned himself. She held him at a light jog that the horse could hold with ease for hours. His gait was steady, and Eleanor easily held an even posture. She glanced over her right shoulder for a quick look after a few minutes ride, but already the coulee had disappeared into the land. In each direction, the ground stretched unobstructed, seemingly flat. She lined her eyes on the hills on the horizon, the western one between Smokey's upright ears. It was as if he, too, had his sight on them.

Eleanor breathed deeply, the scent of budding poplar and green newness intoxicating and heady. Here she was, riding a horse, alone, across the land just as she had imagined doing. She had made the decision on her own to help Snake Woman, had worked out a plan when it seemed impossible, and now was carrying it out. She felt alive and more herself than she had ever felt before. The memory of her first night came to her, how she laid in the grass and knew that she had come home. Now she had come home within herself, within her own mind and body.

She shifted the satchel so it rested snug in front of her on the saddle, supported in the crook of her arm. No wind had yet risen. The steady thud of Smokey's hooves, a bird call, the occasional squeak of the saddle leather – these were light sounds that would easily be drowned out in the wind, but not today. And behind these other sounds was something else. Faint, but she could hear it. Or was it more a feeling? Was it the hum of the stillness? It was something else. Her dream memory arose. The high, discordant voices. That was the sound she heard now, faint but palpable, and once she identified it, she knew it for certain as the sound in her dream. She knew at the same time that the sound came from inside the satchel.

She realized then that the sound had been present but unacknowledged for some time, ever since she had set her eyes on the hills and ridden toward them. It was first discordant to her ears and set up an unpleasant sensation that reminded her of the chills in her body when a mosquito crawled into her ear. This sound was no longer like that. Instead, her body relaxed into a sensation of calm joy, as if warmed by sun emerging from cloud. She began to hum with it, searching for the note that blended with the one coming from the satchel. With the sound, the sense again arose of having arrived home within herself, to the comfort of belonging, to completeness. The sensation was both new and entirely familiar.

Abruptly, the sound ceased. Smokey snorted and raised his head, perked his ears forward and looked to the right. He gave a soft nicker that vibrated through his whole body. Eleanor tracked her own eyes to where Smokey stared. Plumes of dust rose, just the sort that a buggy might send up from dry grass. Smokey stopped of his own will and stood entirely still and attentive, his neck upright and tense. Eleanor's curiosity matched the horse's. Perhaps it is antelope, she thought, knowing that it wasn't, for she knew by now that antelope did not cause the dust to rise in such a way. Cattle maybe or horses, she thought. Some horses that escaped are roaming free. That's what sends up dust like that. She had no sooner accepted this explanation than the form of two horses emerged, one pulling a small buggy, and one the long-legged Scalliwag. Smokey whinnied a full-blown greeting of both relief and welcome.

Eleanor sat paralyzed. She was not supposed to meet anyone. How would she explain to Constable Whyte and what must surely be Miss Lily Hamilton, what she was doing out here on Carl's horse, carrying a satchel. She was supposed to be in school. Just run, now, she told herself. Full gallop. *Don't be silly*, countered another voice. *The Constable would be after you in an instant and Smokey could never outrun Scalliwag.* But he's going to see me and ask what I'm doing and whatever I say will arouse suspicion. *Keep calm and distract their attention. It's a spring day, full of the longing and yearning that comes with the season. You're a young woman in the spring of life, full of the same longing and yearning. It's not unreasonable that you would borrow a friend's horse to ride out over the land, on your first spring back here.*

Eleanor had little time to wonder about this voice that spoke so clearly to her, that sounded like Snake Woman. Constable Whyte and Lily Hamilton had seen her when she spotted them and now rode directly to her.

"Why it's Eleanor," he called, now quite a distance in front of the buggy. "What in the world are you doing out here? Is anything wrong?"

"Hello, Constable Whyte," Eleanor said casually, and with feigned pleasure at this unexpected encounter. She hoped her pounding heart and dry throat would not betray the ruse. She waved to the buggy and called, "Hello, Miss Hamilton. How good to meet you again." Eleanor smiled at the Constable. "Everything's fine. Carl brought Smokey to school today, and it was such a glorious day. Really, I don't know what came over me. I feel rather silly now, and I expect I'll have a great deal of explaining to do to Miss Jensen and Mother and Father, but I just simply had to get out and breathe in this air." She spoke quickly, imitating Hattie's non-stop chatter that could leave a listener breathless, and, Eleanor hoped, gave no opening for interruption. "But really," she continued, "this is so fortuitous. I was planning on getting a message to you on my return, which will be very soon. But when Smokey and I crossed the coulee this morning, there was a woman standing in the flat bottom area, just a bit west of where Mr. Pacey mines his coal. Well, I thought that was very unusual, but it wasn't until I'd ridden up the other side and gone aways that I said to myself, 'Now wasn't it a woman who took that item from the museum – a native woman – and didn't that woman in the coulee have dark skin like a native?' So I said, 'Eleanor, as soon as you return you must find a way to get word to Constable Whyte, or to Miss Hamilton, to Lily.'" She nodded at the woman who sat now alongside Constable Whyte and listened. "And now here you've both come along, and really, it must be less than an hour's ride, maybe a bit more, to the coulee. That woman seemed to move very slowly. I'm sure you could find her easily."

Eleanor stopped. Waited. She fixed her attention on the Constable. Miss Hamilton's head had tilted at that slight angle that suggested she listened less to Eleanor's words and more to the feeling behind them. *Keep your mind away from her*, the voice inside warned, and now Eleanor heard it distinctly as Snake Woman's. Smokey and Scalliwag had sniffed noses and exchanged snorts and snuffles of greeting. Now they stood relaxed, while the small gray horse on the buggy, oblivious to the others, rested with one back leg hardly touching the ground, his necked drooping forward. Smokey half-heartedly nibbled green shoots near his feet. A fat fly buzzed around his ear and he flicked it to discourage its attentions. Has time stopped? Eleanor thought. How long are we to wait in this awkward silence?

"You wouldn't be the first one out on the prairie to fall under the spell of a spring day like this, Eleanor." Constable Whyte's voice broke the spell. "You're not the sort of young lady who would make a habit of it. And your news is very useful, isn't it Lily? We'll go immediately to investigate. I've felt sure the person who took that bundle would eventually come this way."

Constable Whyte drew up the reins and turned Scalliwag to the north. "But you should come with us, Eleanor, and you can show us exactly where you saw the woman. Besides, look at that bank of dark clouds in the northern sky. We'll have one of our famous prairie spring blizzards by tonight."

Constable Whyte was friendly and likeable. What am I doing? Eleanor questioned herself. Lying to my friends, assisting a thief, carrying stolen property. She could not even allow herself a thought of how she would explain her behavior once the day was over. The urge to confess everything arose.

But when she spoke, it was in a voice of clear confidence. "You'll find her easily. As I said, just west of Mr. Pacey's diggings, where the trail goes into the coulee. But really, Constable Whyte, I've wanted to do this since coming to the west and may never get such a day again. I want to ride a bit farther on my own. Then I'll turn back, and we'll very likely meet up later. I'll be so curious to find out about this woman. Don't you think it's quite extraordinary about her being there?"

"I really do. Ride carefully, and don't go too much further. Come on then Lily, Miss Hamilton. We might be close to solving the mystery."

"What's that satchel you're carrying, Eleanor?" Miss Hamilton asked, and her head still had the slight angle, her eyes fixed on the front of the saddle.

"Oh, I'm trying this out as a school bag. Quite the wrong shape and size for riding a horse, or even for walking – but it does carry a lot of useful things. I'll likely go back to my other one. I'm sure this is quite impractical. Good-bye then, I don't want to keep you." With that, Eleanor pulled up a reluctant

Smokey's head, for he had begun to follow Scalliwag. She waved her hand in farewell but did not look back, urging Smokey to a casual lope. Sitting straight and looking left to right along the horizon, she hoped she gave the impression of an enthused young woman who had done a daring and reckless thing. Finally she gave a quick glance over her shoulder. Constable Whyte had already gone a good distance toward the north, but Miss Hamilton's buggy had not moved. Eleanor knew the woman had not taken her eyes from her. When she looked the next time, the buggy was moving, but not following Constable Whyte. Miss Hamilton, instead, drove after Eleanor.

Eleanor leaned forward and coaxed Smokey to a faster pace. How far did she have to go? She aligned her eyes on the tallest hill, held it between Smokey's ears. Would this pace tire him too much? Miss Hamilton's small horse could not possibly keep up with Smokey. But why was she coming this way at all?

When Smokey's neck grew dark with sweat, Eleanor slowed him to a walk. Behind her she could just make out the dust of the buggy and horse. She turned to the left where a depression in the land held clear melt water and let Smokey drink his fill, then resumed the easy jog of earlier. Little time passed before the dark thumb of an upright stone appeared on the horizon. At the same time, the ringing hum resumed from inside the satchel. Or is it inside me? she wondered. With the sound, the feeling returned that she was where she belonged, had come home to herself. Though she regretted her deceit, she accepted it as necessary. The image of Snake Woman came to mind, leaning against her stick, her leg swollen and bandaged, a calm resolve in her face. This is no mad woman, Eleanor thought. This is a woman who has been willing to take great risk in order to do what is needed. This is the kind of woman I want to be.

When she reached the small coulee and the cluster of rocks, Eleanor could no longer see the dust or buggy. Miss Hamilton's field glasses might enable her to see where Eleanor had gone, but the girl was no longer worried. The song from the satchel grew stronger the closer they came to where she would leave the bundle. Eleanor's purpose had grown clearer along with it.

She dismounted and found she nearly collapsed, her legs stiff and numb from unaccustomed riding. She carried the satchel in both arms, still in the manner that she would carry a baby, and walked gingerly to the base of the rock pile. Just as Snake Woman had described it, an opening at the bottom showed a large dark space. She suddenly felt reluctant to leave the satchel at this place, just as she was reluctant to leave Snake Woman that morning. *But you must.* It was her own voice that spoke to her. *This is the task you have been given.*

She pushed the satchel between the rocks and gave a strong shove to its end, sending the bag sliding into the cavern. The motion raised dust that tasted old and dry. The satchel only just fit between two rocks, gritty with hardened lichen. Green blades sprouted in thick, haphazard clumps along the base of the rocks. But in the opening between, nothing grew, and the earth lay pale and dusty.

Eleanor looked into the enlarged space beyond the opening but could see nothing. No sound came from the bag now, and its silence felt sad, with the sorrow of farewell. Eleanor chose another stone that lay in the pile and pushed it into the space where the bag had disappeared. She smoothed the ground at the base, tousled the grass blades to knock dust off, then stood to survey the hiding place. No one could detect this, she thought with satisfaction, and stepped back a few paces. Smokey crunched grass to her left, a meadowlark cheered its greeting above, and her work was done. She felt weary and sighed deeply. Just as she reached for Smokey's reins to begin the ride back, a movement at the rocks stopped her. From out of a dark crack above the hidden satchel emerged a large snake. It slithered slowly in a curved path to drape over the warm rock. The snake raised its head slightly, swayed left to right, turned and slid back into its den.

CHAPTER 35

SMOKEY WAS TIRED and did not hold his head so high or prick his ears forward, yet he was keen to be heading homeward and kept a steady jog. The clouds had slid along the western horizon from the north and began to fill over the remaining blue. As the sun was covered, the air cooled quickly, and a wind rose at the same time.

Eleanor was not sure how much time had passed. At what place was the sun in the sky when she left school? She wished she had paid closer attention. Would Carl wait for her there? Would he ride to where she met the wagon each day and wait there? She felt a flood of appreciation for Carl. He had asked so little when she requested the use of Smokey. He'd simply agreed.

I'll ride to where I usually get out to walk, she decided at last, hopeful that Carl would wait if she arrived late. If early, she could ride toward school and meet him en route, or there. She wrapped her sweater tighter and let Smokey choose the direction, knowing he would guide more surely than she could without a landmark such as the hills. When the horse raised his neck and his ears pointed forward, she strained her eyes where he looked and detected dark bumps against the sky. It's the wagon, she thought. They're waiting.

By the time Smokey reached the southern coulee rim, Eleanor could make out the wagon, Hattie waving and running on the other side, Adam and Carl sitting in the grass, and the small buggy of Miss Lily Hamilton.

Hattie ran to meet her first as Smokey picked his way up the grassy side. "Thank goodness you're back. You're probably in a lot of trouble, but never mind. Miss Hamilton told us you saw the woman and sent Constable Whyte to where she was." Hattie walked beside Eleanor with her hand on the stirrup. "Eleanor, you're crying. Whatever is the matter? Don't worry. You aren't in that much trouble," Hattie said in alarm, just as they reached the others.

Eleanor slid slowly from Smokey, patted his neck, and handed his reins to Carl. "Thank you, Carl. Thank you for trusting me with him. He's a great horse." Her breath caught. She hadn't even realized she had been crying. "Hattie, I'm freezing. Can I borrow your cloak?" Was she freezing, or frightened, or relieved? She didn't know. Didn't know how she would explain this day. Being cold seemed a good choice right now.

Carl took Smokey's reins and said nothing. Hattie ran to the wagon for a blanket and draped it over the shoulders of Eleanor, who kept one hand on Smokey's neck for balance. Beyond Carl stood Lily, Adam, and Lydia.

"Miss Jensen was worried when you didn't come back, Eleanor," Lydia said.

Eleanor ignored her. "Lily, Miss Hamilton," she said and tried to find her casual voice of a few hours earlier, "Please, excuse me. I'm just very cold. You were quite right, I should have come back with you and Constable Whyte. It did get cold faster than I thought."

"Come on, Eleanor, we'll drive you home in the wagon." It was Adam. He put his woollen jacket over her shoulders and left his arm there. She stood still, shivering.

"I want to know what happened," she said between sniffles. "What happened with the woman, Miss Hamilton?"

Lily held her head at that angle again, but Eleanor no longer cared. "I followed you a ways, Eleanor," Miss Hamilton replied, but the smooth, warm quality of her voice was missing, "because I wanted to urge you to come with us. You rode very fast. I almost thought you were trying to outdistance me. At last, I gave up and came back this way. I had to circle to the west to bring the buggy across the coulee. Your friends can tell you the rest of the story."

Hattie seized the moment. "We just got here to see if you were coming when Constable Whyte rode up from the coulee. There was an old Indian woman riding behind him. Constable Whyte said she likely had a broken leg. She didn't speak much English."

Lydia broke in. "She looked a bit crazy in the head, this big grin and pointing to the west. 'Reserve. Home,'" she kept saying.

Hattie continued. "Constable Whyte is taking her, and

he'll be staying at our house tonight. We'll find out everything and tell you tomorrow."

"Tomorrow it will be too snowy for school." Eleanor felt warmth and calmness now. The numb feeling in her legs and feet had gone. She moved away from Adam's arm and returned his jacket. The blanket she wrapped more tightly at her neck, and the gesture recalled Snake Woman. "Adam, thank you so much for your offer, but I feel warmer and the walking will be good. You need to get home. Carl, thank you again. I'll see you next week."

Carl gave his half grin. "If you like, Eleanor. Do you want a ride on Smokey?"

This brought a surge of laughter, and she raised her hand in protest. "Good heavens, no. Not a for a few days, I believe."

Which brought more laughter. "The best cure for saddle stiffness is actually a good walk," Carl said, smiling.

"Where's your satchel, Eleanor?" asked Lily Hamilton.

"The one you forgot this morning?" piped Hattie. "Didn't you find it?"

"As I said, Miss Hamilton," answered Eleanor, already walking away. "It wasn't the right thing to keep. I hope you don't mind if I keep the blanket until next week?"

"Of course not," piped Hattie. "If there's snow tonight, we'll come and pick you up tomorrow."

"Not if there's a lot of snow," Eleanor called over her shoulder. She clutched the blanket tighter and strode briskly, surprised at the limberness that returned to her legs.

The image of Snake Woman on Scalliwag, behind Constable Whyte, brought a grin to her face. When she imagined the woman feigning stupidity and an inability to speak English, she laughed out loud. First I'm shivering and crying. Now I'm warm and laughing. Once, she stopped and looked over her shoulder. The sky was an even, pale gray to the south. The Sweetgrass Hills were charcoal lumps, small and far.

Uncle Bernard, she thought, I hope you come soon. I've got a good story for you. When she thought over what she would say to her parents, it didn't seem so outrageous after all. The story of the old native woman would be of more interest than her own spring adventure. Miss Hamilton will even forget about that satchel, she thought. But I will never forget.

By the time she reached the sod hut and the first flakes of snow were falling, Eleanor had already imagined how she and Uncle Bernard would manage to visit Snake Woman.

◇◇◇◇◇◇◇◇◇◇◇◇◇◇◇◇◇◇◇

Snake slid, slowly and happily, back out onto the rock where he had waited much of the day. Rock, too, had been waiting. *Years, Snake. I've been waiting years.*

The song of homecoming, the song of greeting, had sounded strong all day, growing in strength, until finally there it was, humming and throbbing and pulsing just beneath Snake's body. Rock hummed contentedly and all the earth and grass, the gentle undulations of the land rolling to the Sweetgrass Hills, sang. The river, curling and winding, sang. Far off, the mountains sounded a joyous chorus. All rejoicing.

It's always this way for a homecoming, thought Snake, *and this homecoming is especially sweet.* Pounding its rhythm beneath the rocks that warmed Snake's body was the ancient promise, still beating, humming, singing. All the People of Napi's land, two-legged, four-, winged, finned, and the sliding ground-hugging ones like Snake, all heard the promise sounding again.

Napi's ways are a mystery, hummed Snake, *but Napi stays with us. Forever.*

◇◇◇◇◇◇◇◇◇◇◇◇◇◇◇◇◇◇◇

ACKNOWLEDGMENTS

So many factors, known and unknown, influence a story's coming into being.

For those not yet recognized, I offer my gratitude now, and also acknowledge, with apology, that I may never recognize them. The following I do recognize.

Thanks to Carolyn Jackson and everyone at Second Story Press for giving *Napi's Dance* a chance, and for being such a pleasure to work with through the process.

I've often read authors' expressions of immense appreciation for their editor's guidance. Now I know why. Thanks to Colin Thomas for being thorough, helpful, and firm. Thanks especially, Colin, for good humor and the many deep belly laughs, essential to navigating the challenges of the process, and for your kindness and sensitivity while holding me to the required course.

Deepest appreciation to my friends at Yasodhara Ashram,

for encouragement to find and express my own voice and potential; and for offering examples, tools, and skills on how to do that.

So much thanks to Tom Wayman, writing teacher of passion, skill, and knowledge. Your well of expertise, enthusiasm, and encouragement has nourished this small group of east-shore writers for many years. You always guided us to bring the best of ourselves to our writing.

And to the constant core group of writers along the shore of Kootenay Lake, I am so grateful. Beth MacLellan, Doreen Zaiss and Wai Yin Fung (and those who have joined us from time to time over the many years our group has met) thank you. Your companionship in writing has nurtured commitment, perseverance, learning, and delight. Your support and friendship is a treasure.

I am grateful for the knowledge in the books of Hugh A. Dempsey and for his commitment to collecting and recounting the stories of the Alberta Plains People. I am also grateful to Betty Bastien for her book *Blackfoot Ways of Knowing*, a valued inspiration during the research for *Napi's Dance*.

ABOUT THE AUTHOR

ALANDA GREENE was born in Calgary, Alberta, the youngest of four children. Her father, born and raised in the southern prairie, gave her many gifts, but two were especially significant: he nurtured a connection with the natural world and he told rich stories from the Blackfoot nation of the central plains, stories learned from his native friends as he grew up. She spent her restless adolescent years riding her horse across the hills southwest of Calgary, imagining what it would be like to gallop through that land with no fences to contain it, the way it once had been. She later moved to Kootenay Bay, British Columbia where she spent twenty-four years teaching at the local school. During this time she wrote many articles for education magazines, completed a Bachelor of Education, and wrote and illustrated a book for middle school educators. After taking creative writing courses, she finally settled into exploring the questions that had stayed with her since childhood about the land and history of southern Alberta. From that exploration came *Napi's Dance*. Alanda managed the small bookstore at the Yasodhara Ashram in Kootenay Bay for several years, and she is now engaged with managing the ashram land.